THE
REGULATORS

By Ben Bruce

WWW.BENBRUCE.CO.UK

First published in Great Britain on Amazon Kindle Direct in
2018 by Ben Bruce

Cover design by Sean Strong

Edited by Elizabeth Love at Bee Edited.

ISBN

9781999846923

To Vicky,

Thanks for the patience. Sorry you didn't marry a teacher.

Enfidha-Hammamet airport shimmered like a silver beetle, wings unfurled in the middle of the Tunisian scrub, basking in the late autumn sunshine. Fountains danced playfully outside the quiet main entrance overlooked by the tower, a slim grey cone, that rose up inside a traffic roundabout as if wrapped in an elegant silver dress from which anyone could see the goings-on across the whole airport. It was the perfect example of the creeping modernisation that had seeped into the northern African countries as they sought to make the most of the riches of their European neighbours to the north. It had gone so well, but then the terror attacks on British tourists, just a few miles down the coast, had all but put pay to that.

It was a perfectly functional, modern, clean structure built just before the financial crash of the late 2000s. Originally named after then Tunisian President Zine El Abdine Ben Ali, the airport was renamed once he was ousted from power in the Arab Spring. At its peak, it attracted over two million visitors a year, but the change in attitudes towards Muslim countries in the west, and the fear that had gripped them after several high-profile attacks, meant that those days were now a thing of the past. Like so much of the optimism of the early 21st Century, it was slowly being snuffed out by fear and paranoia, and that kept Mehdi Chedli a busy man.

True, he wasn't nearly as busy as he had been before the Arab Spring, and the rules had changed somewhat since the people had begun to get ideas above their station. Before, it had been a clear line that had been drawn. If you went against the state, you were an enemy of it, and you could be stopped. Mehdi had revelled in stopping people. As a senior officer in the secret police, it was easy to make people acquiesce. The reputation that the organisation carried was often enough to silence most who dared to think that way. Of course, there were those who needed a little gentle persuasion. Others, just persuasion, gentle or not. Some simply wouldn't learn, and now, couldn't learn.

Today's world, he reflected, was markedly different. Now the enemies of the state were more subtly distinguished. Championed, hoisted into positions of power all over North Africa, ingraining themselves into the systems. They were of little concern to Mehdi. Power corrupts, and corruption paid his bills. All of them would come to see things in a similar way to him at some point, and it was true that, with no political ideology of his own, he was able to adapt to any new taskmaster.

In this new era, terrorism was the prime concern, and that was harder to weed out than groups of organised opposition, who had to be vocal and court the people because they had forever needed them. The terrorists kept themselves hidden, knew not to take risks. Some of them knew the inner workings of the security forces better than most, given that they had turned from the state after the change in power.

Those people were traitors, and he despised them the most. He left nothing in the locker, as the Americans who had trained him in his earlier days would have said, when it came to punishing those who had abandoned the state and turned to terror. There were many he had taken into his office, deep inside a broken-down factory in the centre of Hammamet, who would never see the light of day again.

The person he had been ordered to meet wasn't a terrorist. He was a professional, like Mehdi. That made him much more dangerous.

His car rolled into the vast but near-deserted carpark. It was a delight to drive a German Audi Avant that seemed capable of handling everything that he had asked of it so far. It looked the part as well, stylish, betraying an interior that had been specifically designed to withstand gunfire and small explosions, having been reinforced by his technical team with bullet-proof glass and an extra coating of Kevlar inside the vehicle's shell. Not quite a tank, but the next best thing.

It was as much a part of the new Tunisia as he was now, and that was reflected in the way he chose to dress. Smart-fitting Italian suits made him look more like a catwalk model, showcasing the definition of his body, building up to a chiselled chin, and deep brown eyes that could be as kind as they could be cruel. Mehdi Chedli had adapted, and now he was thriving.

He pulled the car up where he had been instructed. Despite the unseasonal time of year, Mehdi felt the desperation of the place. It was deserted. Barely a soul in sight. Reaching down, he found the briefcase he was to deliver to the contact. As he did, there was a tap at the rear driver's side door, and he looked to see a man with shaggy hair, scruffy beard, and a pair of aviator sunglasses on. He was much paler than Mehdi, clearly not a native to these parts. To look at him, he looked like he might have come from the eastern parts of Europe, or maybe even central Asia. Despite the attempts to disguise his appearance up this close, Mehdi instantly recognised him as his contact, Erik Andryiv, and released the anti-hijack system on the car so that Erik could let himself in.

"You don't mess around, do you?" Mehdi raised an eyebrow as the other man entered the back of the car. His eyes scanned warily in the rear-view mirror until he was certain that his new passenger wasn't carrying a weapon. Not that there would be any benefit to killing him, he convinced himself.

"The job is the job." Erik shrugged. "It is all I am interested in. Sooner I am finished dealing with you, the better."

"So, the gun for hire doesn't like being seen with an agent of the government." Mehdi smiled, attempting to assert himself on the conversation.

"I just don't like dealing with people who pretend to have motives or beliefs that aren't as they appear. You pay me, I do a job. You, however, are a snake, and you can turn, and you can bite, for you have no grounding, no beliefs on which you anchor yourself," hissed Erik.

"My god is your god, don't ever forget that," Mehdi cautioned back

"My god will not forget either." Erik shot a look at Mehdi through the rear-view mirror, his gaze steely, no chance of hiding his contempt.

"Careful, you'll hurt my feelings."

Erik smiled back at Mehdi. A crooked and disconcerting smile that even the seasoned agent felt betrayed some kind of ill intent. "We wouldn't want that," he went on.

"No, we wouldn't." Mehdi suddenly felt that the conversation needed moving on before something escalated out of nothing. Considering his position, and the logistical disadvantage he had being in the front seat, he decided to set the pace. "Business. This briefcase has the keys to our locker in London. Our operative there has arranged for the equipment you requested, and our contact within the UK government has assured us that you are no longer on any watch lists. Should you find a problem at any point, it will be dealt with quickly on their end if you call this number."

Mehdi twisted and handed a small card with a London phone number on it before carrying on with his instructions. "There's a tablet computer with maps and schematics of all the potential sites, as well as timing schedules and other valuable information for you. Although now, rather than a briefcase, I wish we had brought you a duffle bag or something."

Mehdi passed the briefcase backwards to Erik, who took it, clasping his hand over Mehdi's and holding him for a moment, forcing the security agent to look him in the eyes.

"Thank you. For everything. Until we meet again."

Erik smiled, released the grip, and slid out of the car. Mehdi wasn't used to being spooked, but there was something about that man, something inherently evil, that unsettled him.

While Mehdi may have been good at intimidation through brutality, Erik had something else. He was just scary. Mehdi watched him walking away and breathed a sigh of relief. With a bit of luck, whilst Erik would be able to finish his mission, he might not find extraction from the UK so easy. After all, when he hit his targets, everyone was going to be looking for him.

2

Barry Vernon had every reason to be pleased with himself as he sat behind the smart mahogany desk in his well-appointed office, closing the lid on his laptop. He had beaten the system; he had played the game and won. It really shouldn't have surprised anyone who knew him. After all, Barry Vernon was the smartest person that Barry Vernon knew. The phone call he had just taken confirmed that for him, once and for all.

His lawyer had been brief. The CPS had considered the case and decided that since it couldn't be sure what money had gone missing – even though it was fairly sure some had – there was no realistic chance of a prosecution. It meant that the shell companies, of which he was a silent partner, would face no further probing and that the links to the companies where the money had gone would remain unnoticed. Barry Vernon could begin to think about that early retirement. Somewhere hot. Somewhere easy going. Somewhere without an extradition treaty. Just in case.

He was, of course, a cautious man. That was probably why he got away with it. That necessity to take the extra precaution, that need to never feel complacent or comfortable. A little part of him knew he might never feel completely safe

11

ever again. There was still that slight nagging in the back of his mind, but he figured that sooner or later, as with everything, he'd get over it. Time's a great healer and all that.

He pushed back from his chair, contemplating his next move. It was going to be, in many ways, the one that he would feel the most regret over. At least in the short term. He was heading to the airport to get that flight out of the country and start his new life. It meant leaving his wife and his kids behind. The kids – he would contact them and tell them where he was. They were all adults now. Grown up and flown the nest and capable of making their own decisions. He knew that, with a few gifts sent their way, they would forgive him, and their relationship would pull through. After all, they were his kids, and money talked.

His wife, Jenna, was a different story. They'd been married twenty-seven years now, and certainly, for the most part, they'd been good. In the early days, they'd been great, but like so many people, as age had caught up with them, that spark had gone. Now he had the chance to find it somewhere else. He was no fool; he knew that any young gold digger that showed an interest in him was doing it as much for the money as they were anything else. He wasn't a looker, not anymore. Back in the day, he might have classed himself as handsome. He had never been tall, but in his youth, his hair had been smart, his clothes trendy, and he had remained fit. But age, most noticeably an expanding waistline and thinning hair, had put pay to that. He was now a short, fat, bald, middle-aged man, but in the end, who the hell cared if they were only after his money? He wasn't looking for a soul mate now; he was looking to feel good.

He knew Jenna wouldn't truly understand what he had done. He reassured himself that she would never, ever be able to live a life on the lamb, living off what, in truth, were stolen monies. Jenna Vernon was a good, honourable lady. Too good for him. He was doing her the biggest favour of all, he surmised.

He took one last look around the office, drinking in his surroundings. This had been the epicentre of his enterprises, both criminal and legitimate. He'd spent the last eight years here, pushing his brand to the position where he'd been given the trust to look after public funds. That had been an incredible honour, one he had originally revelled in and embraced.

He'd never thought this would be how it would end, that he would be the one who was on the take, but here he was. Like so many good men before him, when the chance came, it became irresistible. At first, he had just wondered if he could get away with it, and then, he had realised that he could. In doing so, he made himself a criminal. He let that concept resonate around his head for a moment. A criminal, albeit one who had got away with it. He sighed, then stood up. Time to go.

The laptop, on which so much of his work had been done, was quickly slipped into his briefcase and his coat slipped on. He stepped out into the office. Louisa, his secretary, sat opposite. She had no clue what her boss had done. He often wondered if he should have told her. Perhaps Louisa was one of those girls who was seduced by bad boys and money, but he had stopped that little fantasy in its tracks. Pretty as Louisa was, she wasn't worth the stretch. He smiled at her as he went to leave. She was on the phone, and she waved at him, urgently, trying to catch his attention.

"Mr Vernon, I've got a call for you."

"Tell them I've gone fishing," he replied, before adding, "Have a nice weekend."

And then he was gone. Out of the door. A free man, a new man. In seconds, he was out in the street. That's when it started to hit him, the magnitude of not only what he had done, but what he had succeeded in getting away with. The sun seemed a little brighter, the air a little fresher. He felt seventeen and full of bluster.

Had he been a little less preoccupied with that, he might have noticed the tall, muscular man in the black leather biker jacket with the cropped brown hair hanging up his phone as he spotted Vernon. He might have noticed that, as he reached the corner to turn towards the multi-storey carpark, the tall man was following him, rapidly closing the gap between the two. But he didn't, and he was blissfully unaware, basking in his own brilliance, just the split second before the man's hand clasped him firmly around the top of his elbow.

"Barry Vernon." The voice was gruff, uncompromising. It should have been a question, but there was no doubt the man knew who he had in his grip.

"What…" Barry stammered for a second trying to compose himself. "Who are you?"

There was no answer.

"This way." The stranger pulled at his Barry's arm forcefully, directing him towards the far reaches of the carpark and a plain, inconspicuous white van.

The pace was brisk. Even though Barry prided himself on being in decent shape for his age, he found himself quick-stepping alongside the stranger just to keep up with his assertive strides. He wanted to ask more questions, but he knew that silence was the smarter move right now. If he was in immediate danger of being killed, he would be dead already. There would be time for a man of Barry's expertise to talk himself out of trouble later, of that he was sure.

As they approached the van, a sliding door on the side of it opened, revealing another man inside. Shorter than his companion, although that was to be expected, given the law of averages. Certainly, around the six-foot mark himself, if not passing it. He had wavy black hair curling on top of his head. He scowled at Barry who was thrust in his direction, but his eyes still twinkled. He was enjoying this, every split second of Barry's confusion and fear.

The first stranger pushed Barry towards the van, releasing his arm. "In," he ordered.

Barry stumbled forward into the grasp of the other man, who hauled him into the back of the van before Barry could even think about attempting to escape. The door slid shut. The first man walked round the cab of the van and got into the driver's seat.

At some point on the journey, the smaller man in the back placed a hood over Barry's head. Barry had at first felt the panic strike him as his sight was taken, but then his analytical brain began to contemplate why that had happened. Whoever they were didn't want him to see where they were going, or who they were going to see, one of the two, and therefore, that meant he was probably going to live. As long as he didn't do anything stupid, of course.

With that thought implanted in his mind, he relaxed and then began to consider who had taken him. There was no doubt that this wasn't law enforcement. No agency in this country would ever adopt such draconian methods as lifting someone off the street and bagging them. Certainly, not one he had ever heard of. Even the SIS was scared of its own shadow to a certain degree now, following its implication in the rendition cases with the USA. No, this was something else.

That left private enterprise, which meant that he had probably been earmarked as an asset by someone from within the criminal fraternity. That had always been an issue with the scheme he had set up, especially once investigations began into what he had done. He had pulled off a plan that had worked and made him money. Why wouldn't someone want him to replicate that?

As the drive went on, he became increasingly convinced of this being the likely outcome. So, what should he do when the inevitable "offer" was put to him? There was little doubt he would have to take them up on it. The sort of people who lift you off the street in this manner aren't accustomed to being told no, and even less accustomed to accepting it. It was, therefore, a case of making the deal work for him.

It was a massive inconvenience, nothing more. He could carry out the rest of his plan; he'd just have to wait a while. He let out a silent sigh of relief as he thought about never having left a "Dear John," for Jenna. That would have thrown a real spanner into the works had he returned home and needed to explain that one away. It had eaten at him at first. It had almost seemed like an act of moral cowardice, but now he saw it as inspired.

The sound of the van's engine changed as it entered a tunnel, or perhaps a large building. The echo of being inside was unmistakable. Then they had stopped, the engine cutting out. Still, no one spoke to Barry, and he waited patiently. The door slid open. The darkness inside his hood was alleviated a little as some light crept through the material from above him.

Someone reached under his arm and pulled him up. Probably the shorter man, as the grip didn't seem as firm and the movements less forceful. Barry felt himself led across a hard floor, for what seemed to be an eternity, before the grip on him was released. He stood still, waiting.

The hood was removed.

Barry stood in a tall room, surrounded by a circular wall that rose ten feet above him. Powerful lights shone down from the roof, backlighting five shadowy figures that sat at the top of the wall above him. It made it impossible to make out anything, other than their outline. As he strained to look, the power of the lights stung his eyes.

"Who the hell are you lot?" he demanded, attempting to seize control of the situation. As if he had a chance.

"Barry Vernon," began one of the figures that loomed above him. Her voice was stern, clear, crisp, and was amplified through a hidden speaker system, allowing it to reverberate through the chamber. "You have been found guilty by the Vehmic court of money laundering and the proliferation of public funds."

Barry was taken aback. It was true, he had done all those things, but he had made good his escape already. "Guilty? Excuse me, but I was investigated, and they found out I didn't do it. I wasn't found guilty, I was found innocent."

"Perhaps your understanding of the law isn't as it should be," the woman replied plainly. "Mr Vernon, you weren't proven innocent. No case was brought against you because of a lack of evidence."

"Exactly," snapped Barry. "I had no case to answer."

There was a silence, and Barry tried to seize the initiative. "I think I want my lawyer now," he added.

The voice came again. A little irritation now. "Mr Vernon, let me explain a little about where you are."

Barry span around looking at the figures above them. They seemed to be growing larger. Maybe he was getting smaller, but the dynamics were shifting.

"We are not a normal court system," the lecture continued. "We exist to punish those who believe that they can operate with impunity. Those in power, or, like you, who believe they're in power. We apply the law in a common-sense manner, removing the need for jargon, for technicalities, and for lawyers. We punish the guilty, regardless of privilege."

Barry Vernon swallowed. This was not what he expected. The saliva had gone from his mouth, and he croaked as he began to speak, trying desperately to assert himself. "Well, one thing I know, and correct me if I am wrong, but it's innocent till proven guilty in civilised western society."

"Then perhaps you think we're not civilised. A small price to pay," the voice taunted him. "We work on a guilty till proven innocent basis, and rest assured, we've done our homework on you. We invite you to put forward the case in your defence, and if you can refute our allegations, then, of course, we will let you go with our humblest apologies."

"And if I can't?" Barry's mind raced at the potential outcomes. He had been so close.

"Well, we know you cannot, and in your case, Mr Vernon, there are two choices. You can return the money, which we know you have most of squirrelled away where Jenna would never see, and, of course, most importantly, spend it. Or you can spend the next fifteen years in a private prison facility, invisible to the outside world."

Barry's head snapped from side to side, like a rabbit in a trap. His eyes widened and darted around looking for an escape that wasn't there.

"Yeah, and yeah…" he stammered. "About that, what's to stop me telling the papers about all this? I mean, come on, who do you think you bloody are?"

"Oh, you absolutely could, of course. Many, who have stood where you are, have threatened to do exactly that. Some have even tried, but you've never heard of them or us, have you? And given the extent of our network, we're in a far more capable position to damage reputations than you will ever be. After all, who would you even level your accusations at?"

Silence dripped across the chamber. Barry felt it weighing down on him, piling more pressure on his shoulders. Resignation set in. He knew what he had done, and apparently, so did they.

"Now," the voice came from above once more, only now, it seemed to be coming from all around him, closing in on him, strangling him. "If you would like to begin your defence."

* * *

The tall man, Jack Quinn, took the phone from his ear, clicking it off. His partner, the man with the curly hair, Adam Morgan, looked at him quizzically.

"He took the money option, didn't he?"

Jack shrugged. "Paying back every last penny. Probably take him the rest of his life, but he made the right choice."

The two of them turned and began to walk in unison towards a silver saloon car parked at the opposite end of a small parking lot.

"No kidding." Adam shook his head as they went. "Bloke like him in one of our prisons. He'd have a heart attack if someone stole his dinner. Wouldn't have lasted a week."

"I'd give him two," Jack replied bluntly.

"You're generous," laughed Adam. "Anyway, come on, I need to get back. Laura wants me to get the cot out. Fancy giving me a hand?"

"That's a two-man job?" Jack raised an eyebrow at this partner.

"Oh, come on, you've had kids. You know that cot means all sorts of other junk. I'm just figuring this stuff out. I need a veteran head to guide me through."

Adam's not so subtle challenge brought a wry grin and half-hearted chuckle from Jack. "Fine, but you gotta call me sir."

If there was a senior in this partnership, Jack was it. The two of them were equals in rank, but he had been a Regulator longer than Adam by a good couple of years. They were both now seasoned veterans, with over twenty years' work in the organisation between them.

They both came from different backgrounds. Jack was a former Royal Marines Commando, who quickly found that his talents were going to waste. He didn't believe in many of the conflicts at the time, and the idea of "For Queen and Country" was one that lacked any meaning for him. He joined the army to fight for what was right, and sometime in 2004, he realised he wasn't.

Adam had started with a similar mindset but a different route. He had been a good old-fashioned bobby on the beat, who had dreams of changing his patch, of being able to make a real difference. All he had found, however, was a never-ending trickle of ASBO teens, drunken wannabes, and the same old faces who seemed intent on being arrested for the banalest reasons ever.

Promotions into CID had done nothing to sate his appetite. The tipping point had been the death of fourteen refugees inside a refrigerator lorry on the A5. The police had been unable to extradite the criminal gang behind it, and they had continued to send more people into danger whilst living like kings. Adam found himself open to making a difference in a more effective way.

For them both, whatever their route, there was one shared belief that made them a team now. Justice was not something that old men in wigs got to decide, arguing over different interpretations of the law. There was a grey area between guilty and not guilty that people were smart enough to weasel their way around. It needed people like Jack and Adam to bring justice to their door. It needed vigilantes.

In America, vigilante groups had often gone by the way of the gun, and perhaps the most notable of which were The Regulators. They were a group that came about during the War of Regulation in the late 18th Century, as settlers in the new world began to find that corruption was a regular problem so far from central government. In Europe, things were slightly different, albeit with often similar, brutal results. In Germany, the Vehmic courts were established and served to bring to justice those that the law would not. They were outlawed in the early 19th Century.

Not that they ceased to exist. The Vehmic courts were by now too deeply established, and they moved underground. However, now they needed a specialist force to help them investigate and police. The Regulator name was taken, and slowly, potential recruits were groomed and brought in, and the courts now had the power to extend their arms covertly.

The mantra remained the same. They were still focused on stopping those who were corrupt and seeking to abuse the system, those who had beaten, broken, or simply used the system to their own end.

There was always a lengthy list of people who had broken the law and got away with it. Some were career criminals who had engineered themselves into positions where they were almost untouchable. To Adam, they were the ones that gave him the most satisfaction.

Jack took much more pleasure from the people who had abused their power and often stumbled into, but then embraced, their criminality. For him, theirs was a betrayal of the people, and therefore far more unconscionable. A criminal owes you nothing, and you expect nothing in return. When politicians, lawmakers, peacekeepers, and so on became corrupted, it ran the risk of destroying the whole house of cards. It was far more grievous, and despite their original good demeanour, there was never any sympathy from Jack.

Barry Vernon had been one such criminal. A man who didn't know what he was doing until he had done it, but then kept on doing it. Jack felt a bitter pang knowing that tonight Barry would go home and climb into bed with the woman who he had been about to abandon. His wife deserved better, but she also didn't deserve the heartbreak that would come from knowing her marriage was a sham. In time, if she was smart enough, she would figure it out herself, Jack reasoned. It wasn't his job to deal in people's relationships.

The two men climbed silently into the car before driving away.

3

The streetlights flickered, reflected on the water below as David Webster walked along the banks of the Thames, Southwark Bridge straddling the darkened waters behind him. David saw his breath cascade out in front of him and huddled down his tall, lean frame to try and generate a little more warmth inside his smart black trench coat. He felt the cold on his bald head and grimaced, wishing he had brought a hat, even though they made him look like some sort of character from a 1930s mob movie.

Purposefully, he moved along the footpath and towards a bench. On it sat a woman, blonde hair to her shoulders, similar age to him, late forties, her eyes lost across the water to the opposite bank. A slight smile etched on her face gave her a look of calm assuredness.

David sat next to her.

"A little dangerous to be sitting all alone at night by the river?"

The woman, Lowri Graves, didn't turn her head. Her smile remained in place. "It's even more dangerous to be sitting next to me," she cautioned.

"Don't I know that," he retorted.

"I have some work for you." Lowri moved on, barely missing a beat.

"Anything interesting?" David looked at her hopefully.

"Something someone has pulled out of the more official channels, which instantly makes it our problem. You'll find the details in the usual place. Password has changed," she explained casually.

"You love change, Lowri. What is it now?"

"The hotel we stayed in that first weekend."

David raised his eyebrows. "And if I can't remember?"

"You can." Lowri smiled, then stood up and said nothing more. She turned and walked off down the river in the opposite direction to where David had come from. David watched after her for a moment before turning to look across the river. He shook his head, sighed, got up, and walked away in the opposite direction.

* * *

Frank Knight was not a happy man. He knew his night was about to get a lot worse as well.

He had been hoping that tonight might go more smoothly. It was a night shift with no raids planned, no surveillance in operation, which would normally be a chance to catch a few winks until a call came in. If one came in at all to his department.

Frank Knight was an Assistant Director for the National Crime Agency. Working for the NCA was a job he loved, but it was a job that had begun to take a toll on him, mentally and physically. He wasn't the young man he once was, and he was tiring. He knew it, although he would never admit it, not until it put him on his back, anyway. That wasn't his way. It was manifesting itself though. He was getting tense; he was seeking less confrontation.

That's exactly what he had done earlier that night when an order had come in for him to pull the plug on an ongoing operation into a young upstart in South London who had begun to make a name for himself as a small-time, going on big-time, gang leader. Frank had seen a chance originally for one last tilt at stopping someone before they became something worse, and in doing so, now he realised, he'd made a rod for his own back.

He'd been so keen to get this one last big notch on the belt that he'd put his most tenacious, most dedicated officer on the case. Thea Watts. Thea was everything Frank believed he once had been. Only Thea was better. There were stones that were still molten that she would turn over in her quest to get jobs done, and Frank knew she wouldn't let him down. She would lead his team to one last victory, and when it was done, he would get out before the job killed him.

That was all before tonight, however. Within an hour of being in the office, he'd had a call from the assistant to Home Secretary saying that all ongoing investigations into their suspect, Reuben Arrowsmith, were to be suspended immediately. No reason was given, which meant someone else, someone with fewer scruples, was now taking an interest in the case. Probably Five, he mused to himself. Bloody spooks always liked to step on the toes of proper law enforcement.

Frank Knight ten years ago would have been incensed. He would have argued his case, then gone to his boss and fought to get it back. This was his last big hurrah, after all. But this wasn't Frank Knight ten years ago; this was Frank Knight now. He had no interest in being caught up in political wrangling and posturing. The possible detriment that could have to his position now, the pension pot he'd built up—No, tonight it was better to sit this one out and do as he was told.

The moment he had hung up the call, however, he realised the flaw in his plan. The raging storm would soon be unleashed on him, and him alone, for letting this one go so easily. He cringed.

Thea Watts wasn't Frank Knight ten years ago; she was more. Perhaps in that moment, Frank's vanity finally slipped, and he realised that he had never been in Thea's league when it came to tenacity. He would have argued the toss, he would have been angry, but Thea would be apoplectic. There was a criminal out there, one she was working to put away, and someone was about to do something that would probably circumvent the law to stop it happening.

Now he waited for her to find out. He had sent an email to the whole team. It had been a little cowardly, he knew that, but it at least meant that Thea's anger would be contained to his office, where he had remained since he sent it knowing that, soon enough, she would be in.

He wasn't wrong.

"What the hell is this?" The door had barely opened before Thea fired off her first question, words bursting forth with incandescent rage. "We're dropping the case?"

Frank let her enter and stop before he answered, swallowing hard as he did.

"Look, Thea…"

"No, you look, Frank," Thea sliced into his sentence, cutting it dead. "This guy is a shit. He's a nasty, vicious, ambitious shit, and he's going to keep on being a shit until someone locks him up. And that someone, Frank, is going to be me."

Thea's face did not hide the raw emotion. Frank felt a mixture of sorrow for her, fear. There were few people out there who would ever be able to go toe to toe with Thea when she was like this.

"It's done. Everything on Arrowsmith is dropped. That's come from way, *way* above me, so there's no point in arguing the toss." Frank hoped that something in that might placate her, or at least focus her anger somewhere other than him.

"Fine, tell me who I go see to argue the damn toss." Thea's gaze pierced into him, and he felt himself wilt under it.

"It's… it's no one in this building, and it's no one you're going to be able to convince. It's dropped. Trust me, there's nothing you or I could do, or I would have done it. Go home, have a drink, get over it," he offered.

"You know what, Frank, grow a spine, and you'll be a decent cop one day," Thea seethed, spinning around and storming out of the room before the final words had even had a chance to settle in Frank's head. She slammed the door shut, leaving Frank to flounder for a moment in the accompanying silence.

"Thea!" Frank shouted after her, standing from his chair. "Thea! You get back in here, Goddamnit."

She had insulted his professionalism, insulted his past, which was all he had left now. For a moment, he had wanted her to come back in, so he could remind her that he had been a decent cop once. When she didn't, when the door didn't open, and Thea didn't return for his admonishment, Frank sat back down and sighed a little sigh of relief.

4

The morning sky over the North London suburb of Harrow Weald was grey with clouds that slipped across it, dampening the light that somehow found its way down from the early winter's sun.

In the bedroom of a more than modest traditional bay-fronted, detached property, Adam Morgan lay awake staring at the ceiling. He looked across the bed to where his wife, Laura, lay and then down to her belly, in which was their child. A daughter, according to the sonographer who had carried out the scan. In three months' time, he knew this child was going to rip apart everything he thought he had ever come to know about life.

Laura, as if sensing his gaze, opened her eyes, murmuring something he didn't catch that was probably unintelligible anyway.

"Morning, you pair." He bent forward, kissed her forehead. She wiggled across to him, laying her head on his chest.

"Mmm. Morning to you, too," she yawned

"Is she awake yet?" Adam's hand slipped down to Laura's stomach, searching for a movement.

"No, not yet. Having a lie in I think. I'm sure she'll be up and trying to kick her way out before too long," Laura said croakily, her eyes now closed again.

"Chip off the old block," suggested Adam.

"A proper little Action Madam. Next time, I think we should pad my uterus." Laura's hand reached down and joined Adam's.

"Who says there's a next time?" Adam said. "I've got to decide if I can handle the shitty nappies and sleepless nights first before I commit to any more."

"You'll handle them? Can I have that in writing?" A smile spread across Laura's face.

"My share," Adam corrected himself. "I'll handle my share, of course."

"Hmm. We'll see." Laura clearly wasn't convinced of the integrity of Adam's promise. She felt his body move. as he silently mimed, "We'll see." Despite not knowing exactly what he was doing, she knew full well she was the butt of something. She slapped him lightly, playfully across his chest.

"How about you go get some practice in and make me some breakfast?" she proposed.

Adam bent down and kissed her head once more.

"Sounds fair practice to me," he agreed. "Just don't expect me to wipe your arse next."

Laura shook her head, eyes still closed, as Adam eased himself out from under her. She snuggled down into his groove, feeling the warmth of the bed. He slipped on a t-shirt before heading to the door, then turned back.

"You best not be falling asleep again," he cautioned, smiling. Laura said nothing.

* * *

Jack Quinn's morning routine was different. He sat alone in his spartan kitchen, a bowl of cereal in front of him. Perfect silence as he ate. No TV. No wife anymore. No kids running around. Solitude. Just Jack and his thoughts.

As with all good things, it couldn't last forever, and the serenity of his morning routine was snuffed out as his phone shot out its ringtone, alerting him to an incoming video call.

Jack picked up the phone to see a picture of a young boy looking glumly at the screen, thin, dark hair gelled at a severe-looking angle, and the name Calum beneath it. Jack's son.

He answered, and Calum's face in real-time came up. He still didn't look happy, but his hair was messier, and it suited him better, not that Calum could ever see that.

"Son," Jack said firmly, with only the slightest hint of warmth.

"Alright, Dad," Calum replied.

"What's up?" Jack cut to the chase. His son wasn't given to phoning without wanting something. Neither was his daughter, for that matter.

"I just wanted to warn you that you're probably going to get a call from Mum about Kat," Calum reported.

Kat was Jack's daughter. Whereas Calum was a quiet and reserved child, Kat was anything but. She was tempestuous and fiery. His ex-wife had often bemoaned that Kat was too much like her dad, which probably explained why, ultimately, she had divorced him. She couldn't divorce her daughter, however, nor in fairness could she stop loving her, but they continued to butt heads on a near-daily basis. Calum often gave Jack a little warning. While Jack appreciated it, he knew it was as much because Calum felt he might get his sister in further trouble and curry some favour with his dad, which only served to disappoint Jack. He didn't want his son to be a creep. He wanted him to deal with his own issues and not be concerned with what others were doing first. All the same, he would listen intently to what Calum told him this time, as he had all the others.

"What's she done this time?"

"Mum will tell you," Calum said, which Jack knew meant only one thing.

"It's a boy, isn't it?"

"Dad…" Jack was protective over Calum and Kat, but there was a level of protection for Kat that Calum would never have to worry about.

"It's alright," Jack breathed with resignation. "It's almost always a boy."

* * *

It didn't take Jack long to find her. Like most teenagers, Kat was a creature of habit, and therefore far more predictable than the sort of people he was used to finding. She walked the same route to school every morning, picking up the same friends in the same places, and walking at the same casual pace teenagers who don't really want to be going to school adopt.

Jack had got in his car and followed the route, finding her halfway between home and school. She was with her best friend Sasha, but that wasn't all. Five boys danced around, chests puffed out, all aiming to give themselves the best chance of landing the prize. Jack was pretty sure in this case it was Sasha. Calum had said this was a problem about a boy, which meant that territory had already been marked. He quickly locked eyes on one of the five, who was slightly more laid back and had less need to puff his chest out. He knew he was in already; he didn't have to work for it.

Jack hated him instantly. He was the tallest and the broadest of the group, not that he was broad in a man's sense. He would be, in years to come, and he would be a handful, but he still had enough of his youth about him to ensure that, next to Jack, he would look positively lightweight.

He wore a permanent scowl that suggested that, despite the fact he'd snared the interests of Kat, he remained constantly pissed off at a world he didn't, and would never, understand. He exaggerated his walk making it full of attitude, the sort that suggested people give him a wide berth. It would have been more for his protection than he would ever have wanted to admit, but Jack saw right through him.

Jack coasted the car up alongside them. None of them noticed, and he wished that he had taught Kat to always monitor her periphery a little better. It was a talk that could happen on another day. Right now, it was working in his favour, and she was soon going to learn the lesson.

"Kat," Jack called as casually as he could muster from the car, arm draping itself over the edge of the window. He knew it would appear as uncomfortable to his daughter and her friends as it felt to him, but he stuck with it, even forcing a grin.

Kat turned to look at the car, feigning surprise as she did so, even though she knew the moment she heard the voice who it was calling her. She'd half expected it, since the argument with her mum that morning, but she had hoped that her dad would be away with work somewhere. She figured the odds were in her favour on that outcome, but today, she was to be disappointed. She hid it well, smiling back, much more at ease than her dad.

"Hey, Dad, what's up?" she called back breezily, turning but not stepping towards him, feet planted for now.

"Need a lift?" Jack offered.

"I can't, I'm with my friends," she countered.

"That's alright." Jack was quick to try and negotiate back. "I can fit Sasha in." Jack flashed a wave towards Sasha, Kat's friend.

"Hi, Mr Quinn." Sasha returned his wave. Now it was her turn to look awkward.

Jack continued his proposal. "Come on, hop in. You can forewarn me how you've pissed off your mum before I get a call this afternoon and it becomes my fault."

Jack thought that making it a chance for Kat to help him would give her a reason to join him the car, but there was one fatal flaw in his thinking. Jack didn't understand teenage girls.

Kat huffed. "Calum's a little grass. I swear, I'll kill him. Little…" Her words fizzled out as she tried to suppress her anger, and Jack, realising he had lost the initiative, reverted to his default setting of chastising dad.

"Hey, don't even think language like that."

Kat rolled her eyes and let out a half-hearted and completely unbelievable, "Sorry."

As they had spoken, the scowling youth had made his way towards Kat, stopping next to her and slipping his arm around her waist. Jack couldn't help but notice, as he knew he was meant to. It seemed, whoever this kid was, he was keen to make his point.

Jack tried one last attempt. "Come on, save you walking. Hop in."

"She's alright, mate," the boy said, his head tipping back as if flicking the words at Jack and summarily moving him on.

"Isaac," Kat hissed and turned to look at him. Now she looked like her dad, anger etched on her face. Not that Isaac would recognise it, or understand why she was angry, but Jack understood. She was angry because she knew that, with those three words, Isaac had escalated the situation out of both of their controls and set Jack on a single course.

"I know she's alright," Jack said firmly. "Are you intending on staying that way?"

"What you on about?" Isaac asked, turning to Kat. "Who is this wasteman?"

"I can get out now and show you if you'd like." Jack now had forgotten the call or wanting to find out what was going on. He had done his reconnaissance, and he knew the root cause of the problem. His ex-wife was right to be angry. This kid was trouble. For himself maybe, but trouble none the less.

"Dad, for God's sake," Kat moaned, hoping that one of the two of them might listen and back down.

"Oh, that's your dad?" Isaac smiled, thinking he'd seized some sort of upper hand. Turning back to Jack, a grin widened on his face. "Hey, mate, you know your daughter is peng, yeah?"

"No idea." Jack shook his head before opening the door to the car and stepping out in one fluid motion.

Isaac was probably used to being the big fish in the little pond, like many teenage boys blessed with an early growth spurt. His confidence was born from the fact that more often than not, people backed away from him when confronted. Jack was not backing away. In fact, he was heading right towards Isaac, giving Isaac no time to think. Although, if Isaac had taken a week, he probably wouldn't have come up with a way out of this one.

Stepping backwards, caught out by the speed and directness of Jack's strides, Isaac stumbled, landing square on his rump and forced to look even further up at the mountain of a man who now stood over him.

"You see that? You see that?" Isaac looked around to the people watching on, some of them laughing now at him. "This bloke assaulted me. I'll have you done, mate, you hear, done. I'm just a kid."

"I know." Jack finally felt like smiling.

Kat rolled her eyes. "He didn't even touch you, Isaac. Jesus Christ, wasteman yourself."

And with that, Kat was gone, arms folded, striding angrily, leaving Jack and Isaac standing in her wake. Sasha trailed after her, keen to spend the rest of the walk to school discussing the drama.

Jack watched her go, then turned to Isaac. "Thanks for the help," he smiled before he turned, got back into his car, and then started on the journey to work. As he drove away, he cast a glance in the rearview mirror. He saw Isaac, still sat on the floor, berating his friends as they sniggered at him.

5

Valentin Mamedov was intrigued, so he read the email again. It was a rambling diatribe that heralded the arrival of The Dawn of Albion, a new right-wing group that claimed to be made up of "patriot crusaders, ready to bring the law of the sword to those who threaten our way of life."

The seven poorly worded paragraphs it contained were full of vitriol and hyperbole to the point where they were almost too good to be true. They complained in depth about the mainstream media and its bias for an agenda promoting the devaluing of the British way of life. His paper was named, as were the BBC, *Guardian* and so on, as being part of a liberalist elite that sought to force their abominable views on decent folk, which made Mamedov laugh. No one could force a view on people; it wasn't in the interest of any media outfit to do that. What they simply did was take a section of it and enhance the message, shout it out that little bit louder so that people found a voice they accepted and took it on. The idea that he was shaping a narrative was ludicrous. If you didn't like his paper, you didn't buy it, and you didn't share his views. Valentin Mamedov wasn't in the business of changing people's opinions. There was no money in that.

It saved particular attention for politicians and not just those on the other side of the house. It was particularly scathing of the mainstream right-wing politicians, even those right-wing politicians that many would label extreme. They seemed to be a target for the email, which would play out well in the pages of his decidedly left-leaning newspaper, *The Inquirer*. It was almost as if there was no one out there that wasn't a target, like they wanted to upset the world and then some.

In that respect, it was perfect. His readers loved to hear stories of those on the opposite side blaming some mass media conspiracy or venting their spleens in uncontrolled and excessive fashion. They liked the idea of the right-wing side of the political ravine being somehow less intelligent than the left. One of the highest shared articles his paper's website had ever published had been a study that had decreed left-wing voters to be smarter than their right-wing counterparts. It had become an often-thrown insult in the war between the disparate political sides that had been fought out on the battlefields of Facebook and Twitter.

The rest of the email was a direct threat to those they saw as the enemy. Anyone who was in the way of their agenda was an enemy of the people and would be removed. Bloody vengeance would be sought. There were links to videos of right-wing demonstrations, all of which Mamedov knew were nothing to do with this new group. He didn't care. It would all go down well in his comments section, as his loyal readers took incredible joy in picking apart the inconsistencies in the email.

This, of course, would be a story that he would lead with today. Something about the rise of the alt-right and a new dangerous strand of them. He didn't think the threat was that real. There were so many who talked the talk and never walked the walk. The language used suggested someone not capable of getting to the politicians and media that they had targeted, but that wouldn't stop Mamedov pushing the threat as real. It would be given the right angle, the right headline for his website. The more clicks he could draw to his article, the more people he could get signing up online to his membership scheme, the richer he became. That was why he did this. It was why anyone did anything.

Valentin had grown rich on such ideas. As a result of getting rich, he'd grown. He was never a big child, average at best, and that had followed him all through his early years growing up in Moscow. His wasn't a tale of eastern European woe, however. Valentin had come from a rich family that had been well positioned within the Party in the later years of the Soviet Union and, as a young man, he had helped engineer their transition into the new age.

Valentin had been a journalist, a good one as well, in that he wrote what he was told and he wrote it well. In the new Russia, he had seen an opportunity to set up a paper that offered the first real free press in Russia. With the support of two of his father's former Communist Party comrades, the money had been found to do just that. Valentin had been very careful to ensure the paper had an editorial tone that appeased not only the new identity of Russia, but also the old identity, those who still wielded the power. Some of that power you didn't want to cross. Ex-members of the KGB were still pulling the strings. They weren't used to being questioned, and Valentin knew this. He used this to his advantage, and his empire grew. So did he.

Now, over twenty years on from the start of his endeavour, Valentin weighed a good eight-stone more than when he started. With four ex-wives and countless mistresses, it had been no impediment, so there had never been any reason to do anything about it. Living well meant getting fat. Living well was enjoyable. As long as he was rich, it wouldn't hinder him. Even the baldness that crept through his family and made the much firmer physique of his father look more severe hadn't dented his success with the ladies. Money talks, that much he knew.

The bed he lay in was further proof of that. It was a huge, super-king size, lavished in silk sheets, adorned with a

pile of eight plush pillows and inhabited by both Valentin and
Mishka, a girl he had met a couple of weeks previous whilst on
a business trip to Sochi.

Mishka was the sort of girl that Valentin loved. She
was a cliché, in that she was tall, lithe, and blonde, and that
meant a lot to Valentin. When she was on his arm, he fitted
some sort of ideal of what he should be. A powerful man, with
money and success, who attracted just the right sort of woman.
It was, of course, all a transaction. She got what she wanted out
of it, which was to be lavished with gifts and admired by others,
whilst he got what he wanted, the kudos of a beautiful woman
and all the perks that so obviously entailed.

As he looked at her, asleep on the other side of the bed,
Valentin felt a moment of exquisite joy. Here was a beautiful
girl in his bed, and he had an excellent new story just drop into
his hands. He was at the peak of his powers and nothing, no
one, could stop him.

* * *

Adam Morgan looked at the bleak, 1950s office block
that stood in front of him. It was, like so much of the building at

that time, a concrete monstrosity that had weathered into a dour and grimy looking complex of grey towers, interjected with sorry-looking windows coated in a film of whatever London kicked up and threw at them over the years. He often couldn't believe this was the place where he worked, on one hand, but on another, he knew it was perfect. It was so mundane, so innocuous, so weak looking that it was the perfect cover.

He walked up to the entrance, subconsciously pressing the button labelled in a plain font, BONAPARTE INTERNATIONAL. A matter-of-fact but warm female voice seemed to speak at a great speed, yet with perfect clarity. "Good morning, Bonaparte International."

"Morgan," Adam replied.

"Come right up." The intercom line went dead. The hum of the electronic door lock releasing sounded his invitation into the building.

Inside was no grander. A small entry hall led almost immediately to a narrow flight of steps that were coated in a cheap-looking lining, designed to give the impression of a light wood. At the top of the stairs stood a mottled glass door, through which daylight cascaded down to light the stairway. He made his way up, through the door and into another room.

This room was a small six-foot by six-foot square, one door at one side, one door at another, and a small metal pad next to the door he was yet to pass through. In the corner of the ceiling, looking down on him, was a small camera. Next to the door that stood in front of him was a small pad, made up to look like nothing in particular. He reached out and pressed his thumb against it, a green light arising from the bottom of the pad, reading his print with a mechanical whirr of machinery coming from its insides.

Adam knew what was happening on the other side of the door. It was a well-established routine, and he played it out in his head as he waited to be allowed in. The owner of the voice that had guided him this far, Meg Tanner, would be behind her desk, watching a computer screen spew forth his details. It would link his thumbprint with the vast array of information it had stored on him in its database. After a moment, a green CONFIRMED would appear under a small passport style picture on Meg's computer screen, and Meg would release her grip on the pistol that hung on a gimble below her desk. Her hand would move to a button on top of the desk and activate the doors.

Regular as clockwork, Adam heard the sound of electric locks letting go again, followed by the clunk of electromagnetic deadbolts dropping into place, so the door could be opened. Adam, needing no further invitation, stepped into the room.

He smiled as he entered. Meg smiled back at him from behind her desk.

"Morning." Adam nodded his head slightly.

"Morning, Mr Morgan," she replied as he reached yet another door that led to the main floor for the office.

The other side of the door was the main room of the Regulator's London Field Office. It was a windowless room, open plan, that went on for a good sixty feet both in depth and width. The light was dim overall, with smaller points of light illuminating the various workstations around the room, all spotted from the ceiling, with adjustable controls on the desk that allowed the occupier of that spot to set it to their personal preference.

On the left-hand side to anyone walking in through the main entrance were a row of offices behind frosted glass doors, which were used either temporarily for different meetings, or permanently, such as the one used by David Webster, Station Chief. Aside from him and his two direct subordinates, the rest of the team worked in the open plan. From analysts, like Mo Younis, who was currently reviewing a stream of data from what looked to be a Facebook profile, to field operatives, like Jack and Adam.

Mo spotted Adam walking in and stepped up from his desk, beelining over to him. "Hey, man," he said casually.

"Alright, Mo, what gives?"

"Got a feeling your partner is going to be running late."

"Late? What's he done now?"

Mo laughed. "Seems he ran into one of his daughter's would-be beaus and made him look a proper pussy 'ole, to use a phrase that's been thrown at him on WhatsApp all morning."

"You're kidding? You can get into WhatsApp now?" Adam raised an eyebrow. "Don't tell Jack; he'll have you snooping on Kat all day, every day."

"Don't I know it," Mo chuckled before carrying on. "Listen, about Jack, yeah. He's alright, isn't he? I mean, since the divorce, it's not like he's lost his edge, is it?"

Adam pulled a face to show he wasn't particularly comfortable with the question. "He's fine, yeah. He's fine."

"If you say so, boss. I mean, you're the one alongside him if things go to the wall." Mo had never been afraid to voice his views. "It's just his metrics – they're not what they were when we analyse."

Metrics were something that had been brought into the Regulator's performance review three years ago, and Adam still questioned their usefulness. Sure, they could tell you if there was a delay in your reactions, if you were slower than normal, but they couldn't tell you why and they led to speculation, just like Mo was doing now. He was also forced to silently admit that Mo was a good judge of characters. That was his job, after all, to be so immersed in whoever he was profiling that he could tell you what they were thinking. Jack had been doing a lot more thinking recently, which wasn't like him.

As they talked, Jack came in from the parking garage. They both looked over to him and nodded as he approached.

"I trust him," Adam said to Mo quietly. "He's had my back all this time; I've got his too. He just needs to adjust to the new scenario."

Mo nodded his assent silently as Jack sat down at the desk opposite them.

"Morning," Adam said to Jack.

"Been a good one?" Mo asked with a wry smile.

Jack looked at him and shook his head. "Jesus, Mo, you know everything."

"Your name is tagged; your families names are tagged. Anything happens, and someone talks about it, I know," Mo went on.

"That's scary." Jack raised an eyebrow before turning to his partner. "Weekly brief in ten?"

Weekly briefing was something that Webster liked to do with all his teams. Theirs was scheduled first thing on a Monday. It was Webster's chance to get them focused on what they needed to be focusing on, not that they ever worked a normal working week.

"Looking forward to it immeasurably." Adam smiled back.

"Course you are," Jack replied.

* * *

David Webster was in his office well before his allotted shift began. It wasn't uncommon for anyone in the field office to be eager and early, such was the transient nature of the threats they dealt with. For David, it was part of a mantra which stemmed from being prepared and extended beyond just punctuality.

He loved the understated efficiency he had created in the neat workspace. Having helped with the design when the office opened, even now he found his eyes drawn to the desk as he entered. That had been his plan, to leave the walls a bare gunmetal grey, edged with stainless steel, that gave offered no distraction. It made him the focus.

He sat down at the desk, a sleek, black, modern affair, and powered up his workstation before settling down to read the daily intelligence reports with the coffee he brought in with him. The early arrival gave him all the time he needed to be prepared so that when, finally, Jack and Adam arrived for their briefing, he was fully prepped, ready to lead.

"Good morning, gentlemen," he greeted them without standing up. Adam and Jack took a seat each opposite David.

"Sir." Jack nodded.

"Morning, boss." Adam was far breezier, and it drew a questioning glance from Jack, which Adam returned with a nonchalant shrug.

David got straight down to business. "I'm putting you all on a new assignment that's been passed down to us from the Vehm."

"Anything interesting?" Jack asked.

"Could be. Seems that an upcoming South London mobster has suddenly received the backing of a lot of people in powerful places and has hired himself an international mercenary to carry out a job over here. Someone inside the corridors of power has removed said mercenary from the watch list to allow him safe access into the country and pulled an NCA investigation into the gang. We need to know what's happening and who's pulling the strings."

"What's the angle? Why use the gang banger?" Adam asked.

"That's the question we need answering. The guy is Reuben Arrowsmith. He runs a crew out of Peckham. They have pretty much got the entire area eating out of the palm of his hand, working under a mandate of fear. There have been seven murders in the last two years that NCA have tried to pin on him but, so far, no one is talking, despite a number of these crimes being less than discreet."

"Reap what you sew, people," sighed Adam.

"We're not going in there to raise the community spirit," David remarked.

"What are we there for then?" Jack wanted to know.

David turned his computer screen around to show Jack and Adam a picture of Erik. "This is Erik Andryiv," he explained. "Russian paratrooper by his former trade and now a gun for hire. His work is usually political, for whoever is paying the right money. Governments, terrorists, he's not fussy. There's no real reason for Arrowsmith's crew to be hiring someone of his calibre. It marks a real operating change for them, and the financing of this seems to have come from sources both within and outside of our country."

"A real multinational operation then?" Jack went on.

"Still doesn't explain why he's doing the hiring." Adam was still puzzled by that.

"Working theory for me?" David offered. "I think whoever it was sees Arrowsmith as both a good security for their asset and a perfect foil for when it goes off. We need to get to Arrowsmith and find Andryiv. It's imperative that we put this story together. I don't care how you do it, but find out what's happening, stop it, and then we can think about tying up the loose ends."

6

A bored looking barman smoked a cigarette idly behind the bar of the Cock and Fiddle, as nonplussed by the smoking ban as he was by his job and current crop of customers. He sagged against the bar as limply as the ash from his cigarette, his tall frame slumped on bony arms that never came close to filling the white shirt he wore.

It was the middle of a Tuesday afternoon in the Cock and Fiddle. The pub was a sorry sight, as were the motley array of people in there. An uninspiring sixties pub dropped in the middle of a housing estate that had been left behind by progress. The name was some not so subtle attempt to raise a smutty giggle that now fell flat. The whole thing was a relic from a bygone age, outside and in.

Despite the time of day, there were still enough to justify opening. A couple of elderly gentlemen sat hunched over a game of dominoes, waiting for one or the other to accuse their opponent of cheating before getting into a snarly, spittle-infused argument. It would no doubt end with one or the other standing up too quickly and displacing some aging joint. At the other tables were an assortment of should-know-better alcoholics, all set in their daily routines. One man, who had originally only ever drunk orange squash but now devoured five pints before 2 p.m. as he read his paper, sat in a corner on his own. Two others sat working in unison on a joint venture, setting up a selection of rollups that would last them the day, well before the point where their fumbling fingers could no longer be trusted to do the job. A couple involved in a far too obvious affair cosied in the corner. He still in his work shirt, her in her best pearl necklace.

And at the bar, the worst of them, Stephen Owens. Stephen made the barman's skin crawl. He was one of those down on his luck barflies, oblivious to the awkwardness he inspired in others, who littered every pub the land over. He was always in there, even though he rarely had the money to get himself more than a couple of drinks. Yet, despite his many personal flaws, somehow, he always seemed to find someone who would get him a drink, or lend him a tenner till his horse came in.

A few months back, he'd been in the pub almost every day. It had been unbearable. Where the money had come from, the barman didn't know, but he sure would love to find out and thank them for all the joy they'd brought him.

Now Stephen was here, end of the bar, nursing a beer, waiting for some poor mark to come in and engage them in conversation, before the inevitable, "go on then, get me a beer," came up, as if he was doing them a favour.

The door opened, and the barman looked up, seeing an athletic-looking, mixed-race man, cropped dark hair, leather jacket, walking into the pub confidently. He knew him in a flash, and he knew this meant trouble. Reuben Arrowsmith, a man whose name had suddenly been on the lips of all the scumbags and villains that entered his pub. Stephen saw him too and smiled that ever confident, ever hopeful smile.

"Reuben, drink?" Steven asked.

"Guessing you've got some money then, Stephen?" Reuben asked.

"Ah, yeah, I mean, I've got, you know, some." Stephen shifted a little, like a kid who just realised they forgot about a test that day. Now he was the uncomfortable one.

The barman stopped what he was doing. He'd seen people kick off in pubs before, and he wasn't ready to involve himself in this one.

"Define *some*," Reuben shrugged at Stephen, bobbing a little on the spot.

"Well, I'm a little short, man, just a ton init, you know, I mean, yeah." Stephen was trying to find his feet again.

A hundred pounds short, the barman mused to himself, a little relieved. That's not the end of the world.

"I suppose in some ways, given you're three weeks late, I should be happy that you've got this, really, shouldn't I, Stephen?" Reuben pondered.

Stephen shrugged. Smart enough to say nothing it seemed.

"Ton short?" Reuben raised his eyebrows, reiterating the point.

"Yeah, yeah, I mean, I can get you that tomorrow. I can get it you today, stick it on my tab or something…"

The barman began to edge away at the word tab. He knew Stephen's tabs; they were all written up in the office upstairs, some a few years old.

Reuben reached out his left arm, placing a friendly hand on Stephen's shoulder. "Nah, you know what, let it never be said that I'm a tight arse."

"Yeah, no, of course not." Stephen looked relieved.

Bang!

The sound of the shot made everyone look around stunned. Stephen's eyes widened, and he looked down at his chest where a small, but devastatingly deep, hole had been opened. Blood already cascaded down his stomach. He looked up once more at Reuben, now seeing the smoking pistol that protruded out of his right hand. Stephen slumped to his knees.

The couple having the affair bolted up and raced to the door. Before they could get there, a huge blond-haired man with a sawn-off shotgun stood looming in front of them and stopped them in their tracks. He shook his head once, letting them know that the door was out of order.

Reuben leant into Stephen and whispered.

"Let it never be said, though, that I'm a mug. You do not take liberties with me. You hear? You do not."

Reuben put the gun up to Stephen's head, placing the barrel between his eyes, and then fired again. Stephen's dead body dropped to the floor. Reuben turned to the room.

"Does anyone here know who I am?"

Reuben scanned the room, no hands. Then he spied the barman, hand timidly raised, shaking in fear. Reuben walked over towards him slowly, then, quick as viper strike, he brought the butt of the gun and wrapped it around the barman's chin, sending him crashing backwards into a shelf of glasses.

Reuben turned once more to the group.

"Anyone else know who I am?"

No one knew who he was.

"Good." Reuben nodded to the big blond man. "Hold the fort, me and this boy here have to sort the CCTV."

With that, he grabbed the collar of the barman, from whom blood was spilling out of his mouth and the few gaps where teeth once were, and dragged him out of the bar area into the depths of the pub.

* * *

Wiretapping premises like Reuben's was decidedly easier in the modern world than it would have been years ago. In the past, a team of covert operatives would have had to infiltrate the premises and secrete hardware in locations that, whilst offering the optimum in audio and visual coverage, could also remain hidden. All of this would have to be done quickly, silently, and invisibly. Whatever work was needed to do this would also have to leave no residual trace. No mess, no debris, and, to the uninitiated, no clue that anyone was listening in.

Now, however, it was down to one person, Polly Swenson, a 28-year-old computer science graduate from a small town in East Sussex, who sat at a computer terminal, miles away from the site, completely safe from being spotted as she set up the bugs.

Reuben, like most criminals, was extremely cautious when it came to his base of operations. People wanted to take from him and take him out on a pretty regular basis. He needed to do all he could to minimise the risks. There were cameras covering every angle of the site, all of which had cost him a small fortune and fed back to a central terminal in his office. There, the footage was recorded onto an SSD and stored until it might be needed.

Originally, the system had been wired, with the cameras on top of poles. Reuben had invested in a wireless system after a rival gang cut the wires and then helped themselves to his safe. For the purposes of Reuben's enterprise, that was perfectly acceptable. Until now.

Reuben was not a foolish man. He had seen the reports of security cameras and baby monitors being hacked; he knew that there was a security flaw in them and he changed his passwords methodically. Always randomly generated, always memorised for one week only, always changed the following week and always only known to himself. It was as foolproof as he could make it.

It couldn't stand up to Polly Swenson, however. Using an algorithm she bought on the dark web that purported to have been designed by Israeli intelligence, tweaked to suit her own purposes, Polly very quickly managed to not only tap into the system but also ensure that every time Reuben entered the password on his terminal, it would automatically update hers.

That had given them a complete overview of the site and everyone who entered or left. It didn't, however, provide sound. That was provided by using a variation on what had become known as the Speake(a)r method, whereby a computers headphone could be used, through remotely manipulating the sound card, to receive audio, as well as play it back. A subroutine had been uploaded to the playback unit, and as long as it wasn't being used to view footage, if the headphones were plugged into the jack, sound would be monitored. Even if the system was turned off, or in standby, audio would still be picked up, as the subroutine would deceive the user into thinking the machine had powered down when, in truth, it was simply in hibernation.

It took Polly Swenson all of an hour to put everything in place and for The Regulators to have eyes and ears across everything Reuben did.

7

Heathrow airport was alive with people, in stark contrast to the airport Erik left in Tunisia three days before. The world's sixth busiest airport. Nearly seventy times busier than Enfidha-Hammamet and more than three times as busy as Dusseldorf, where he had spent three days laying over. There, he continued his preparation with the help of some brothers-in-arms who had holed up in the city, awaiting the orders that would send them to work. He didn't know what their jobs would be. Somewhere else, on something else. Knowing anything else could be dangerous.

It was there he had watched the news from Tunisia and seen the shell of a burning Audi Estate on the highway near to the town of Sousse. He had felt nothing as he contemplated the end of the last man to have seen him before he left for Germany. Probably the only person who knew he had flown there, other than himself. He was merely a loose end that had needed tying off, someone whose confidence could not be trusted. Therefore, he had to die, even though he had been instrumental in getting them this far. Mehdi's God, no doubt, would take that into consideration, against all his other crimes. Erik doubted that would be enough to save Mehdi from eternal damnation, but then, he was sure he wouldn't be spared himself either.

Erik was no soldier of faith, that much was true. He didn't even know what his faith was anymore. He had dabbled with the Orthodox Christianity that prevailed over much of Russia but had been intrigued to learn more about the other cultures he had come across the more of the world he travelled, especially as so many of the people who Erik fought were fighting for one god or another. In the end, he had come to a simple conclusion. There was probably only one god, and man had made up his own interpretations to better suit his position. So, he was freed from church, freed from the organisation of it all, allowed to pursue his path in the knowledge one day he would have questions to answer.

Being a mercenary meant he had little honour when it came to the jobs he took. The jobs with a political motive, he enjoyed them the most, because people's motives were so open. It gave him an insight into the kind of people he was working for. Most of them thought they were changing the world for the better, missing the point as they perpetuated the cycle of misery by taking up arms. He accepted the irony of his own role in that, but he had a skill, and he needed paying.

He was clean and efficient in his actions for the most part. He was a professional, and for that reason, he knew he was always going to be one step ahead of those he faced. For him, it was a process, not an emotion. That was what separated him from his clients. That was what kept him alive.

The team this end worked hard over the previous months to ensure his passage from the airport would be a smooth one, but as he entered the carpark, he still had no idea where he was going after. All he knew was that the final directions would be delivered to him there. It was a system that ensured, should he have been intercepted before making it to London, the security of the mission would remain intact. Certainly, long enough for it to be successful.

The car was in the slot where he'd been told. A grey Focus, the most popular car in the UK. Perfect for someone who wanted to blend in. He got in, took his ceramic Glock pistol from inside his sleek leather travel bag, and dumped the bag behind the passenger seat. He was never a man who travelled with much. A tactical decision to allow him to be less lumbered at all times. That was why the locker that Mehdi Chedli had arranged for him at Heathrow had been so crucial. He needed to ensure he had some form of protection the moment he arrived, and he had been very happy to find the contents of the locker just as it should be. A credit to the

72

Tunisian secret service, he mused. He reached into the glove compartment where he anticipated finding the tablet. It was empty.

Erik sat back in the seat, taking a moment to process the information. Something was wrong here. The people behind this didn't make mistakes.

A sharp knock on the window snapped his train of thought. He turned quickly, reaching for the gun as he did so, to see a mixed-race man at his window. Reuben Arrowsmith, the contact he was meant to make later. He peered in through the window, face nearly pushed up against it, smiling, holding a tablet. The tablet that Erik wanted.

Erik nodded, and Reuben took his lead, opening the car door and taking a seat. Erik kept the pistol trained on him, and Reuben raised an eyebrow.

"Hey, come on now. There's no need for that. We're all friends here."

Erik scowled back. "Is this how you treat all of your friends?"

"I'm just here to ensure that you get to where you've got to be. Appreciate the local knowledge."

"I'm a professional. You and the people you work for, or with, hired me because of that fact. I get to where I need to be."

"I get the feeling here, mate, that we're not on the same page, so let's start again." Reuben offered a hand out to Erik. "Welcome…to…the…U.K…"

"Are you taking the piss?"

"No, I'm paying you. You want professional courtesy, we can have that. Perhaps one day we'll even be friends."

Erik stared at Reuben for a moment, completely still. "Perhaps."

"There, much better. Nice flight?" Reuben wasn't flustered.

"I've had better."

"Well, how about we get you back to the safe house, set you up with anything you want. You've got some time to, you know, kill. Want some girls, boys, booze, drugs? You name it, we'll get it."

Erik's stare didn't change, no hint of warmth, no hint of a change of mood.

"We'll look at your girls."

"Good man," Reuben beamed. "On the house, too, of course."

"Of course. And the targets. I need to see all you have on them. Movements, security, family, everything."

"You'll have it, my friend, you'll have it all. Come on, let's get back, show you my manor, son."

Erik took one last look at Reuben. He had to admit, the confidence of the man was admirable. He was a charismatic and driven young man, that much was for sure. It would almost be a shame to kill him when the time came. He started the car and, following Reuben's instructions, headed towards the South London safe house.

* * *

The area outside of the secondary school heaved with relieved teenagers making their eager escape home. Dashing for cars, buses, bikes, or simply scarpering on foot, free from their lessons for one more day. Calum Quinn had his head down, neck tucked into his shoulders, silently making his way home, praying to avoid anyone and everyone. He was not to be successful.

"Oi, you little scrote!" his sister's voice cut across the babbling chatter that enveloped him.

He looked up, at first failing to pick her out in the crowd, but then he quickly noted a parting in the pupils as she beelined towards him, her rant continuing.

"What are you doing grassing me up to Dad?"

Calum sighed and turned on the spot, trying to walk away from her, but she was too set on her course, too immersed in her anger to give up.

She reached out, grabbing his shoulder and spinning him around. "Well?" Kat demanded.

"What? You'd rather he found out off of Mum?"

"You ain't got no right!"

"Sorry. I just wanted to warn Dad."

"Yeah, well, he came along and embarrassed me in front of Isaac."

"Who's Isaac?" Calum shrugged, looking over Kat's shoulder to where a group of tall boys stared angrily at him.

"It doesn't matter, alright, just keep the fuck out of my life, yeah?" And with that, she shoved him, as an exclamation, before turning around and storming back through the curious crowd, who had stopped to watch the siblings squabble.

Calum shook his head to himself and turned again, head down, walking away.

* * *

Thea had spent the day under a cloud, storming through all her possible plays to try and get the case reopened. First, she had phoned everyone in the chain of command that she knew, putting forward her argument for the case against Reuben Arrowsmith to remain ongoing. Without exception, they had told her it was outside of their hands, and when she had reached the top of the chain, as far as she could take it, she became angrier.

She'd spent the rest of the day driving around the patch where Reuben and his gang operated, hoping to find him. Even just someone in his gang would do. She had no real plan of what would happen after that, but she was sure she'd come up with something, find some way to open the case again, but it was never put to the test. No one was about. In fact, the streets had been remarkably quiet. Not even a solitary associate on show.

It was dark by the time Thea made it back to her flat. She opened the door and stepped inside, switching on the hallway light, chasing away the darkness from the hallway. It was a small, modern flat. A thin corridor connected the main entrance of the property to the bathroom, bedroom, and then finally the open-plan living area, which looked out over the nearby Park Hill Park in Croydon. She walked through to the living area and froze.

Sitting on her couch, calmly, was a woman with blonde hair down to her shoulders, somewhere in her forties. She looked comfortable as if she had made herself at home. A glass of water, half drank, sat on the coffee table in front of her, neatly placed on a coaster.

Thea stared at her, making a quick decision on whether to launch into an attack or wait and ask some questions. Her fingers clenched around a set of keys in her pocket, working the shaft of one forward between her middle and ring finger, ready to strike if needed.

The woman spoke. "Good evening, Thea. I'm Lowri Graves"

Thea cut her off quickly. "I don't really care who you are. I don't even care why you're here."

Lowri shrugged, a smile on her face, attempting to placate Thea, to reassure her. "Well, I feel…"

"You feel you should tell me anyway. Yeah. Great. I'm getting a drink. Want one?"

Thea turned her back on Lowri. This woman wasn't an immediate threat in a physical sense, she was sure of that. Maybe further down the line, but she'd have to cross that bridge in due course. For now, she wanted to set the pace.

"No, thank you," came the response from Lowri, who added, as if by way of an apology, "this won't take long."

"Great."

"I want to ask you for your help. I'm here to ask you to keep your head down."

"Because you want Reuben Arrowsmith, and you pulled the plug on my operation?"

"That wasn't us who pulled the plug. We would be delighted if you got Reuben, but someone else has other ideas. If you're side-lined, we need to be able to get to him."

Thea took a bottle of red wine, removed the lid, and let it pour out into a glass before turning and asking the burning question. "Are you going to bring him to court?"

"No. Probably not, but we'll stop him all the same."

Thea took a big gulp of wine, swallowed, then spoke. "Then thanks for popping by. You know where the door is."

"I understand you're angry. This was your case."

"Is. It *is* my case."

"You're not going to get a conviction, Thea. Not for the good stuff anyway. Maybe you'll get him on a small mistake, driving offence or something pointless; but the murders, those that are done and those that are to come, they're never going to stick. He's far too clever. There's a ceiling level for justice, and he's exceeded it."

"Says you. I know that I can crack this."

"Your life is in danger if you do. They will see you as a threat as well, and they will get to you," Lowri stated matter-of-factly.

"Do I look like someone who scares easily?"

"No, I guess not, but what would it take for you to feel you were wrong? How many bodies do you want to rack up by his hands, before you admit that us going after him was the better way? Because, believe me, if we do it your way, he will kill again, and then those bodies are at your feet as well."

Thea's face wrinkled in disbelief and disgust. "Don't lay this on me; he's the one doing it."

"And we're the ones stopping it."

"Circumventing the law is never the best way to do anything. It makes you and them the same."

"Do you think the families of any of his victims agree? Would you be happy to have that conversation with them?" Lowri pressed on with her argument, hoping to get something to resonate. She'd seen plenty of people like Thea, who had let professional pride get in the way of ending a case.

"That's such an ill-informed point of view. It's bloody populist crap. We have rules and laws so that we become the better people. If not, how can we govern? No, it's not the way we do things in civilised society, and if I see any of your people, God knows who you even are – I don't care, to be fair – but if I see them, I'm taking them down."

Lowri smiled, taking a moment. She cocked her head slightly to one side, then stood, offering a hand to Thea. "Well, think about it for a while, please."

Thea looked at the hand, then back at Lowri, making no effort to take it, simply raising her eyebrows in question.

"I was like you once," Lowri went on. "I understand where you're coming from, but eventually, something will happen, and you'll realise that there is no other way sometimes. It's not the sort of decision you can make lightly, but we can't fight these people by our rules, because they find it too easy to subvert them. Sometimes, we need to take them on at their own game. Otherwise, we will always lose."

Lowri paused, then walked calmly out of the room, Thea's gaze following her firmly all the way out of sight, waiting till she heard the door open and close. When she did, she took another big gulp of wine.

8

The salmon sizzled when it slipped back down into the pan as Reuben switched his attention to the mixture of mange tout and asparagus stir fry that was to accompany it. He smiled with genuine joy as the meal came together. Cooking was one of the things that he took real constructive pleasure out of. It was his release and something he knew he was damn good at. Nisha told him so all the time, and he knew that she was about to tell him the same shortly when he presented this to her.

Some days, he wondered if he would have had a decent life as a chef. He didn't believe for one second that his being a chef would have changed the world for other people. After all, there were a whole host of other bad people waiting for him to stumble and take his place; and were he not there, one of them would rule this manor. That's just the way it was. But maybe there would have been something for him in the quiet life. An honest living, bringing people a little bit of joy.

The money soon made him forget such low-key ambitions. No, cooking was something he enjoyed and shared only with those he truly loved. Nisha Hart, waiting patiently in the other room, was top of that list.

Nisha had been his girl now for two years. She was everything he ever wanted in a woman. Her hair was a wildfire of frizzy light brown waves, tinted with blonde highlights, accentuating the edges and making it seem alive, almost glowing in his eyes. Her eyes were dark, sultry, and captivating. The first time he'd looked into them, he knew that he was going to fall under her spell, and no amount of machismo posturing was going to allow him to pretend otherwise. She was a good few inches shorter, and that appealed to his need to be the man of the relationship, at least in other people's eyes. Away from any judgemental glances, however, there was no doubting that Nisha could hold her own, and Reuben would be the first to admit, with more than a hint of pride, that Nisha was his equal. Sometimes, she was even more. She was everything.

He put the vegetables into a bowl, arranging them carefully, moving them around with the tips of his fingers, briefly holding on till the heat began to tingle, and then, when he was satisfied, he turned his attention to the salmon, taking each of the two fillets in turn and putting them on their own individual plate next to the bowls of vegetables. He stepped back, admiring his handiwork briefly and then picked both plates up and made his way through the flat to the dining room.

The flat itself was a very modest, unassuming affair. It didn't immediately conjure up the images of a successful gangland boss, but this was all part of the plan. Reuben was a planner, and his plans now meant that keeping a low profile gave him the plausible deniability he desired. His money was invested in numerous sources. Some legal, some fronts, and some downright illegal, but all of them were turning a healthy profit, which he, in turn, invested into more schemes. He drew enough on which to live comfortably, but he left enough on which to soon retire lavishly. For all the talk of millennials being doomed to a long working life and not being afforded the opportunity to break the chains of work, Reuben was living proof that, with a plan, albeit one that broke many laws, you could beat the rat race.

The dining room and living room were separated; that's what Reuben wanted. He had dreams of being a family man someday, and he was determined in the narrative of being the sort of unit who didn't all sit around in front of the TV and eat dinner together. He wanted his kids to be better than him. That wasn't to say he didn't think he was good. He knew he was, but he wanted them to be able to do it without having to break the rules. Reuben would run the gauntlet of jail and death for as long as he had to, but there was no way he wanted that life for his kids, if and when they came along.

The dining room was a small, compact room that linked the hallway and kitchen to the living room. It had a small cabinet in one corner and a square table for four in the centre. Two places were set, at one of which Nisha sat. She beamed on seeing him.

"Oh, God, yeah, this definitely looks worth the wait. You've outdone yourself again, babe," she enthused.

"Well, you know, them years in college weren't wasted, girl. I can get me some fine ingredients and that, I mean, look at this, cordon bleu, à la Arrowsmith." He set the plates down before taking his seat.

"You're a provider, I know that." Nisha breathed in the smell of the food before taking up her cutlery and beginning to tuck in.

"Nish, you know it, I look after what's mine."

"Speaking of which," Nisha got down to business. "You know that skank from NCA was around at the laundrette again?"

Reuben raised an eyebrow. He did not know, but then, he trusted Nisha to be his eyes and ears more than any of those directly in his gang. For him and her to be fair, this was their gang.

He shrugged. "Looks like desperate times call for desperate measures."

"Girl's clutching. She asked me how I live with myself knowing what you do and where all our money comes from. I told her I live just fine."

Reuben laughed at Nisha's brass. "That's why you're my girl, no turning your head."

"No turning yours either, boy, we straight up."

"Straight up."

Nisha paused for a moment, maybe just to chew a piece of food, maybe just building to the moment, Reuben couldn't be sure.

"She showed me a picture."

"Let me guess, someone's face with a hole in it?"

Nisha screwed her face up. "Yeah, I mean, like, what, she thinks 'cause I'm a girl, that'll make me fold up? Plain sexist."

"Would have helped if I didn't tell you everything first, wouldn't it?"

"She might have done a bit better."

"That's why you're my partner. My equal."

"Till the end."

"The bitter end."

* * *

Her blood was boiling even more now. The anger she had felt when Frank betrayed her had put her near the point of no return, but now the interloper in her house had left Thea beyond redemption.

She stepped out of the lift into a smart-looking corridor in an executive block of flats. She wondered briefly how much the rooms here cost. They were certainly more expensive than hers and certainly far too expensive for two regular working girls to be living opposite. But these weren't two regular working girls. They were an integral link in the conveyor belt for finances for Reuben Arrowsmith's business model.

Both, technically, were registered as masseuses. Both also worked from home, running a host of online fronts, including moving money through virtual games systems, like World of Warcraft. Thea knew all this, she knew it very well, she just could never prove it, try as she might.

She paced her way to the first door, on her left. It was the penthouse that belonged to Ursula Nisevic. Ursula had come over to the UK eight years ago from Croatia and had quickly found her get-rich-quick scheme as an escort. She had worked under so many different pimps and madams over her time here that she couldn't name them all now. Eventually, she found her way onto the radar of Reuben three years back.

The story on the street was that Reuben hadn't been interested in her skills in the bedroom. He'd been quietly impressed with her business-like mind when he'd first spoken to her as she entertained his table at the club she danced at. He'd told her to come see him some time to talk about business opportunities. Ursula passed that off as just another punter wanting to arrange a private meeting without having to give up an extra cut to the club owner, and she was more than happy to oblige. She had been very surprised when, turning up at Reuben's office, she was greeted by both him and Nisha. This was, indeed, just a business opportunity.

Ursula was smart, however. She'd seen a chance to do something that rewarded her for something other than what was between her legs. She now had a whole list of imaginary clients, all of whom paid her cash, all of which she declared. Thea had seen the books. Had her massage job been real, she might as well have installed a revolving door on the apartment, but it wasn't. Ursula hadn't had so much as a single client since she joined Reuben. It was all a front.

Her loyalty had been repaid, Thea admitted as she pounded on the sturdy door to the penthouse. "Ursula," she bellowed, hoping to make herself heard through the thick door. "I'm here to make a deal."

There was a moment of silence before a slightly muffled, yet obviously annoyed, eastern European voice shot back from inside the flat.

"Is it a deal where you fuck off and leave me alone?" Ursula's accent turned the "u" in fuck into an "o," which only served to add to the peeved tint to her voice.

"Entertaining? No, course you're not. You can't entertain clients who don't exist." Thea mocked.

"I'm at the door now," Ursula barked back, louder this time, so probably truthfully. "The only person I entertain right now is you. You going to pay me, or you going to fuck off?"

"One-time deal. New identity, new job, I can even get you a house, immunity, a British passport."

"A job? A house? A passport? Are you kidding me? I got a job. I got more money than you, believe it or not. And a house? What do I need a house for when I got this place? My God, girl, are you thick? And a passport? Come on, I can get a new passport every week, whatever country I want. You got nothing better to say, then you can fuck off." Ursula accentuated the last two words, really making sure that Thea got the point.

Thea stood for a moment. She knew Ursula was right, it had been a vain hope, but one she had clung to on the way here. Maybe Ursula had a bad day, maybe she had fallen out with Reuben and this was just the moment that she had been looking for to get out. That wasn't going to be the case today, so she turned her attention to the door opposite.

She pounded on the next door, waiting to hear from Marianne. Marianne was Hungarian. She was slightly newer than Ursula, but no less formidable and no less deeply rooted into Reuben's network. Thea knew there was little chance she would be turned either, but right now, doing something was better than doing nothing.

"Marianne, come on. It's Thea Watts, NCA," she called out.

"She's gone out, you fucking idiot." Thea turned back towards Ursula's door, where Ursula now stood, cigarette in hand, dressing gown on, her blonde hair tied up.

Thea sighed; "Jesus Christ, Ursula. This is your life?"

"I love it. It's better than yours." Ursula dropped ash nonchalantly into a small plastic pot plant outside her door.

Thea slammed her fist slowly onto the door, looking at Ursula, who eyed her with bored indifference, before making her way slowly away, only slightly crestfallen and barely hiding it.

* * *

Inside the penthouse, Erik watched through the security monitor that was wired just inside the door. He saw the female NCA officer, as she'd identified herself, walk away and saw the girl from the apartment opposite eyeball her all the way back to the lift. He lowered his Glock, letting the tension slip away, before moving back into the darkened apartment that for now, at least, he called home.

* * *

Adam and Jack wasted little time as they began to piece together the workings of Reuben's team and what had transpired up to this point. Already, in a corner office of the Regulator's building, a flowchart of pictures and evidence had been assembled on a wall. Centre stage was a photo of Reuben and, just below him, was a photo of Erik with a big red "?" between the two. On Reuben's left was a picture of Nisha and, on his right, a picture of Kevin Fisher, the big blond-haired man who had been with him in the pub. A tangled string pieces connected different snippets of information pulled from the NCA resources and appropriated from Thea's investigation. So far, they were still drawing a big blank in terms of motivation, and both knew this was going to be a key part of the jigsaw as they moved forward.

"Someone has to be bankrolling him," Adam concluded after a prolonged period of silent staring at the smorgasbord of the information in front of him.

"Probably," Jack agreed.

"Who?"

"No idea."

Adam sighed. "I think we're going to need a more hands-on approach here."

"I'm glad you think so," Jack smiled wryly at his partner. He wasn't used to the procedures Adam liked to use.

He didn't doubt they worked, but he was very much an "actions speak louder than anything" man. "When do we start?"

"Tonight? We should pick up someone on the edges of the group, someone who might not be missed too much, should it come to that, but who might give us an in."

"Someone who works under Fisher then. He's involved in everything that's going on here. Although to be fair…"

"You'd simply lift Fisher."

"Why not? If Reuben knows what's happening, it's fair to say he will too."

"We tip our hat too soon. Anyone targeting someone that high up in the organisation is going to set alarm bells ringing. Better someone disappears who won't be missed too much. Someone who they know could be in trouble."

"Any favourites?"

"How about this guy?" Adam stepped forward and pointed his finger right between the eyes of a stocky man's mugshot with tightly curled dark hair and a dour expression on his face. "Yannick Burtin."

"What's his story."

"Far as anyone could make out, he's a Frenchman who came over here in the late nineties, worked freelance for different gangs across the city, so not really known for his loyalty. Has a few debts as well, so it would be feasible for someone like him to be a target for someone he owes to."

"Any idea where we might find him?"

"No, but I know a man who will."

* * *

Mo was working hard at his terminal as Jack and Adam approached. He never looked up but gave a slight smile of recognition as they stopped at his desk.

"I think you guys are going to love me," he beamed.

"More than we already do?" Adam asked.

"Oh yeah. I think I've got a lead on how Erik Andryiv managed to get into the country unimpeded."

"That's lovable." Adam nodded.

"Totally. Flowers for you in the morning," Jack added. "What have you found?"

"Well, it looks like someone hacked into the UK Border Agency database and removed all the flags on his profile, allowing him to simply slip through. They tagged a couple of other people on his flight to ensure that no one really had time to give him a second glance."

"Can you find out who?" Adam asked.

"Yeah. You see, it looks like whoever did it was a hacker. Not some government spook at GCHQ, but a nerd in his basement. Now, that could have been for a couple of reasons; maybe this is a private job, and someone just needed to hire a guy for the gig, or perhaps someone thought that doing it off the books meant that they had an extra layer of plausible deniability."

"So how do we find out who did it and, more importantly, who ordered it?"

"That's the geekier bit. Now, a fair chunk of the people who do stuff like this, they're pretty pissed off at the world. Chip on the shoulder and all that. I mean, why else would you learn how to hack government systems if you were a happy, law-abiding citizen?"

"Other than you, Mo?" Adam joked.

"Other than me, and if they're anything like me, they're also quite smug when they pull something like this off. They love for their community to be able to see their efforts, so they leave tags."

"Tags?"

"Yeah, little bits of random code, totally benign, but just there so that if someone else stumbles through, trying to do something similar, they'll see that and realise that such and such had been there first."

"Can you find the tag?"

"Already did. What you need next is someone who knows whose tag it is. Problem is, these people are super secretive. They only share that sort of thing with people they trust, their own community, and you've got to be absolutely shit-hot at what you do to be a part of that."

Adam laughed and placed his hand on Mo's shoulder. "Want me to blow the smoke up your arse now?"

"Would you?" Mo sniggered.

"Who is it?" Jack asked

"Kristian Glover. He's a 24-year-old dropout. Lives off the grid, he thinks. At number 146 Valley Road, Streatham."

"Brilliant work, Mo," Adam enthused. "Think we need to split our forces. One of us take the nerd and the other head off and pick up Burtin."

"I'll take the Frenchman," Jack said. "I think the subtler approach with our computer friend is what's needed."

"You're probably right, although I don't want you to think I'm ducking a fight. I mean, I can take the Frenchman."

"I know you can, big guy, I know you can," Jack mocked.

9

Yannick Burtin hated England. Genuinely hated it. The people were dull; the buildings were bland and uninspired. The weather, even though it wasn't that far removed from the weather he'd been used to in Paris, was still somehow more miserable. The thing he hated most was his situation. He had gone from being a man with lofty ambitions and a plan to have it all to this shell of a man, working for some two-bit crook in darkest South London. He owed money to people who should be lacing up his boots, all because the cards hadn't fallen right in a few games of poker.

The cards hadn't fallen right his whole life, he was forced to admit on reflection. He had grown up in the banlieues of Paris, the bastard child of an Algerian immigrant mother and a French policeman father who had turned his back on them both as soon as she announced her pregnancy. Maybe that's why he hated the police. It was sure a sturdy enough excuse, he reasoned.

Life there had been hard, but he had found a way to cope then. Boosting cars had been his forte back in the day, and many a night he spent whizzing around Clichy-sous-Bais with a string of Gendarmes in pursuit. Sometimes they got away;

sometimes they got caught. Getting caught meant taking a beating from the officers, who were far more interested in meting out street justice than they were in taking people through the system. He wondered at times if any of the officers who struck him had been his father. He'd never even seen a picture of the man. He never wanted to.

Yannick had made his way to London more by chance than design. He came over on the Eurostar, just to see what it was like. Why wouldn't he? It was, after all, right on his doorstep. He had been seduced, to a little degree, by the idea of the British gangster. A stylish, cool and yet ruthless myth that, even now, he had never managed to find replicated in real life. The Krays, they may well have been a real thing back in the sixties, but this current batch of criminality made statements in different ways. Fear was the only form of respect that mattered, and while that had been an indispensable part of what happened with gangsters back in days gone by, the romance that followed their story had never really been replicated in this modern day and age.

He found little odds and sods of work over the years, but he found that his reputation needed building again. By the time he came to London, car crime had moved on, due to improvements in technology. Yannick had to reinvent himself as something new. He was angry at this, and he channelled that anger into making himself something of a hard man.

It worked to a degree, but Yannick was still bitter that it only played to one of his strengths. He was unappreciated. His quick French wit was slowed by the coarseness of the English language, and he was seen as one dimensional. He couldn't go home, however. That would mean admitting failure and starting over once more. He knew he didn't have the time for that now.

No, he took his fate with a typically Gallic shrug of the shoulders and got on with it. It wasn't the life he wanted, but it was the life he had, and he would continue with it until the right opportunity presented itself. It was bound to, sooner or later.

He heard the knock at the door of his modest flat and rose from the armchair he had been sitting in, reading Le Monde, one of his best links to his homeland. He put it down and sauntered to the door, checking the security feed of his camera as he approached. He saw a big guy with brown hair standing at his doorway. He could have been German, not English, Yannick thought, as he pressed the intercom.

"Hello?" he asked.

"Yannick Burtin?" the stranger asked.

"Oui." The inflexion at the end had the effect of turning it almost into a question.

"My name is Jack Quinn. I'm here to make you an offer."

"What sort of offer?"

"The chance to do the right thing, maybe even go home."

"I am home."

"Sure, you are."

The stranger looked up at the camera, saying nothing more. Yannick sighed and realised that he wasn't going away. Not without some mild interest, he began to unbolt the door, wondering what the stranger might have to offer. He didn't get the chance to finish that thought. The moment the door came ajar, Jack charged, dropping his shoulder. The corner of the door struck Yannick flat across the nose, putting him down on his back, out cold.

When he came too, Yannick's head was spinning. He went to raise his hands to his face, but he couldn't. He was tied, or more accurately, taped, to his armchair. Arms, legs, torso, even his head, all held in place. Opposite him was the cropped-haired stranger who had called himself Jack Quinn.

"What the hell do you want?" Yannick growled.

"Answers."

"Fuck you."

"Wrong answer." Jack stepped forward and landed a firm blow right in the solar plexus of Yannick, drawing the air out of him. Yannick naturally went to double up, but couldn't, the tape holding him in place.

"Let's try again."

Yannick glowered at Jack.

"I want to know what you know about the man Reuben has hired. The professional."

"What professional?"

Another punch, this time, just off centre and lower, into the soft tissue. It was harder. Yannick wondered how much Jack held back.

"The one that came into the airport the other day. What's your boss planning?"

"He doesn't tell me what he's planning."

No punch.

"I believe you."

"So, I'm useless to you."

"No. Not at all. You might not know what he's planning, but you know how I can find out. Where is this man?"

"I don't know."

Another punch. Again, harder.

"Guess."

"There are a number of places he could be at. I would think he's in one of the girl's flats. That's where people usually hide out."

"Which one."

"Any. It doesn't matter. Rueben has so many, he can just move them around. If they find you sniffing about, he will be moved. Stupid fucking Englishman."

Another punch, this time to the jaw.

"I told you the truth, man!"

"I know, but I didn't care for the editorial. Now, I'm going to get to the crux here. I can let you live, that's well within my mandate. It's what I'd like to do. I can also end you, or I can take you from here with one phone call and put you in a hellhole for the rest of your days. What I'd really like to do, however, is send you back to France, where you will live out the rest of your days as a law-abiding citizen with a normal job, working the doors or something. Shouldn't be hard for a guy of your physique to do that. Most importantly, you'll be free of all that debt you owe. No more looking over your shoulder, but that's all contingent on your doing as I say from here on in."

"Which is?"

"I need you to find out what house he's in. I'm going to let you go, and you're going to do all you can to find out, and then you're going to tell me. Do that, I'll get you a ticket back; I'll give you an SIA licence for door work, which will help you back home. I'll even give you a fucking reference. You can go home, Yannick, and you'll be alive. But you need to find that house. Not try – find. What do you say?"

Yannick looked at Jack and thought.

* * *

"It's bloody cold," Frank grumbled to himself as he walked around Watermeads Nature Reserve. He was on his third lap of the area now, following a route that took him past the local football stadium, then looped around on itself as it was intercepted by the River Wandle. He had never been here before, but he felt like he was becoming a little bit of an expert on the area now.

His strange choice of walking route wasn't accidental. It had come as an order from someone who wouldn't give their name but had used a valid security services code when they had contacted him. Probably a good way to weed out any surveillance, he reasoned. Still, he hoped sooner rather than later, whoever was meeting him would be satisfied. At least his pedometer score today would be high.

A man approached in the opposite direction. It was dark; there were no streetlights here. The main illumination came from the floodlights that rose above the stadium, but by this point, Frank was on the opposite side of the nature reserve. They only offered a scattered and faint glow, and he struggled to pick out any features on the man at first. He could tell he was tall and athletic, certainly someone who could have been a part of British intelligence.

The man approached; Frank saw the man more clearly. Dark short hair, a slight five o'clock shadow, thick nose and a stern brow. It had to be his man.

They walked past each other. The man didn't even look at Frank. More walking then.

"Don't stare next time." A coarse whisper came in Frank's ear. He hadn't even heard the man come up behind him. He looked, it was the same guy. Frank felt the man put his hand on his back, pushing him forwards. "Keep walking."

Frank did as he was told. He felt his heart race. What was it they wanted with him?

"Give me your phone." Frank didn't feel any power to say no, and he passed it to the man.

"What…" he began, but he was quickly cut off.

"Just listen," the man said. "You can call me Bowen. Has your phone got a QR reader?"

"Yes," Frank stuttered. He had always felt in control of situations the whole way through his professional career. Not now.

"Good." Bowen pressed his thumb on the phone's fingerprint scanner, unlocking it.

"How did you?"

"Just listen." Frank heard the irritation in the voice. Bowen pulled out another phone which had a QR code displayed on it. He used the scanner on Frank's app, then passed the phone back. "This will install a covert communications device on your phone. You work for me now. I don't have to tell you that this goes no further."

"Of course, but what do you need me to do?"

"We'll be in touch."

The man quickly turned and walked the other way, head down. Frank stopped, watching him disappear around a corner, enveloped by the branches.

* * *

"He's going to do as we want," Jack said over the phone to Adam.

"You think we can trust him?"

"No. But I think we can scare him. Have you got to that kid yet?"

"Just outside now," Adam answered. "Mo's running a sweep on his property; reckons he's probably got all sorts of surveillance. If we can, I want to catch him unawares. Get into his head a little bit."

"Makes sense, I'll leave you to it. Got some finishing off to do here." Jack was gone, and Adam hung up his phone.

He was sitting in his car, a smart Mercedes estate with tinted windows, looking at Kristian Glover's house. It was a two-storey semi, probably built sometime after the turn of the 20th century. The houses on that side of the road were all very similar, whilst on the other, a block of modern apartments lined the way. Adam wondered what might have been there originally.

The street was fairly busy with cars, vans, and even a bus route trundling up and down it, despite it not being one of the main routes through the area. It all gave Adam even more reason to be cautious on his entry. A spooked kid running down the street raising hell wouldn't go unnoticed here, so he wanted to make sure his entrance was as covert as possible.

His phone rang, and he switched it to video mode. Mo appeared on the other end.

"You're the bearer of good news, right?" Adam quipped.

"Always," Mo replied. "I've managed to get into his system, and I've looped his cameras. He has a number of motion sensors on the stairs, but they're all currently updating their software, as if by magic." He winked, acknowledging his own role in the magic.

"Great, and he's definitely in there?"

"I'm looking at him now. He's completely engrossed in his computer, second floor, back bedroom. Blinds are down as well; it's nice and moody. God, he's so cliché."

"Suits me fine, thanks, Mo. I'll speak to you after."

Adam clicked off the phone. He checked the traffic. All clear. He got out of the car and crossed the road, making his way quickly but confidently up to the door of Kristian's house.

The door to the house had an old Yale lock. Adam took a small device from his pocket, not much larger than a regular key, but with a larger handle, cylindrical and about the width of an AA battery. He placed the thin end of the device in the lock, pressing a small button on the top. A light hum came from inside the device. Then with a faint click, the door swung open. Adam walked in.

Inside the house it was silent. The downstairs was completely empty, save for a small TV and a little chair hidden from outside view behind a net curtain. There was a dining room behind the living room in which on one side was a small table that certainly hadn't hosted many dinner parties. No one was about, and Adam began to climb the staircase that stood right in front of him.

He crept slowly, looking for the motion sensors Mo spoke of, but not seeing them. He guessed if Kristian had had any sense, they would have been screwed under the stairs themselves, moving with the floorboards, out of sight, but still equally as effective. He hoped Mo's updates were still in progress.

He made it to the top of the stairs. In front of him was a bathroom that looked in desperate need of a good clean. Off to the left were three doors. Two to the front and one to the rear. It was the rear one he wanted. From inside the darkened room, he could make out the unmistakable glow of a computer monitor, tinting the walls in a ghostly blue light. He stepped up to the door and walked in, bold as brass, as if he owned the place.

Kristian didn't see him at first, headphones on, eyes locked firmly on the screen, but something must have triggered a sixth sense in him. Some primordial survival instinct that worked still, even in the meekest of humans. In fact, probably more so in their case, given the survival of their ancestors to this point. He looked up quickly, shocked. He tried to get up and get away, but the headphones caught him. He raised a hand feverishly to pull them away as his legs flailed around frantically. He tumbled to the floor from his chair, and Adam stepped over him.

"Hello, Mr Glover. Huge fan of your work" He offered a hand to the stricken form on the floor. He was a tall, thin man with blond hair that was a little longer than it needed to be, but he'd still made the effort of combing and styling it. He wore a grey zip-through hoody over a white t-shirt and bootcut blue jeans. He looked up agog at Adam, not knowing what to say.

"Don't worry," Adam went on. "I'm not here to hurt you, I'm here to help you. Save you, if you like."

"Wh… Who are you?" Kristian stammered.

"I'm Adam Morgan, and I'm here to talk to you about a little job you did on the UKBA system last week."

"I don't know what you mean," Kristian said defiantly.

"Yes, you do. Look." Adam reached down, wrapping his hand around Kristian's wrist and hauling him up to his feet. "We can mess about with this, but the truth is, if I want you to talk, we both know I'm going to be able to do that. I don't want to go down that route. I know you're just a good kid who's been mixed up in something that's about to go way beyond what you expected. I assure you, I'm on your side."

"You're on my side? What, are you some sort of spy or something, from Mi5? Ain't my side." Kristian almost sneered.

"No, I'm just a private citizen, concerned about recent events. You can check me out, I'm sure you will. I don't work for our government, but I think you have been."

"What?"

"Or at least someone inside the government. You were told to remove someone's flags on a flight into the UK, and you did. You left your tag in there, that's how we know."

"How do you know what my tag is?"

"I know a lot, Kristian. What I don't know is who got you to do it."

There was a pause.

"If I tell you, they'll kill me."

"They probably said that, but you know what, that's just something they say for dramatic effect in TV shows to build tension. Think about it logically. Once you've told me, there's no benefit in killing you. In fact, killing you would only serve to slow them down from their new primary focus, which would be killing me. They're far more likely to want to kill you when they find out you left a trail, which, if I found out who you are, they're going to find out sooner or later. Your only chance now is to tell me who they are, so I can get to them first and save your bloody life, kid."

Kristian stood silently, running through Adam's logic in his head, checking it to make sure it made sense.

"How do I know you won't kill me?"

"I told you, I don't want to. I don't need to. I'm not a bad person, I want to stop the bad people. The person whose flags you cleared, did you do any research on him?"

"Yeah, of course, I mean… I had a look. I was curious."

"So, you know that he's a pretty bad bastard. You think the side you want to be on wants him in our country?"

"I told you, I don't give a shit about this country. I don't give a shit about anyone. I wouldn't care if the whole fucking place burned."

"Yeah, course, big words." Adam looked a little disappointed. "But we both know you wouldn't ever back them up. Behind that screen, fine, it's easy to plot and fantasise about doing this, that, and the other. Bringing about the end of the civilisation, whatever. But if I were to ask you to take a gun and put a couple of bullets into some innocent passer-by, you wouldn't. It's not easy killing someone, you know?"

"That's not… I'm not…" Kristian stammered.

"That's right, you're not, but the hombre you let in, he is. He is pure evil. A man who kills for money, no questions asked. He's here, and he's going to hurt someone. And then, when that's done, they're going to shut up shop and tie up any loose ends. Hell, they should have done it sooner, because here I am talking to you. Right now, your only chance is tell me what you know, and then I can hide you away until the dust settles and we bring these people down. If you don't, I won't help you, and they will kill you."

Kristian paused for a moment, weighing up all his options. Then the gates opened, and he poured forth his story.

"I don't know a lot about him, just that his name was Bowen. He told me he was a part of a faction that worked its way inside the government and wanted to bring the whole thing down."

Adam watched as the kid slumped to his knees shaking as he sobbed.

"He might not have been lying," he said as way of comfort.

10

"Bowen has been in touch," Reuben told Fisher.

The two of them sat alone in the office room of Reuben's yard. It was on the second floor of a portable cabin overlooking a car yard that doubled as one of the many legitimate fronts of Reuben's empire. Cars came here to be scrapped, fixed, modified, whatever. There was always a cash payment, and the money noted in the books was always more than the customer paid. A perfect agreement for both parties.

"What did he say?" Fisher asked as he sat opposite his boss, sipping on a glass of Grey Goose. The two of them retired upstairs while the others got into a card game at the suggestion of Yannick. That came as no shock. The only surprise had been that, for once, he was winning. Perhaps the Frenchman's luck had changed.

"He wanted to check to make sure our boy was all settled in. He thinks the first hit should go down by the end of this week. All the prep their end is done, we just got to keep him safe 'til then."

"Shouldn't be a problem, if he does as he's told."

"He's pro ain't he; he's not going to mess about."

"No, of course."

Reuben shifted forward in his seat, sensing the pensiveness in his second-in-command. He trusted Kevin Fisher, the two of them had been through a lot together. The development of his whole empire had come with "Fish," as Reuben referred to him, backing him to the hilt.

"What's up, man? What's bugging you?"

Fisher squirmed in his seat. "Nothing, I mean... I don't know. I guess don't like doing work for other people."

"You and me both," nodded Reuben.

"Can I ask you? Do you trust him?"

"I'm not going to say I do. Them at the top of this as well, all of them. Never trust someone you ain't ever looked in the eyes."

"So, what are we doing about it?"

Reuben sat back, pleased he'd read Fish right and pleased that his man had his senses still finely attuned to what was going on. The right back-up could save your life time and time again.

"We need to wait a little. They're not going to show their hand until the endgame's in sight. When they do, we pull the plug first. I mean, come on, we know we're being played first, so we need some precautions put in place. Some leverage. They came to us thinking they could use us Fish, but they can't. First sign of them deviating from the plan, don't matter what it is. We end it. We end them. You don't even need to ask me; you just pull that trigger. Trust."

"I will, but you know they're going to come at us hard if we do that," Fisher urged.

"Then we're going to have to come harder. Don't sweat it unduly. I get that you got our best interests at heart here, that you want us to stay alive, man."

Reuben took a silent slug of Grey Goose and looked at Fisher. If he hadn't have known him better, he might have accused him of being scared, but Reuben knew there was a world of difference between scared and prepared.

* * *

Calum survived another day at school. That was, at least, how he saw it. He'd even managed to negotiate the end of school crush quickly, using a pre-planned route he'd been working on over his time there, designed to miss classes that were always released early and skirt nearer to those teachers who took a perverse pleasure in keeping their kids in just a little bit longer. It was all there to keep interaction to a minimum, to get him out of there as quick as possible and to get him on the walk home away from the throngs. Away from trouble.

Now he was away, out in the quiet suburban streets, dodging the main roads, where there was always the chance of groups of people, or kids hanging outside of shops who might want to shout something. It didn't matter what they said, half the time he never heard it. It mattered they said it.

He was hunkered down inside his coat, which he always wore regardless of the temperature. It made him look a little bit bigger than he actually was. It also helped him hide and pass through unnoticed, back to the sanctuary of his home.

It wasn't easy being this way when your dad was like Jack. Calum Quinn was sure his dad must see him as some sort of a failure. Why wouldn't he? How could he love this little weasel of a kid, who couldn't be further from what Jack was? He hadn't inherited his dad's strength or courage, although it never occurred to Calum that strength was something which could be earned through hard work and courage was simply pretending not to be scared. No, it was easier for him to believe he was a disappointment. Years of hiding behind his dad, letting him be his shield, had left him unprepared for the independence that had been thrust on him, seemingly out of the blue, when he reached secondary school. He'd had to fend for himself and he couldn't.

At home, it hadn't been any easier. Kat embraced taking charge of her life completely. Calum didn't know why. She had always been even more protected by her dad and, if anything, she should have felt even safer in his shadow. Again, the teenager in him couldn't relate that she might have wanted to break free and be her own person and not what her parents wanted, even if her own person was more like her dad than she would ever care to admit. He just simply couldn't see it from her view or anyone else's. All Calum knew right now was how he felt and most of the time that was wretched.

The last twenty-four hours hadn't been any easier. His sister was angry at him, and he sort of understood why, if he was honest. That guilt made him feel even worse than her anger, as did his steadfast refusal to apologise for what he had done. Calum simply couldn't bring himself to admit he was wrong. It wasn't in his nature.

The blissful feeling of escape that enveloped Calum was suddenly ripped away from him as he walked past a figure that he didn't see until too late. An arm grabbed the scruff of his collar on the big coat he hid in and spun him around, the ripping of the seam serving to punctuate the terror that he suddenly felt.

There was no time to think, no time to get away. Calum raised his hands in a pitiful palm-up gesture to block whatever was coming, but he scrunched his eyes tightly shut, meaning his outstretched palms were little more than minor obstacles that his attacker overcame quickly. Clubbing blows came from his right hand in quick succession to the side of Calum's head. As he held onto the coat, Calum tried to spin away, sending both of them into a slow, shuffling, spin as the blows rained down.

Finally, Calum's legs gave out, and he stumbled to the ground. It wasn't over, and a hard kick struck him in the gut. He gasped, his body tensing, eyes wide open in pain and terror, just in time to see the boot once more come down, this time on his head. The blow was softened by the hood of the coat that was still up and stopped the full force getting through. It gave Calum the chance to get his hands around his head and hope for the best.

Eyes closed, he yelped in pain as each kick came in. One, two, three… and then he lost count, blind to what was happening, just needing it to be over, praying for it to stop.

Then it was.

There was silence, save for heavy breathing and Calum's sobs.

One last hard kick to the ribs, and then Calum heard footsteps sprint away from him. It was over. The attacker was gone.

Calum lay on the floor, his head spun, his torso hurt in so many places. He cried and waited for someone to come and find him.

* * *

The office was quieter by the time Jack got back. The day shift was over, and whilst there were always people working, the night shift was decidedly smaller than the day. Those involved in active investigations were usually there all hours like Jack was, but anyone who was working on something less than immediate was encouraged to keep normal hours. It kept them fresh for when, as it always did, the proverbial hit the fan.

Mo was still there, of course. He was pretty much an ever-present, only going home to sleep. Mo often said that all he needed was a desk, a computer, and somewhere to go and pray. The office offered all of that; therefore, he didn't see the need to head home and just to do the same thing he did at work. He lived alone, Jack knew that much. Beyond that, Jack's knowledge of Mo was limited. He'd never asked, and Mo had never told.

Jack felt the phone ringing in his pocket and pulled it out. He glanced at the caller ID. Isobel. His ex-wife. He put the phone back in his pocket, careful not to send it straight to voicemail and risk angering her. Better for her to think he was busy and unable to get to the phone than being deliberately evasive.

Mo intently looked at his computer screen as Jack made his way to the desk. "Working hard?" Jack asked.

"You bet. I'm delving into the mind of Kristian Glover, and I've got to say, it's fascinating."

"Adam's patched you into his machine?"

"And Kristian's coughed all the relevant keys. It's a real treasure chest, man. You wouldn't believe the shit this kid's been up to."

"Or understand it," Jack admitted, looking at a screen that was full of, as far as he could tell, nonsense and gibberish.

Numbers, letters, symbols, snippets of phrases, nothing that made any sense to him.

Mo laughed, eyes still on the screen. "No, maybe not. This is my world."

"Have you been able to get anything useful yet?"

"I'm still piecing it all together. What I've got here is a record of everything this kid has done. I need to try and tie that into anything else that might have happened. Chances are that he wasn't the only bird in the nest and there were a few others doing jobs for them."

"That could be an issue," Jack looked on.

"How so?"

"Well, say you've got a load of people who you had do work for you, and you find out one of them has turned grass on you. What do you do?"

Mo looked up at Jack. "I stop the rest of them having that chance."

"Yeah. Exactly."

Jack pulled his phone out of his pocket again and went to dial Adam. Before he could, Isobel rang again. This time, he had to send her to voicemail, he had to prioritise. Her call cleared; he got on with the job of dialling Adam.

"What's up?" Adam asked.

"You think your boy there might run off to the people he worked for?"

Adam's voice became hushed. "Might do, I don't know."

"You've got to make sure he doesn't. Mo's working on the theory that there might be other kids out there doing the same. If they realise we've got to one of them, they might get spooked and shut up shop on any other leads we might find."

Jack heard Adam inhale, mulling over the possibilities.

"Yeah, and we can't lift him either. His disappearance would definitely be picked up," Adam thought out loud. "Want me to housesit him?"

"I've got a better idea. He needs to still be online, or people are going to twig, and there's no way me, you, or any other field ops are going to know what the hell he's doing on that thing. No, we need someone who can sit in with him who speaks the same language as this guy."

Mo looked up at Jack, eyebrows raised. Jack nodded back at him. Mo shrugged, a little smile on his face.

"I'll leave you to sort that out," Adam said. "I think I can guess who you're thinking of."

"I'll get him to you." Jack hung up the call and turned to Mo. "You good with this?"

"Do I get a gun?"

"Probably."

"Then I'm good with this."

"Good man, Mo."

Jack stepped away from the desk and took his phone out. Isobel had left him a voicemail. He listened to it, then quickly made his way out of the office.

11

Calum lay in the hospital bed, asleep, exhausted from the attack. Isobel sat on a chair next to him, her baby in pain in front of her. Her eyes were red from crying when she heard the news.

Jack saw her through the door to the room before he saw Calum. He saw the worry on her face, saw the way her normally immaculate auburn hair had been left half-hanging out of a lazy bun in her rush and how she was dressed only in her tracksuit bottoms and a loose sweater. He knew he loved her still. Seeing her like this made him stop outside the room for a moment, scared to go in and to confront the pain he knew he was going to come face to face with.

Swallowing his pride, he opened the door.

Isobel saw him, turning at the sound of the door opening, and gasped, a small sob of desperation coming out of her. Jack knew she was angry at him for not returning her calls right away, for sending her to voicemail. So angry that, when she did leave the message, she signed off with "*Be there if you care for your son.*" Isobel knew full well that Jack cared for his kids more than anything in the world. That wasn't why their relationship had failed. It had failed because she felt he cared

128

more about his job than he did her and she knew she deserved better. That had been made abundantly clear to Jack.

Now though, Jack could tell she just needed someone, anyone, to unburden to. To let out the pain that she'd had building inside herself since she first saw Calum's battered and broken body. She stood up and flung herself forward into Jack's arms, and he caught her, holding her close, himself not sure what to make of the moment.

Jack's eyes crossed to the bed where he saw his son. He saw the injuries, and he felt a flash of rage. Someone had done this, and that someone would pay. He made that solemn vow instantly and silently, then he closed his eyes and breathed in his ex-wife.

They stood silently together, her in his arms, for what seemed like an eternity.

* * *

For three hours, Kristian's head rang with the questions that Adam asked. What more did he know about Bowen? Had he been asked to carry out any other tasks? Was he aware of any other people working for Bowen? How was he to contact him? Kristian, who up until tonight had felt in control of the situation, suddenly found that he knew nothing about what was going on. He had been approached with such confidence by the man who had called himself Bowen that he felt no fear in dealing with him.

Kristian recounted the story to Adam as best he could. Bowen found him on the dark web, in a secure chat server where people discussed, but rarely ever enacted, their dystopian dreams about bringing down the entire system. Kristian had been very vocal about his hatred for "the man," and the way the world was. It was a broken system, and, to his mind, everyone knew it. There were just precious few who felt they could do anything. An armed insurrection would never work, that much was clear. So, it was left to people like Kristian, he had claimed, to carry out guerrilla cyber-attacks. And so, the meek shall inherit the Earth.

It was this ambition that Bowen apparently found impressive, and he had asked Kristian if he could do a couple of simple tasks for him. He wanted to get someone into the country, someone with what the government would call a radical agenda, simply because it didn't fit with their myopic and ordered world view on things. He wasn't the terrorist they made him out to be; he was just a man who spoke out against the corruption of the west, which was something that Kristian was more than happy to believe and get on board with. So, he did as they asked. Nothing more, nothing less.

Now, here he was, going over and over the same story, telling the man who had broken into his house exactly that. It didn't seem to matter how many times he said it, how many times he had to repeat the same small parts of information, this guy simply didn't seem to believe him. He kept going over the same old things, breaking it all down and making Kristian relive the whole thing over and over again. How could he be in this much trouble? All he had done was let someone into the country. No one person could be that big of a deal, could they?

Finally, the questioning stopped. Kristian sat on his chair, by his desk, where he always sat. Morgan, the man who had come into his house, squatted on the far side of the room looking at him intently. Kristian wanted to know why he was staring, but he simply couldn't find the courage to ask. He was as scared now as he had ever been.

"You know…" Adam stood up and walked towards Kristian, who felt his whole body tense up. "I don't think you're a bad a kid."

Kristian didn't feel any more relaxed. His wide-eyed gaze walked around the room with Adam as he slowly paced out a semi-circle around the cowering hacker.

"I think you're a good guy really. I don't agree with your politics, but hey, most of the people out there, most of the time, don't agree with each other on politics. It's really not a reason to fall out, is it?"

Kristian said nothing. Adam went on.

"Nah, we need to cooperate more. I mean, I can see where you're coming from. People get screwed over, people get pushed out, people like you. There isn't a way back in either, so what are you meant to do but, you know, burn this mother fucker down?"

Adam looked at Kristian, who felt Adan's eyes prying into him, trying to read beneath the surface. There was nothing other than apprehension and fear.

"So, if that's true, and I want to believe it is, that you had no choice about doing this, that the world left you no choice, why won't you just tell me what else you did? I mean, you know we're going to find out."

"He told me not to talk to the police," Kristian sniffed.

"I told you," Adam bent down and looked Kristian right in the eye. "I'm not the police. I'm a concerned private citizen. I'm here to stop what you've done hurting lots of innocent people. You can help me or hinder me, but I will stop it. If you help, your life is going to be a lot better after this day."

"Help how?" Kristian moaned.

"Tell me something. Anything. Get me to this Bowen, because we don't know who he is, and if we don't know who he is, we're going to struggle to stop him."

"And you can protect me if I do?"

"Better than I can if you don't."

Kristian looked at his computer. "I can leave a message on the chat server to let him know I need to ask him something."

"Do it." Adam motioned to the computer and Kristian sprang forward. Then Adam stopped him. "Wait, what do you have to do?"

"I've got a list of codewords that I can add to my name on the chat server, and if he sees one of them, he gets in contact."

"You got that list?"

"Got it? No, I mean, it's in my head."

Adam nodded, and Kristian felt relief. He was being trusted. "Fine, do it, but anyone comes through that door trying to shoot me, then I shoot them, then I shoot you."

Kristian said nothing but turned and began loading up a page. Adam's phone rang. He answered.

"I'll be right down to let you in," he said quickly, eyes always on Kristian, before hanging up. "Is it done?"

"Yeah, I just have to wait now, I guess. I never had to contact him before.

"Okay, good. Come on, we need to go downstairs. I got a friend you need to meet. He's a grade 'A' geek like you. You'll love him."

* * *

In a darkened office, somewhere deep inside the Palace of Westminster, a smartly dressed man somewhere in his late thirties, athletic-looking for a civil servant, with a strong jawline, broad shoulders and thick, powerful arms, pushed back from a laptop and pulled a phone out of his desk. It may have been considered odd, given that on the desk already was a landline phone and two mobiles, both his personal phone and his work one, all the calls to and from which were logged by GCHQ. Just in case.

He scrolled through the third phone and selected an app. It had no icon, no name, just the greyed-out logo that sits on an iPhone screen when an app hasn't been fully downloaded. He pressed it. A keypad appeared, much like the normal keypad on a phone. He dialled a number and waited for it to connect. The app was a former pet project of the NSA, a VoIP based system that was used for encrypting calls between existing mobiles. It had been bastardised by the people he worked for, made more robust and deviated somewhat from the original NSA setup, just in case they ever wanted to listen in and had a backdoor. You could never be too careful.

It took a little longer to connect the call than normal. One of the things you had to put up with using this sort of tech. Soon enough, he heard the sound of a ringtone on the other end. Not like the domestic calls one might normally expect. More like the sound an international call makes. Then there was an answer.

"Hello?"

"Glover, hit the panic button," the man said into the phone.

"Understood," the voice at the other end said.

The line went dead. The man at the desk put the phone back into the drawer and went back to the computer screen and whatever work he had been doing before.

12

"Man, you've got to tell me who you are!" Kristian's face had lit up somewhat once Mo had explained to him how he had tracked him down. "I mean, you know, I won't tell anyone, but I need to know, you know?"

"You know I can't do that buddy," Mo smiled back. He liked Kristian. The kid was caught up in something he didn't understand. He'd made a bad choice, a really bad choice, but his true character was coming out now, and Mo hoped that Adam could see that. "But, I swear, I only use these super powers for good."

Kristian laughed. Even Adam felt a little more at ease, and he was hopeful that Mo's intervention and his charming disposition might allow Kristian to start to trust them. After all, one of the good guys, in Kristian's eyes, was on their side.

Mo kept him talking, kept him moving along at a nice pace and stopped him from dwelling on anything. Adam didn't understand most of what was being said, the two of them may as well have been talking Esperanto. It was an alien world to him, but he knew Mo was making progress just by the body language of the two men. Satisfied, he decided to patrol the perimeter, checking through the windows of the house, then taking a walk to the end of the garden.

Once Kristian had sent the request, Adam quickly put in a call to get a drone out and in place above the house, to give them first warning should anyone approach. The problem was that the house was on a residential street, so should it be simply a one-man approach and not a tactical assault. Any warning they would get might be too little, too late. Still, he felt a lot better with an infrared eye in the sky above them.

He walked to the front window and looked down the street. It was quiet. Night was now fully set in, and the street lights in the area left little swathes of luminescence that disturbed the cover of anyone looking to make their approach. There was also still a steady, if not regular, flow of traffic as people buzzed to and from home, work, or wherever their place of leisure was to be for the evening.

At the back of the house, looking out from the window in the room where he had first come across Kristian, it was a different proposition. The garden was overgrown and lined with unkempt trees. Clearly, Kristian wasn't an outdoorsy type. It was perfect cover for anyone who wanted to get as close to the house as possible without being spotted. Still, with the IR camera on the drone hovering overhead, Adam still felt a degree of security.

"Morgan, this is Raf," a voice buzzed in his ear from the hidden comms unit he'd put in to keep him plugged into everything that was going on.

"What's happening?"

"I've got one body making their way towards you, out the front on your side of the street. He just crossed the road about fifty yards down. Male, about six feet."

"Copy." Adam's voice remained impassive, and he walked calmly towards the front of the house.

Looking out of the front bedroom window, he saw a figure approaching and pushed himself up against the wall by the window to try and make himself as flat and as small an object to spot as he could. The man was six-foot-tall with cropped hair, but just as Adam was beginning to worry, he turned left and into the next-door house.

"Target is heading up adjoining drive," Raf commented in his ear. "Looks like he's got a key, he's gone straight in. Must be a neighbour."

"Thanks, Raf, excellent job. Keep watching," Adam said, relaxing from his temporary sentry post.

He turned and made his way downstairs again. He'd barely reached the foot of the stairs before Raf was back again.

"Car pulled up, about thirty yards south. Can't see how many occupants. No one moving yet."

Adam was nearer the front door now, so he stepped to it and opened it a crack. He could see south down the road to where a grey Audi had parked up, just in the shady spot between two lamps. Textbook. There were at least two people in there, of that Adam was certain.

They sat in the car. Not moving. Waiting for something clearly, but what? Adam scanned up and down the road but saw nothing.

"Is there any other traffic inbound?" he asked Raf calmly, making sure not to raise his voice, in case he panicked the others.

"Roads are clear, backup should be with you in just a couple of minutes," Raf said, as Adam cursed the distance.

Still, there was no movement in the car.

"Hell are they waiting for?" Adam could feel his body tensing, he flexed his fingers, tried to regulate his breathing to keep his heart rate down, ready for when they came.

The street was now eerily quiet and suddenly seemed devoid of life. He moved away from the window and towards the back bedroom, talking to Raf as he went. "Can you tell me if they move out of the car?"

"Not a problem," Raf said.

Adam walked into the back bedroom where the two others were working. He made his way to the back, took a casual look outside, and then stood calmly, breezily against the back wall as Mo and Kristian continued to discuss something that was far beyond his realm. He wasn't listening either; he was waiting, poised, ready for the attack. He was hoping Mo would notice something amiss, but he was far too engrossed in his primary job.

"I'm just going downstairs, quick sweep," Adam announced. Mo looked at him and saw as Adam nodded his head slightly. He knew it would probably scare Mo a little, that was natural, but he wanted him to be on his guard. He wanted to give him the best chance he could if they got past him.

He quickly descended the stairs, reaching the front door and pressing up against the frame. He peered out of the peephole.

"Are they still there?"

"No one's moved," Raf reported.

They had to be waiting for backup of their own. Two people wasn't enough to storm a room when you didn't know how many occupants were in there, which played into Adam's hands. His own backup was getting closer and closer. They were going to be alright.

Then there was another noise.

Something wooden moved, knocking against something else. It was a brief sound, a scrape, then a hollow, soft thud. Over in an instant. Like someone moving a panel. Like someone lifting a loft hatch.

Adam looked.

The access to the attic was at the top of the stairs, right in front of the door that led to the room Mo and Kristian were working in. It was a simple wood panel hatch. Now it was gone. In its place was a man, hanging upside down, his head and upper torso exposed. Clutching a shotgun.

The barrels were already pointing into the room. Adam shouted.

"Get down!"

The blast came almost instantly. Straight into the room.

Adam raced up the stairs. He fired a burst of shots, hoping to hone in on the sound of the shotgun blast. None of them found their mark, but the volley was a good enough effort to force the attacker to take cover.

From the roof space above them came the sound of feet thumping quickly and heavily on the floorboards as the assailant headed back to the next-door house where he had come from, as Adam pieced together how the attack had come together. The car had been a distraction. The man who had entered next door had made his way through the roof space. This eventuality had been planned for.

Adam was at the top of the stairs now. He looked in the room. The table was on its side, Kristian's computers were dumped on the floor. He could see Mo taking cover against the near wall. Kristian hadn't been so lucky. The shot had found his chest, ripping it open, leaving it a bloody mess. It would have killed him near enough instantly.

"You alright?" he called to Mo.

"I think so."

"Good. Stay there," Adam barked. "Raf, where's that backup? I've got one hostile coming out of next door."

He looked up the stairs towards the attic hatch, which was now shut again. Quickly, he raced downstairs out into the street, his gun trained on the front door of the next-door house. It was shut.

"Backup is seconds away. Hostile heading out the back," Raf's running commentary told Adam that he was already losing ground. Wrong door, toss of a coin. He had expected him to bolt and go for the car outside. Another diversion.

"Shit," Adam turned and was quickly back inside, crashing through the house, out of the back door and into the overgrown garden.

"Which way did he go?" he called into the comm unit.

"Straight down the garden, over the fence…now," Raf replied.

"Get backup round there now!" Adam tried to sprint through the garden, but the wildness which he had earlier seen as his advantage now played against him. It slowed him to a crawl as he fumbled in the dark through brambles and thistles. "Son of a bitch!" he cursed.

He made it finally to the end of the garden and hopped the fence, racing through the next garden, which was much more tidily manicured, and out into the street.

"Where did he go?" he called into his comms.

"He's just reached the end of the street. I think he's got a car coming to pick him up."

"Track that car, find out where it goes and who gets out." Adam shook his head and then let off a frustrated shout, before turning and jogging back the way he came.

13

It had been a long day, Frank thought. He'd spent most of it looking for Thea. He needed to try and bring her back in line. That had been made abundantly clear to him, and now he had his orders.

She'd made him wait. Most of her day had been spent out of the office. She didn't say what she was working on, but Frank knew. That worried him.

It was late by the time she got back. The earlier buzz and activity of the office had been replaced by a much more sedate feel. There were still a few others working late into the night, but compared to earlier, it was almost empty as Frank approached Thea at her desk.

"Evening," he said, a conciliatory tone in his voice. "What you working on?"

"You don't want to know really," Thea said breezily.

"Is that because I already do?"

"Shit, you are a detective after all!" They both laughed, each of them relieved that their earlier tête-à-tête was seemingly in the past.

"Did you find anything?"

"Depends. Are you going to help me, or throw it away?"

Frank pulled a chair and sat at the edge of the desk next to her, leaning forward and looking at her intently. "Listen, you were right, I let my spine go. I bottled it, but I'm not like you, Thea. I'm close to the end, and I can't let all this be for nothing. I've got nowhere else to go after here, just retirement. Me and Joyce, we need that; we need our life after work."

"I get it, Frank. I just want you to be honest with me."

"I will," Frank lied, "and I'll support you. You can do this, off the books, just keep it quiet. Don't let anyone know what you're doing, okay? Just, keep me in the loop. I won't ask any more questions; I won't poke my nose in."

"Plausible deniability?"

"Something like that."

Thea looked at Frank, seeing, for the first time in a while, her old boss. "Thanks, Frank."

"Any time. You want a drink, coffee or something?"

"Sure, I could do with a break. You're buying though."

"Fair enough."

The black limousine pulled up inside the security cordon at Old Palace Yard, Westminster, outside the Houses of Parliament. Bowen waited in the back for his boss, Lord Leighton Mitchell, to step out, before following suit. He'd been the aide to Lord Mitchell for the last eight years. It was a role that also saw him double as a personal protection officer, given his years working in the British Army.

Leighton stood, a stern look on his face as he gazed at the home of British democracy. He smoothed down his jacket, adjusting the lapels with a brisk shake, ensuring that he looked as proper as possible, before quietly stating, "And we're sure the hacker has been removed?"

"Quite, sir."

"And the men he was talking too?"

"They won't be able to find out anything more than they already know. The boy was compartmentalised for this exact reason. What he did, they already know about. They won't learn any more from his computer. The next phases will continue apace."

Lord Leighton Mitchell hummed at this, a pondering noise that played out somewhere between being less than convinced and processing the next phases in his head.

"I still feel we need to try and eliminate that threat. I presume this was one of those bloody private enterprise do-gooders?"

"We think so," Bowen nodded.

"Then find out who has such pet projects. I'm keen to know more, so we can sort this out. People are always reasonable when the facts are presented."

"Absolutely, sir. I'll see what I can turn up."

"I want them found now!" Mitchell spun and snapped at his colleague, prodding a finger into the younger man's chest. "You find them, and you sort this bloody mess out. I've too much to lose here."

"Of course." Bowen bowed his head slightly in feigned apology. "I'll go and make some calls now, leave you to it."

"Don't let me down," hissed Mitchell, before he strode away and into the building.

Bowen watched, before pulling out his phone and dialling a number.

"Tell me we have some workable leads?" he asked, trying but failing to hide his annoyance with how he had just been treated.

"Have you ever heard of the Vehm?"

"The secret courts guys?"

"One of them turned up leaving the house of an associate of Mr Arrowsmith. We're pretty sure that he's unaware, but he might be being played. You need to tip him off and remove the threat."

"Send me a name, and I'll get it cleared up."

"Details coming over now. He should be easy to find; his kid has just been taken to hospital."

* * *

Jack's vigil had been a quiet one. He and Isobel barely spoke. Despite their years together, the time apart had created a buffer between them, an awkward no man's land where neither felt the right or responsibility to talk to the other, to strike up any form of conversation. It would have been forced, they both knew it, done only to stop the silence that sat on the room like a heavy blanket, drowning them all in the quiet contemplation of how their family had fallen apart.

Calum had said nothing. He remained steadfastly tight-lipped about what happened. He had spoken to the police – Isobel had insisted – and told them the bare bones of what he knew. That someone had jumped him, darting out from some bushes, catching him unaware, and that was all he could remember.

Jack knew there was a lie in there somewhere. He'd spoken to far too many people in the past to miss the rather obvious evasive techniques his son employed, even if they had been telegraphed. Looking away, sullen demeanour, the raising of the voice when he said he didn't know anything. It was all so tell-tale that every parent knew them. Isobel too must have known, because at one point, when the two of them were outside of the room, she urged Jack not to push their son.

"Please," she had pleaded. "He's not like you. If he doesn't want the confrontation, don't force it on him. Let him deal with this his way."

Jack hadn't wanted to, it went against what he was, but he accepted Isobel's request and instead let his son dictate the pace. Hospital probably wasn't the place and now certainly wasn't the time, but he knew he wouldn't be able to wait forever. He needed a name. Maybe one day, Calum would be ready, and there would be something that could be done.

For now, he wanted to be Jack Quinn, father, not Jack Quinn, enforcer. All the other things didn't matter, and in the sombre setting, he found time to question himself on what role he had played in this. Had he been too hard on his son, to the point where he had forever damaged his confidence and belief in himself? Had he made him this easy a target? Had he forgotten to let him be his own man?

The thoughts tormented him because he knew there was little he would be able to do now to change the path that Calum was on. So much of his life was set that, for Jack, all he could see was more of the same for Calum. It never dawned on Jack that people could change at any point. For him, once you were on the threshold of adulthood, this was who you were and who you would always be. It was cynical, not that he knew that.

A vibration in his pocket from his phone saved him from any further deep thought. He looked at the caller ID. It was Yannick.

"I've got to take this," he said to Isobel as he stood. She said nothing in accession.

The corridor was near enough empty, just a few people doing odd jobs around the hospital as they prepared for the breakfast rounds to begin. Jack answered the call.

"They have someone at one of his flats in Peckham. I don't know which flat, just that it's in Peckham. They have girls working out of there and a man who lives in each one of the blocks as security. That's all I know so far," Yannick reported, before hanging up. Jack said nothing, placed the phone back in his pocket, and went to walk back to Isobel and his son. As he reached the door, he saw a doctor approaching him.

"Mr Quinn? Do you mind if I have a quick word?"

Jack looked at the guy. Too tall and too broad to be a doctor, despite the arbitrary white coat over his shirt and tie. His face spoke of too many fights, too many missions, too many deaths, and not enough saved lives. A soldier, not a doctor. Not even a field medic.

"We best go someplace quiet," Jack suggested.

"There's a room just through here for families," the fake doctor offered.

"Fine." Jack followed the men calmly through a couple of sets of double doors and into the room. He closed the door behind them and waited.

"So, Mr Quinn, your son."

"You're not here to talk about my son," Jack pointed out, keeping his voice low and controlled.

The fake doctor nodded. "Actually, I am. Your son, your daughter, maybe even your ex-wife. If you care enough, that is."

"You're going to want to choose your words wisely here," Jack warned, noting the slightly smug look on the fake doctor's face.

"You're involved in an investigation. That investigation will fail." The fake doctor was clearly revelling in this. The sick little smile broadened with every word.

"Understood," Jack shrugged.

"Do we have your compliance?" the fake doctor cocked his head as he asked.

"I said understood."

"Mr Quinn. Hospitals aren't very safe places. Do I need to remind you how many people die in these places?"

Jack said nothing.

"Think about the offer. You just need to stall the investigation, that's all. Slow things down. You have, after all, got other things on your plate."

Jack said nothing.

The fake doctor waited for an awkward moment. Then, realising he was getting no further response, he moved towards the door. Jack let him.

"Take care, Mr Quinn," said the fake doctor as he got to the door, opened it, and walked out.

Jack pulled his phone out of his pocket and dialled Raf.

"Raf, I need you to track a guy through the hospital, now." Jack waited five seconds and then stepped out of the room. The fake doctor was already out of sight.

"What does he look like?" Raf asked.

Jack gave him the description as he made his way to the nearest stairwell. Raf worked quickly, a computer program going through the details he had put in, tracking all the footage from the hospital and locating the target.

"He's making his way downstairs, heading towards what looks like the staff carpark."

"Is there a quicker way there?"

"I'm sure I can find you one if you run."

The fake doctor had just reached his car, just grabbed hold of the door handle, when Jack reached him. His arm was outstretched already, and Jack reached down with his right hand, grabbing the fake doctor's wrist.

"I thought about your offer. I've got a message for you and the people you work for," he snarled.

The fake doctor went to draw his arm back, but Jack pulled it in towards himself, at the same time pushing forward with his left forearm into the elbow joint, driving it forward off his back foot, so his whole body was behind it. The two counteracting motions ripped the joint in two, tearing tendons and cartilage so that the fake doctor screamed out in pain and shock. Enraged, he went to swing a wild and loose left-handed shot back at Jack, spinning and pivoting off his right foot, bringing his left leg around.

Jack saw the arm, saw the leg. His right arm came up and brushed away the blow. It was nothing more than a reaction shot, no hope of making it count against a decent for. As the fake doctor planted his left leg, Jack raised his, bringing it down just above the knee joint, pushing down, once more using the fake doctor's momentum, as he continued to spin, to put more force into the blow, hearing the satisfying pop as the man's knee came out of its socket and his whole leg crumpled like a deck of cards, leaving him sprawled and wailing on the floor, a collection of broken limbs and profanity.

"I warned you to choose your words, and you chose poorly," Jack said. "Tell your boss, bosses, whoever, that we will get them. I will get them. You want to pick a weak spot? That ain't mine."

Jack turned and walked back into the hospital.

14

Reuben had been working late into the night. He had wanted to ensure he was prepared. It was what he did. Make sure he was one step ahead of the game. It had been a crucial part of the mantra that had got him to where he was now. Always thinking about how the other side would come at you before they did and finding a way to nullify it before it happened. This one, however, he still wasn't sure he had cracked. These guys had a plan that he was slowly unpacking, trying to figure out where he stood in it, to ensure that, come the end, he was still standing.

It was well into the new day when his phone went off, which wasn't necessarily unusual. Nisha knew he was working late, so she wasn't checking in, but as a lot of his activities took place in the small hours of the day, there were countless reasons why employees and associates might be ringing up to talk to him. It wasn't an employee though; the call was coming through on the scrambled app that Bowen had insisted he install on his phone.

"What's up?" Reuben sounded remarkably breezy given the hour.

"I just got word from one of our sources that you have a leak."

Reuben felt himself go cold at the word. The loyalty of his men meant more to him than most things, and the thought that one could be betraying him broke his heart.

"Who?"

"Yannick Burton."

"How?"

"He's passing off information to a group we're aware of, that want to stop our operation."

"Police?"

"No, a private party."

"And you're sure that Yannick is the one talking to them?"

"Positive. We have proof one of their agents was at his house, and we've seen money deposited in his mother's bank account."

"I need to check this for myself before I do something to one of my own, you get me? This...I gotta do this."

"We expect nothing less."

Reuben swallowed, devastated by the news. "Bowen," he went on.

"Yes?"

"You know what my people mean to me. If you're messing with me."

"I know what your people mean to you. I've been told."

"You know I put a lot of trust in what they say to me. If I didn't, let's face it, you and I wouldn't be talking."

"I understand, but I'm not lying. You check it out, however you need to do it, and then clean up any issues."

"Fine. Got it." Reuben hung up, rubbing his face with his free hand, then slamming that hand down on the table.

* * *

Vic Bartram tied the laces on his running shoe as he went through his carefully rehearsed morning routine. Each day, at precisely 5:34 a.m. – Vic hated doing things at the more regular intervals to which the day was split – Vic woke up, got from the bed he shared, more often than not, with his wife, and went for a quick rinse in the shower. It wasn't a shower designed to clean him, more a brusque blast of chilly water that would sharpen his senses and get his body working faster. Within minutes, he was out, towelling himself off quickly – his hair, now a thin, blade-one buzz cut, needing little to no attention – just merely enough of a dry to ensure he wasn't too damp and, therefore, might chaff with his morning exercise.

Out of the bathroom, he'd quickly snack on a granola bar, while he dressed in his running gear. Simple shorts, tee, and socks in the summer, more Lycra and coverings in the winter. Today, it was light and mild outside, despite the early hour, and shorts and t-shirt had been deemed fine. Dressed, he would come downstairs, sipping on a bottle of water as he began warming up, topping it up just before setting out, muscles stretched, ready for his run.

The route he took was cyclical and followed five different routes, one for every weekday. It was Wednesday today, his hump day and the second longest run of his week, a ten-kilometre run that took him up towards Norbury Park, from his home in Pollard's Hill.

He tried his best to stick to the better areas of where he lived. This part of South London, as with anywhere in the city, was a melting pot of diverse cultures. Some of them, a select few, had issues with his politics.

That, he had long since decided, wasn't something he was prepared to feel guilty about. Vic Bartram was proud of the way he had risen to the top of one of the UK's new right-wing parties. Immigration *was* an issue, no matter what any of these leftie commentators wanted to say about it. Their *Guardian*-reading, quinoa-eating lives weren't touched in the way the lives of others were. They hadn't spent much time with real people and heard their struggles, brought into their stories and became their champion.

It was perhaps true to say that Vic hadn't spent much time with those people either before he had begun his rise to the top. It was also perhaps true to say that he didn't particularly want to spend much time with them now, but he did what he had to because they deserved a voice and they had made him their champion. In doing so, they had begun to provide for him, the sort of life that he wanted all along and, ironically, despite his disdain for foreigners, they too had become integral to his lifestyle.

Now, in a post-Brexit Britain, the war had been won for many on the alt-right, and the battle had shifted towards taking on the left head-on. Vic sensed that wasn't a battle that would be as easily won. He wanted to try and change his tack, but what do you become when your only policies are, to many, a little too racist for comfort? What he really needed, he mused as he ran that morning, was a good old terror attack, something that could be blamed solely on the door of Johnny Foreigner.

He rounded the corner and passed by a small green in Pollard's Hill. He passed this way most days, in fact, it was only tomorrow when his running routes didn't bring him here. It was a quintessentially English part of the world, he thought to himself. True, there were a few foreigners and the like living around here now, but most of them had integrated, so they weren't really the problem. That's how he knew he wasn't racist, despite what his critics said. They were alright, all of them, if they just did things the way they were supposed to be done in Britain.

Vic Bartram kept on running, out of the green, unaware that he was being watched from the tinted rear window of a van parked up so that it overlooked the green. Unaware his actions were being monitored, recorded, and a plan was being made that would give him exactly what he was looking for.

* * *

"We might have narrowed down the location of Erik Andryiv," Lowri informed the room. There was a sombre mood in David's office that morning. Jack had reported in the incident with the fake doctor at the hospital, and it had caused them all to take a step back. So often they operated with a feeling of impunity, that their being revealed had never crossed their minds, but clearly someone knew who they were and a whole lot more as well.

Lowri slid a sleek tablet across the table to David, showing the picture of Erik leaving the apartment. "Jack's source was right. We've found our man."

"Where was this?" David looked at the tablet and passed it to Jack who, after inspection, passed it to Adam.

"Outside of one of Reuben's working girls' apartments. That was where he was holed up."

"Was?"

"The working girl is back in place They're probably moving him around."

"I would," Adam agreed. "Keep him mobile."

"It's not all good news. Your man Yannick may well have been compromised. We overheard part of a phone conversation Reuben took last night; he was talking about traitors in his midst. He didn't seem pleased." David kept the disappointment out of his voice, but Jack couldn't.

"Shit."

"It was always going to be a matter of when, not if."

"I really hoped we could get him out. One less body."

"He's still the enemy, Mr Quinn, don't forget that." Lowri looked at him. She'd been watching his performances lately, and she too was worried he might be losing his edge.

"Of course." Jack took the criticism, and Lowri moved the conversation on.

"Our surveillance has also given us a name. Bowen. We don't have anything more than that at this point, but we think there might be a connection between him and someone within Reuben's gang. We get the feeling they simply weren't picked. There's some sort of element of pre-existing trust there."

"What makes you say that?" Adam asked.

"We're only getting one side of the conversation when they speak, but Reuben said something about Bowen being introduced to him, so there has to be a connection there somewhere. We're digging, but we've found nothing."

"What about the kid's computer?" There was still the hope that Kristian's death hadn't been in vain for Adam.

"Mo's still recovering. Raf is working on it, but he's not Mo," lamented David.

"Anything we can do for him?" Adam felt more than a degree of responsibility for Mo.

"Give him time and space. In the meantime, do your jobs. Get out there and dig something up on Andryiv. Take the pressure off him, and he'll find it easier," Lowri ordered.

"Got it." Adam and Jack stood to leave.

"Jack, a quick word?" Lowri said softly as he went to leave. Jack looked at David and saw the surprise on his face. He had no idea either.

"Sure." Jack watched David and Adam leave and then sat back down. "What's up?"

"How's your son?"

"Hurting."

"And your wife?"

"Ex. She's hurting too. Different sort."

"I'm sorry that they were brought into this."

"Goes with the territory, but the best way to nullify a weakness is let it not seem like one."

"I'm worried it is though."

Lowri watched Jack, looking for a reaction, but she got nothing. He just looked at her impassively, waiting for her to go on, so she did.

"The man you attacked. We could have used him."

"I know. I made a call. Send him back as a message, try and secure the safety of my family. If they think I'm willing to do that when I'm threatened, they know there's no point threatening me. They want me to stop chasing them, so they need to know that hurting my family means I chase harder."

"But we could have chased harder if we had the chance to extract some information from that guy." Lowri leant forward as she spoke.

Jack nodded, accepting her point. "We might, or he might have been a grunt, compartmentalised from it all. It's how we would have played it. I made a call. I stand by it, and if it was the wrong call, I stand by the outcome of that."

Lowri weighed up what he said. It was true, the man probably would have led them nowhere, and so Jack made the right call. That didn't help shake the feeling this was endemic of something more, and Lowri needed to make him understand her concerns.

She pursed her lips as if contemplating something and then said, "I want you to go back home and see your son before you go back out. I want you to get some closure on this if you can. If you can get a name to the police, great. If you have to find who did it and do what you have to, fine. But I need you focused, Jack. Something is coming. I can't have half of you out there, half of you at home. That's not how this works out."

"Now?" Jack was surprised at her orders.

"Now. Get this sorted, so we can move on."

"Okay." Jack mulled it over and found he was happy with her suggestion. Get a name, get it cleared. "I'll talk to him."

15

Mo had woken early that morning, although, to say he had woken suggested that, in some way, he'd been asleep. Mo wasn't entirely sure he could really call the way he had spent the last night "sleep." It had been more a waking nightmare. Cold sweats, the vision of Kristian spinning, holes appearing in his body. Blood spilling out onto the floor and the gun searching for him, the nozzle looking to lock on. In his dreams, however, Adam didn't get the shots off in time to force the attacker back, and the shotgun had swung down in a merciless arc, it's sawn-off barrels looking him dead in the eyes. Then the explosion came, catapulting the shot towards him. He felt it piercing through his face, burning through his eyes, the smell of it suffocating his nostrils and burrowing down his throat. The taste of metal, gunpowder, blood and bone cascading over his floundering tongue. The shot puncturing the parts of his brain, each one of them shutting off as the damage was done, and then nothing. It was only after that that he awoke.

He didn't know how many times he had seen that vision that night, how many times he had died in his dreams, but he knew he wouldn't forget it for as long as he lived.

That thought brought forward an almost crippling guilt. He did live. Kristian did not. He had been there and watched this young man die. His only mistake, albeit a big one, was to get mixed up in something that was out of his control in a way he never understood. How many other kids like that would have followed suit, swept up in the idea of sticking it to the man? There was an entire world of people who believed that was their mission in life. Squads, teams, lone wolves, people with grudges, people who thought it was all a laugh. And was he one of them? Was what he was doing now, with The Regulators, the same thing? Was he actually sticking it to the man? Was he really on the outside? Was he the bad guy?

His head swam with these thoughts. He wanted to go into work and take his mind off it, to keep himself busy, but the instant he thought that, he wanted to be anywhere but work. Anywhere but that place, where the reminder of death and his complicity in Kristian's death would haunt him the whole time he was there.

The phone was ringing. Mo heard it now. He didn't know if it had just started ringing, or if it had been ringing for a while. He picked himself out of his bed, out of his daze and over to the phone. He saw Adam's name. Mo put the phone down and walked into the bathroom slowly, lethargically.

The mirror above the sink showed him his reflection, a man who looked shell-shocked, he thought to himself, almost laughing internally at the irony. *Well, of course,* he thought. He turned the tap on and watched the water run for a moment, contemplating its short freedom from the tap, it's joyful dance in the bottom of the sink, then it's inevitable disappearance into the black hole of the plughole and whatever came after.

Mo knew what came after for him. He was a devout Muslim, always had been, always would be. The problem was, he always felt he was on a path of righteousness. Now, blood had been shed in front of him, and he blamed himself for his part in that. Would that matter when he faced his yawm-ad-din, his day of judgement? Would he find paradise in Jannah, or would this action outweigh everything, leaving him to face the fire of Jahannam?

The question tore at him. It burnt him inside. He had to do something, he had to devote his life from this point on to being a good Muslim, to doing right. He knew that deep inside, but the thought of doing anything, certainly anything as monumental to make up for his part in the death of Kristian, filled him with an even greater dread. The fear of the here and now was far more palpable than the fear of the final day of Earth.

The phone rang again. He ignored it again.

Mo stared into the mirror. He hated the man he saw.

* * *

"I must admit, I'm very surprised to see you here, Lord Mitchell," Valentin Mamedov said with complete honesty. It had been a complete surprise to him when his secretary had called through to his office, explaining that the old stalwart of the left had turned up unannounced at his office and wanted to give him a story, face to face. "You know I've not been doing any actual journalism myself for quite some time?"

"Well, in this day and age, one could quite easily argue most of the buggers out there aren't doing any actual journalism themselves," Mitchell roared with laughter, slapping his own knee in delight at his wit and forcing Valentin to join in, if only out of politeness.

"No," he chuckled, "this is true, my friend, and I must say, it is great to see you."

"And you, Valentin, old lad, but you know I'm right. A lot of these bloody idiots on the other side, some of these rags. Well, they're not journalists, they're bloody toxic."

"Quite," Mamedov agreed, to a point. Their playbook was similar to his, after all. Find a hook that resonates with your audience and turn up the volume on it to drive sales. Simple. It just so happened that their angle was the other side of the political spectrum and, without doubt, dug into the darker side of people's psyches. "They play a dirty game; we've struggled to keep up."

"Well, you've done a fantastic job. Always got your paper with my morning crumpets, and now, well, hopefully, we're seeing a change in the political discourse."

"Really?" Mamedov wondered if this was why the old man was here.

"Yes, I've been quite surprised by it all myself actually. You see, we've been talking to that Vic Bartram. Turns out, he's not such a bad fellow."

"I don't know about that," Mamedov's face wrinkled. Bartram had been quite a bad fellow indeed, where his paper had been concerned. He'd threatened to sue them on a couple of occasions, tried a couple of unsuccessful court cases and injunctions and now routinely refused to give comment to them on any story whatsoever.

"Yes, I know you and he have had your tiffs in the past. Hopefully, that's going to change. He came to me the other week, wanted to talk about a cross-party working group. He's on about abandoning his party's stance on immigration, on Muslims, the whole thing."

"Really?" Now Mamedov was incredulous. He'd long suspected that Bartram, like most of the alt-right politicians, merely jumped on a bandwagon to further his career, but this was a real about-turn.

"Well, perhaps abandoning is the wrong word, but changing tack certainly. He wants to make the party more inclusive, bring the whole thing together, do away with the angry middle Englander thing, even drop their plans for one in one out. Says he's seen that Britain needs to be a multicultural society and is doomed without it."

"Doomed without it? You know I'm going to have to speak to him about that?"

"Oh, yes, of course, wouldn't expect anything less old chap," Mitchell grinned. He too knew that there was no way that Bartram would take Mamedov's call. He was counting on it. If he did, the whole thing would unravel quickly.

* * *

Yannick stood nervously in his boss's office waiting for Reuben to say something. He knew there was a problem, knew that his boss had an issue on his mind, but he couldn't tell what. There was no way that he knew, was there?

"Yannick, pal, I think we have a problem," finally Reuben spoke. It wasn't the words that Reuben wanted to hear.

"What's up, boss?" he asked, trying to sound cool and calm. Nonchalant.

"The safe house that our boy is in, I got word it might have been compromised."

Yannick swallowed. Was this it?

"Who did it, boss?" he asked, eager to find a new patsy to point a finger at.

"I don't know, yet, but I need people I can trust. Fish is my normal goto guy, but I got to take him off on something else, so that makes you next in line."

175

Yannick flushed inside. It felt good to be trusted, and for a moment, he totally forgot that he couldn't be.

"What do you need me to do, boss?"

"I'm moving the boy; I want you to babysit."

"Sure, no problem, boss. Now?"

"Yeah, Yannick, now. He's at our warehouse over in Herne Hill. Just need you to sit on the door, in a car over the road, covert like. Anyone snoops around, you let me know."

"Got it, I'll get over there now."

"Good lad, Yannick, don't let me down," Reuben said, praying that he wouldn't.

16

"You know I'm only ever a phone call away if you're worried, or someone ever tries anything again." Jack looked at his son, trying his hardest not to let himself sound desperate. It was harder than he thought. The natural urge to tear apart, limb from limb, the person who had laid a hand on his son was deep seated within him and had been intensified by the visit of the fake doctor the night before. Now, they were back at Jack's ex-wife's house, Jack's old house, and he had called in to check up on them all, never mind his son.

"I know," Calum mumbled, looking away from his dad, trying to concentrate on the TV that sat on top of his chest of drawers opposite the bed he was currently laid in.

Calum's room was a typical teenager's room. The walls had been painted, obviously, blue by his parents when they moved to the house that now lay solely in the name of Jack's ex-wife. That had been some ten years ago when Calum was still just a little boy, but even then, Jack had known that his son was not made to be like him. Not that he had, at that time, thought that a terrible thing. It was only now, when he wanted his son to stand up for himself and help him fix this, that he felt a disappointment with his son.

That pained him even more.

"Calum." Jack wasn't accustomed to begging, but he knew one last try was worth it. "I want to sort this. I have to help you, bring him to justice, whoever it was. You don't have to be scared."

Calum sighed and strained his neck to further look beyond his dad. Isobel who had been standing by the door, arms folded, stepped into the room.

"We can go back to the police…" she suggested.

"No! I don't want the police," Calum snapped at her. "I just want to be left alone."

Isobel stopped as her son's words bit into her. She had told Jack that she had never been so scared as she had by this. Like Jack, she just wanted to protect her son. She wasn't so worried about revenge. She just wanted to make sure that whoever did this, whoever had beat her son to a pulp, never got the chance to do so ever again. Yet, here was her son telling them no. How could they protect him if he didn't want help?

Jack stood. "Okay, son, no police," he promised. "You get some rest."

He walked out of the room, placing a hand on Isobel's shoulder as he walked by her. She took one last lingering look at Calum, tucked under his duvet, legs curled up, his sad eyes staring mournfully at the TV, before she followed Jack out of the room, closing the door behind her and catching up to him on the landing.

"What can we do?" she asked him, knowing that this was his realm. She might not love him anymore, she might not want to be with him, for the person he had become, but she had to admit, the person he had become, in times like this, could do things she couldn't.

"I'll find him. Them. Whoever," Jack said.

"And then?"

Jack sighed and looked at her. She was looking at him, quietly pleading for him to do the right thing.

"I promised him no police."

"I know, but we need to do this right. I mean, come on, it's going to be some kid, you and I both know that."

Jack did know that. He already had his suspicions. Calum had come to him with the tale about Kat and her new beau. He had then humiliated the kid. It didn't take much to connect the dots, and as much as it burned him up inside, Jack wasn't going to start beating up children. That wasn't him. It wasn't fair. Although, what part of fair had that kid shown Calum? Jack felt his anger rise again.

"If Calum isn't going to talk to the police, it's pointless. They won't be able to do anything if Calum doesn't help them. Putting him through that, Izzy, he's just not made for it. It'd do him more harm."

"But he needs to…"

"He needs to get better. I'll talk to whoever it was. I promise I won't cross a line."

"Don't. He needs you, Kat needs you, both of them, here, not in a prison because you beat up some kid who isn't worth it."

"I know," Jack said quietly. He looked out across the landing at nothing in particular, knowing he had to leave, searching for a reason to stay. "I should…yeah, get out of here. Leave you to it."

"Okay."

He turned, placing his hand on her arm. The action almost seemed clumsy from him, transparent in its intent, such was his normal inability to show affection.

"Are you okay?" he asked.

She took his hand from her arm with apologetic tenderness, which hit Jack with all the subtly of a door slam. "I'm fine. I need to rest that's all, it's been a tiring twenty-four hours."

Jack nodded. "I'll see you around."

He took his leave, walking past her, down the stairs and out of the house. He'd barely made it back to his car when his phone rang. It was Yannick.

"The target is in a warehouse in Herne Hill. I'm sending you the address."

* * *

An hour later, Adam and Jack sat in silence in the car as it made its way towards the warehouse where Yannick said that Erik was holed up. Adam had hoped that Mo would have been there this morning, that he would have had the chance to talk to him, put his arm around him a little and try and coach him through what had happened that night. That he hadn't showed was worrying. Mo wasn't one to duck work, whatever the reason. He lived for it. True, he had been offered the chance to take some time, but Adam had never expected he would. He felt guilty for taking Mo into that situation.

The car pulled into a side street, just short of the warehouse. The warehouse was an old Victorian building, with vaulted roof, that was in serious need of repair, but more likely being left to rot, before Reuben cashed in the land to a property developer when it was time to get out of the game.

They both looked at the warehouse from the car.

"You know this is a trap, right?" Adam sighed.

"Yeah, probably."

"Then is this the smart play?" Adam asked.

As he did so, four police cars, raced up to the warehouse, lights flashing, slamming to a halt outside and spilling the officers inside quickly out. They raced from their vehicles and into the warehouse.

"It's definitely the smart play." Jack smiled.

They waited and watched from a distance. There was no way that they were ever going to set foot into the warehouse. Their intelligence had shown that it had been used solely as a storage space since it had been built. In one corner had sat a two-story office area, but the rest of the warehouse, from floor to corrugated iron roof, was an open space with little in the way of windows and therefore little in the way of natural light.

A perfect place for an ambush.

If they went in with torches, they'd be lit up perfectly for anyone waiting inside to take a shot. Go in without, and anyone prepared with night vision would be waiting. Even if they were equipped themselves, they would have had to scan the whole building and get their shots off, before someone else got to them. It just wasn't viable.

So, the police had been called to a report of an officer down in a warehouse. That ensured that every cop in the area would race to the scene as quickly as possible. Whoever was in there waiting for them would have to think twice about engaging half of South London's police force. and as more and more cars arrived, it certainly seemed that was what had descended on the building.

Quickly, however, they began to peel away, as it became clear the situation wasn't all it had seemed. Jack and Adam waited. They had noted a couple of unmarked cars pull up, but most had left. Only one unmarked car remained fifteen minutes after the first police cars had arrived, in addition to two of the original four. Out of that car had come a lone female officer, CID or NCA, or something like that they had both agreed. She had scanned the area, and for a moment, it seemed like she had looked straight at them, but then she had carried on inside and was yet to return.

"Wonder what they found in there?" Adam was starting to feel intrigued now, his feet up on the dash as he waited for the outcome.

"Must have been someone in there. I imagine they're trying to explain away their presence in a big dark warehouse."

"You reckon they were armed?"

"Probably, but it's going to have been so dark in there. They would have had time to get rid before the police arrived. I'm going to imagine that the cops probably didn't even realise that they were sat in darkness, what with the adrenalin pumping. They'll sweet talk their way out, but it's going to be nice to put a face to whoever it was."

Finally, the last police came out, talking to a man in black overalls, who was all smiles. He patted them on the back as he went, clearly making out like it was all some big joke to tell the family around the table. Jack took a couple of photos as they enjoyed the moment. They could try and get an ID later. The female plainclothes officer followed. She looked less impressed, and once the man had left, she talked briefly to the last two officers, before they got in their car and drove off.

"When she's gone, we'll go," Jack said, knowing it would look conspicuous for them to leave now.

But she didn't go. She looked at them and then began striding purposefully towards them.

"Shit me," Adam said, sinking down in the seat. She approached the driver's side where Jack was sat and rapped on the window.

"I want to talk to you," Thea ordered, rather than asked

Adam looked at Jack, a sly smile on his face. "Sure, what about? The area? Seems nice, though some of the neighbour's career choices are a bit offbeat."

"What's your business with Reuben Arrowsmith?"

"Our business?" Adam repeated the question. "We don't have any. Never even met the guy."

"Look, we can mess about, beat around the bush all day, but you and I have a shared interest in this shit. So, how about we get down to business and talk?"

"What makes you think we have business with Reuben Arrowsmith?" Jack asked.

"The fact I saw you coming out of one of his associate's flats the other day, and now you're here, outside one of his properties, as a shit tonne of police barge through the door."

Jack raised an eyebrow at Adam. The cop was good, and there was no doubting she had character. "I'm all for it," he said.

Adam sighed. "Sure, why not. But not here. Let's find somewhere else. Somewhere off the radar."

"There's a coffee shop in Wimbledon, Giovinco's, you know it?"

"Not my usual spot," Jack nodded, "but we'll find it."

"Fine, I'll see you there in an hour and a half. I want to see who comes around to check in on your handiwork."

"We'll see you then," Jack replied as politely as he could muster.

17

The coffee shop was a typically modern, continental themed affair. Exposed brickwork on the walls. Greys, whites, and browns making up the majority of the colours of anything that was painted. A pristine counter was staffed by two equally pristine baristas, who stood in front of a shiny coffee machine and an array of cups and pots. In front of them stood a wide array of cakes and pastries. It was not the sort of place that you expected to see Jack and Adam, and they did their best to fit in. Merely by their gait and the way they dressed, they didn't strike anyone in there as typical Giovinco's clientele.

They had waited ten minutes for the cop before she showed and introduced herself as Thea Watts, a name that they had both instantly recognised from the case file. Now she was getting down to business.

"I know you know who he is. I even know what, if not who, you are, and if I had you arrested for impeding an investigation, that wouldn't be far off the mark, would it?"

"What investigation?" Jack muttered. The cop was fearless, he admired her for that, but she was out of line. They were, after all, on the same side.

"You think you're above the law, don't you? You think the rules don't apply to you, but they do."

"No, the rules don't apply to the people we're after. That's why we're here, and you're chasing shadows," Jack retorted.

Adam stepped in, his hand on his partner's shoulder, a silent reminder that this wasn't how things were dealt with. "Look, you want to bring Reuben to justice. So, do we. I'll make a deal with you. If we can find anything that's actionable in a court of law, it's yours."

"You said a deal," Thea mused. "A deal suggests that something goes the other way as well."

"You share your information with us."

"I can't do that."

"Think of it as an interagency scheme," Jack offered.

"But you're not just another agency."

"No, but we offer you, realistically, the best chance of stopping Reuben doing more horrific things, and we'll play fair, we always do. If there's something we find that can nail him in a court of law, it's game on. We give it to you, and we disappear."

Thea sat back in her chair and surveyed the two men in front of her. There was an earnestness in them both that she couldn't escape. They genuinely believed what they were doing was right. She disagreed with them; she couldn't hide that. Yet what they said was right. It was as close as she was likely to get right now.

"Your choice is simple." Jack sensed her weighing it up and decided to offer his input. "The more resources you have, the closer you get to putting him behind bars, but right now, you're going around in circles. We know that, you know that, and it could be that you never find that missing piece by playing by the rules. But if you bend them, just a little, maybe that's all it will take for it to fall in place. Otherwise, Reuben stays doing what he does, and you keep chasing him forever and ever. Your epitaph doesn't have to be about this guy. It should be about this guy and the next guy and the guy after that. That happens when we help each other."

Thea nodded. "We find anything actionable, you're out. You break a law, I arrest you. I don't care if you turn the wrong way down a one-way street. You live by my rules, not yours."

* * *

Bowen pulled the balaclava over his face before he stepped in front of the camera. It would have been a shame for the deception to have all come apart based on something as stupid as forgetting where you were and giving away your identity like that. So far, he had been extremely clever. Even Reuben Arrowsmith didn't know who he really was. The only people who knew were either a part of the conspiracy or would be dead before it was over.

He had picked a room in an apartment block which was owned by a number of those involved. It was a perfect location because it stood empty. There was no chance of being interrupted, no chance of any residual sound from tenants coming through, only perhaps the whine of a jet above that would simply narrow it down to somewhere in London, at any given day.

Taking a deep breath for his performance, he stepped around the camera and checked to ensure he could see the red light on the top. Satisfied, he began his speech.

"Fellow patriots, today marks a new era in British politics, one where the false idols, who have stolen the right from true patriots, will be made to pay for their crimes."

* * *

Vic didn't see Erik until it was too late. He didn't have time.

Erik stepped out a couple of yards ahead of him, and Vic's face had shown a burst of indignant anger. His mouth had opened to say something, but the words never came out. Vic's protest was a barely formed notion when Erik appeared, hood of a grey sleeveless tracksuit top up and around his head, sunglasses on, angry-looking tattoos on his arm, machete held in a gloved hand. His eyes widened in fear as Erik brought the blade up and then down in a swift slash across, starting in his throat and scoring its way through his neck, his arteries, and into his upper torso, his skin and flesh cascading open and the blood surging out of him in a violent cloud.

Vic's face froze into a look of fear and disbelief as he tumbled past his attacker, his brain still grappling with the options it hoped would help him survive, even as the blood loss quickly reached critical. He staggered forward, scraping and bouncing across the tarmac, a gurgle from his mouth where there should have been a cry for help. He gasped, his eyes wide, and then Vic said and did nothing more ever again.

Without looking back at the man he had just killed, Erik slipped the machete into a carrier bag and quickly turned and ran from the area. He had spent the previous days scouting out the position of all the nearby CCTV cameras in the area. First, he headed east, towards the main route through the area, London Road. He made sure that the cameras there caught him running. His face was obscured enough to keep him unidentifiable. It was the imagery that he had been ordered to let people see. A white man, neo-Nazi tattoos on his arms. The number 18. A swastika. The right-wing connotations were important, he had been told. It was no problem for him to wear them. Other people assigned meanings and picked sides. He had survived by doing exactly the opposite.

Once on London Road, he darted into a block of flats. He had already disabled the security cameras in the areas he knew he'd need to access, to create a run that would allow him to make his way through the flats and a quiet door that led to an empty apartment. There was no one around as he opened the door and walked in.

Inside was a broken-down mess of crumbling cupboards and faltering walls. It was clear no one had lived here for quite a while. Perfect for what he needed. Under the sink in what was once a kitchen, he found a small duffle bag. Inside was a change of jacket and jeans. Erik peeled off the fake tattoos that ran up his arm, then undressed.

Once changed, he went into the hallway of the flat and used a chair to get him up those last few inches. He reached up and opened the hatch into the attic. Carrying the clothes he had been wearing earlier, he climbed up into the small attic space and found a thick plastic tub that he had previously put there. He took the lid off carefully and placed his old outfit and tattoos inside, then the carrier bag containing the blade, watching not to splash anything on himself as the liquid began to bubble. An acid ate away at the discarded evidence. He placed the lid on the plastic tub again and pushed it further back into the loft space. Then, he lowered himself out, pulling the hatch back over. When he was sure there was no one in the corridor, he left the flat for the final time.

Making his way along another pre-planned route, he burst through the fire exit, over a small wall and into a wooded area where there were no cameras at all. For all the police would ever be able to tell, the assailant who murdered Vic Bartram had simply entered the block of flats and never reappeared ever again.

18

"One of you," Reuben seethed, "has betrayed my fucking trust."

He stood in front of five men, all of whom had been playing in Yannick's card game the other night. They were all standing looking straight at him, impassively, being careful not to show any sign of emotion or fear that might suggest that they were the one he was thinking of. Reuben knew, of course, he had been there, watching the warehouse just like Jack and Adam. He had seen the police arrive, although he hadn't seen Jack and Adam and he had seen that Yannick was nowhere in sight. Then he had left.

Next to Reuben stood Fisher, hands held in front of him, legs a little apart, his gaze fixed on the men.

"Someone dies tonight," Reuben went on. "Someone dies. I don't care if it's all of you. If I must do that to know that I've got rid of the fucking rat, the fucking cockroach, the leech who has been draining my goodwill and shitting on my doorstep, I will. So, here's the deal to the other four of you, listen up, right. I want the rat, so you lot are going to have to sort it out yourselves, and if you don't. I will."

Reuben stared intently at each one of them. They all stood silently. Yannick tried his best to retain his poker face, but deep down, he knew the gig was up.

"You've got half a fucking hour." Reuben turned and stormed up the stairs to his office, Fisher taking one last accusing glance at them all before following him.

Once in the office, Reuben slammed himself down in his chair and poured two large drinks as he waited for Fisher to make his way up and sit down. He shoved the second drink in Fisher's direction, before devouring his in one gulp. He took a breath and then went on.

"I cannot fucking believe that he's done this to me. I cannot believe, after the chances I gave that French, bloody, slug."

"You know it's Yannick," Fisher raised an eyebrow. "So, why didn't you act on it?"

"The other four down there need to show me something. They've been around him and they let him slip past them. They made this happen with their inability to spot the problem. So, they need to fix this, or they're useless to me as well, and let's face it, I clearly can't inspire loyalty, so I need to fucking make them give it."

"You meant it? Killing them all?"

Reuben said nothing. Instead, he got up and poured himself another drink, just as large, but this time he sipped. Still standing, he spoke in a softer tone.

"How long you known me, Fish?"

"I couldn't count it if I wanted to. More than one lifetime, boss."

"Right, and I'm fair, and I believe in my people. I believe in you, and I believe in those four down there to work it out."

"Yeah, but all due respect, that's not what I asked."

"But it's still the answer. I might be making a gamble, and I might lose, but I don't think I will."

"Fair enough," Fisher's wasn't the sort who liked to question his boss, and he knew that what he was proposing made sense. He had shared the same sense of dismay when he found out that there had been people snooping around the flats and even more so when it became clear that they had known what they were doing, which could only have come through inside information. "So, when he fesses, what's the next step?"

"We kill him. Then we kill whoever he spoke to. Once they tell us what they want and who sent them, of course."

Fisher waited a split second, hesitating over whether or not to ask his next question. He eventually decided to. "What's happening with Bowen?"

Reuben pulled out his chair, sat down, and rocked backwards, eyes to the ceiling.

"You know what, Fish, I really don't know. He's a soldier, I know that, but his bosses are going to be pissed off about it."

"Are we still planning on killing them first?"

"I think we have to. I think we're dead if we don't." He sat forward and shuffled some papers across his desk as if examining them, even though they pertained to nothing of note. "I mean, I'll be honest, we're drawing a blank, we've got nothing on these guys yet. That worries me a little if I'm honest."

"Let me make a suggestion."

"Go on."

"The people who Yannick was speaking to, they're obviously connected to this in some way. Maybe from the other

197

side of the coin, yeah, but they're in this game. My enemy's enemy is my friend and all that."

Reuben nodded slowly.

"You think we should parley with them?"

"No, of course not, we ain't snakes, but if we do find them, we damn well make them talk."

* * *

Bowen walked silently into the meeting room where Lord Mitchell was talking to six of his fellow committee members from the Joint Committee on National Security. It was a job that Lord Mitchell had been very proud to be appointed to, but the things he'd learned had shocked him and had spurred him into the actions he and Bowen were undertaking.

Bowen walked over to one of a row of chairs that sat against the far wall and said nothing. To most, it would seem he did nothing, but there was the slightest, barely perceptible sign, a small twitch in his face, only visible to someone who might have been looking for it. That someone would know that the twitch meant that phase one of the operation had been undertaken and, more importantly, had been successful. Lord Leighton Mitchell knew that, and he felt a sudden flush of relief to finally be underway on the mission.

It had pained him that certain people were going to have to be sacrificed in order for their goals to be met. For years, as he played with the idea, he had dismissed it as simply too barbaric. He had seen many people fall foul of the ambitions and desires of others, some mortally, others professionally or personally. It had been a very productive venture for those in control, and now was the time to make a move of his own. He took a sliver of comfort from the fact that Vic Bartram would have died quickly, although of course, there was always more than a hint of remorse directed towards his family.

Now Vic had finally done something noble with his life, not that he would ever know it. In all probability, were Vic looking on, he probably wouldn't agree that it was a move that he would deem noble. Vic was a man who had thrived on division, and everything that Leighton Mitchell was planning, he hoped, would bring people together, albeit in a less than triumphant sense.

In his head, it had been a clear and concise path, but now that the first domino had truly fallen, he felt himself being swept along by it all. Was he really in charge of this now?

Could he call it off if he wanted, he wondered? What would be the point? Then Vic would have died for nothing. No, this was it now. There was no turning back, and he had committed himself to this.

The fear of someone unearthing the plan still existed. With support from people high within the intelligence community that had been actively running interference, both here and abroad, he was certain it would be impossible for anyone to put the pieces together enough to have anything other than an inkling about what was going on. Certainly not enough to bring anyone to justice. Once it was done anyway, it wouldn't matter. This would have such an impact on the public psyche that the direction of Britain would be changed, for the better, forever.

With that idea settled in his mind, he felt the tension ease out of him, and he smiled. It was good to do something for the good of people, even if they would never know, he thought.

* * *

Frank didn't feel good. The NCA was one of the many agencies that had been tasked with investigating the terrorist attack that had left a UK politician dead. It was a huge operation, with officers from every conceivable branch of law enforcement all vying for position, trying to discover the link that would help them blow the case open. So far, they had managed to track the movements of their prime suspect to a block of flats close to where the crime had been committed. That was where the trail had gone cold.

He needed a break; he needed something to fall in his lap.

His phone rang.

"Knight."

"Hello, Mr Knight."

Frank's blood ran cold. Even though he couldn't tell from the screen, he knew now that the call had come through the app Bowen had asked him to install. The voice was unmistakable.

"You need to stall the search."

"What? Why?"

"National security."

"A bloody politician is dead," Frank protested.

"This call might be secure, but think about who might hear you," Bowen warned.

Frank looked around. He was right; there were plenty of people who could easily overhear his end.

"Fine, but this doesn't make sense."

"You need to trust us." For once, there was a softness to the voice that made Frank feel a little better.

"Okay, I'll do what I can."

"You'll be fine, Mr Knight. This is for the country."

The call went dead.

What had been proposed wasn't necessarily a hard job. They had no idea if the attacker was in the flats still, and if he was, they had no idea which address he would be in. Searching an entire block of flats required the ascent of the owners, and a small subsection of the tenants in the flats certainly didn't want police nosing around their property. Tensions were running high, there was no escaping that. There had even been some suggestion by one irate resident that the killing of Vic Bartram was all just a setup so that the police could come into the flats and round up anyone they pleased.

It made Frank's job of stalling his officers search all that bit easier. He could use the pretence of trying to win over hearts and minds. It would buy him some time, for now at least, until he figured out a better way.

"Mr Knight," a young police officer, a woman who could barely have been out of the academy a year, approached him. "I need to speak to you, sir."

"What's up, officer?" Frank couldn't remember if he'd heard her name. There had been so many people.

"Parsons, sir. One of the flats, I was door knocking, and no one answered."

"Par for the course."

"So, I went around the side and had a look in the window. It was meant to be occupied, the list we have has it down as belonging to a Keith Wilson, but when I looked in, the place looked deserted."

Frank panicked for a second. What if this was where they wanted him to avoid?

"I think we can go in there, sir," she went on. "I don't think we're going to step on any toes."

"Okay," Frank sighed, thinking quickly. He needed to stall, but there was no way that he could realistically say they weren't going in. "Okay, I want to just do this right. I don't need to blow this up and run the risk of losing him if he's in another flat and it all kicks off. I mean, that could well be what they're waiting for, cover of a riot would be all they needed to make it out."

Officer Parsons nodded. It seemed to make sense to her, he could see, but he could also see she was a little crestfallen that they weren't going in.

"You did well, Parsons," he added. "Really well, it's noted. Keep the flat secure. No one in or out till I give the word."

Parsons smiled, and Frank felt good again. Briefly. He still had to drag his feet just that little bit longer, but he knew he could make it work.

19

Valentin had barged through the doors and into his office to see a scene of organised chaos as journalists chased leads and stories, trying to piece together the dots of what had happened to Vic Bartram. They knew very little so far, certainly a fair deal less than Valentin.

He quickly spotted his website editor, Mark Noon, and hurried over to him.

"Mark, Mark," he called to him as he approached, trying to convey urgency, but also not get the whole floor looking at him.

Mark was a younger man than Valentin, in his thirties, and had kept himself in far better shape than his boss. Then again, he wasn't nearly as rich, so he probably needed to.

"We are getting some pretty decent traffic on this," Mark reported, figuring that's where his boss would be taking this conversation.

"You ain't seen nothing yet," Valentin beamed. "Come on, my office, gotta show you this."

Valentin hurried them into the office and pulled out his phone, showing Mark the email he had received as he was on his way in. It was the video that Bowen had made, though neither of them knew that.

"This just came into my inbox. A declaration of war from that frigging right-wing nutter who emailed the other week. It's bloody gold dust." Valentin couldn't contain his glee. His face lit up like a child at Christmas as he thrust his phone towards Mark, who in turn took it and began to watch the video.

When it was over, Mark shook his head in disbelief. "This is almost too good to be true. Can we verify it?"

"I don't care, he said it, get it on my website now. Get this everywhere."

"Okay, no problem." Mark took the phone to the computer in Valentin's office and quickly began to upload it through the paper's content management system. As he did, Valentin hopped behind him, watching the progress bar work its way nearer to completion and silently pre-empting the clicks and the ad revenue.

* * *

Mo hadn't planned on coming back to work. He hadn't planned on doing anything, but when he heard about the killing of Vic Bartram, his natural curiosity had got the better of him. He was well aware of who Bartram was, what sort of a person he was. Mo was one of the people that Vic warned of, simply because of the religion that Mo belonged to. As a Muslim, Mo was instantly an enemy of Vic's, whether he bore him any ill will or not.

Mo had wanted to try and find out more about what happened. The news outlets, where he had originally seen the story break, were crawling with talk of a brutal attack by a right-wing terrorist, who had killed a prominent political figure with a machete. He had seen the sinister video of the balaclava-wearing man online, demanding an immediate end to immigration and the repatriation of all "non-indigenous peoples," or more attacks would take place. It didn't sit with Mo.

So, he had begun to dig. He was soon into the CCTV footage of the assailant's escape and he, like the rest of the intelligence community, was convinced that the man that had been identified as the killer had gone into that block of flats. The problem was, he hadn't come out and, for whatever reason, probably planned, there had been no footage inside the flats or in any of the adjoining land.

That didn't add up to him if they were looking at a lone wolf attack. That level of preparation was more than a one-man job unless this guy was as technical as he was violent. This had to be the work of a cell of people if it was a terror attack. That wasn't what he was seeing, though. All the chatter, in all the usual places, was people speculating about the guy's motives. Even when he started to tap into the networks that usually knew more than most about these sorts of attacks when they were coordinated, there was still the same level of confusion one would expect when there was a lone wolf attack. The presence of the video further muddied things. No one online was talking. No one seemed to know what had happened. No one was congratulating one another. It was like they were all waiting for someone to step up and take the limelight in their shadowy underground, but no one was doing so. They were happy to be in the public eye, but where it mattered, where they could coordinate further, they simply didn't exist.

Troubled by this, Mo continued to dig. He wanted to know where the attacker had gone, where he had ended up. If he had escaped from the area, then he would have passed through the gaze of a CCTV somewhere, so Mo worked his way through a net of cameras that he knew eventually would bear fruit.

There was nothing. No one who fit the description passed through. It was hard to get a real look at the attacker anyway; he had obscured his face really well. It was a very professional job in truth.

Too professional, thought Mo. This couldn't be the work of some newly formed faction. This was the work of someone who had been there, done that, before. Someone who would be able to walk out of the scene of a crime like nothing had happened and disappear into the crowd. A hired assassin.

That's when Mo went back into work. As good as his systems were, he had nothing like the computing power he had in the office, and that's where he had found himself, less than an hour after his epiphany, still in his scruffs, unshowered, unshaved, but focused.

As he entered, Mo sensed the heads turning. He wasn't interested in them, or their questions, or their judgements, if there were any to be passed, he simply wanted to get to his workstation and get down to business.

Mo's workstation was opposite Raf's. He knew that Raf would have taken on a lot of his workload, but he also knew he wouldn't have complained. He nodded as he sat down, feeling slightly embarrassed. "How you doing, Mo?" Raf enquired.

"Ask me in a couple of hours." Mo fixed his eyes on the screen and began to work.

First, he had to pull up a face from the database of images that they had logged. It didn't take him long to find it. The next step was to run an automated procedure that would begin to plot various points on the person's face, creating a map that could be rendered in three dimensions. Once the data points were plotted, he began loading in the video files from the cameras he had been scanning, looking to get a match. Happy that everything was up and running, he got up from his desk, walked out of the office, past Meg, down the stairs, and out into the street.

Two hours later, after quickly cleaning himself up, then heading to a nearby mosque to pray for the first time since the shooting, Mo found himself back at his desk as the programme worked its way through the last of the data.

Finally, it presented him with a list of screen grabs that it had identified as being potential candidates. The highest ranked photo, which had scored an eighty-three-point-seven-percent chance of being the same person, intrigued Mo the most. He quickly applied a filter, then another, then another, until finally, he saw what he had suspected all along.

Twenty minutes after Vic Bartram was killed, Erik Andryiv was walking away from the scene of the crime.

20

"I think we have to pass this on," Jack stated. "It's a police matter, not something we can deal with."

"Our evidence is still pretty flimsy," Adam countered.

The two of them were locked in discussions with David about how best to proceed now that Mo had linked Andryiv to the killing of Bartram. All three were uneasy about the implications of people within the British government being involved in such a crime, but there was no doubt that this was too big a coincidence to ignore.

"We can always continue working it up, whilst passing it on to Watts. We promised her, and if we can give her something early on in the relationship, then it might be what we need to convince her to give us something back if she hits a wall," Jack went on. Something about Thea Watts had resonated with him. He knew she would see this through and she would do all she could to bring it down on the right side of the line. He didn't necessarily think that was a bad thing.

"I guess," Adam conceded, "but I still think we're dealing with something more. I don't see why they would go to all that effort just to off a bloody racist. I mean, who actually gives a shit about him?"

"The far-right do," David said gravely. "He's already becoming some sort of bloody martyr for them. Who knows where this could lead. The papers are already full of the usual rhetoric."

"And that's why I'm worried. Say we hand them Andryiv, without joining the dots, and he goes down fighting? Where do we go then? Are we just playing into their hands?"

"Feels like a waste of a good assassin." Jack wasn't convinced.

"It might, but it's a damn good back up." Adam wasn't done. "There has to be a phase two. Andryiv is too good just to be used on one half-baked racist and then get binned. So, if we close the net, are we running the risk of not getting to the head of what's coming?"

"And if we don't, are we running the risk of letting it happen?"

"There's a case for both," David had to agree, this wasn't a clear-cut choice, "but I think we need to do all we can to try and get to Andryiv, and if that means co-opting, willingly or not, the assets of the NCA, I think we have to do it."

"Fair enough," Adam accepted the order.

"I'll call her now, set this all up," Jack said.

The two of them left David behind and made their way out of the office, down to the carpark, Jack on his phone. Thea picked up.

"Thea Watts," was her stern and short answer.

"It's Jack Quinn. I think I have some intel you're going to want to see."

"What's it about?"

"We're not on a secure line here, where are you?"

"I'm just waiting to meet someone. Who's going to be listening?"

"Maybe no one, but better safe than sorry. Can I come to you?"

"Sure," Thea said. "There's a carpark at a drive-through near where I'm at. I'll send you the details."

"I'll be there soon."

* * *

Frank did his best. The wheels turned slowly as he made calls to all the wrong people in order to find out if they could set something up with a local community leader. To ensure that people were happy to see the police go into unoccupied flats. Finally, contact was made, and Frank made a point of rejecting the earliest possible time, opting for the second.

The meeting went well. Frank had pondered sabotaging it, but he knew that would cause more trouble in the long run and that he had only been told to stall the investigation and not start a bout of civil disturbance. Vic Bartram's views hadn't been popular in many parts of London, and in this block of flats especially, most people didn't fit in his demographic, creating a definite resistance to any move to help the enquiry. The process moved slowly, but it had moved along in the end. The longer the police were interested, the worse it was for the people who really had things to hide. The residents eventually agreed, and all the empty flats were opened so the police could carry out their search.

It was underway as Frank contemplated what to do next. He hoped this would be the end of it, not just this case, but his covering up of whatever was going on. He had drafted his retirement letter. It was time, he told himself, time to let other people play this bloody game and for him to enjoy life. This certainly wasn't enjoyment. Every bloody phone call now filled him with a dread that he hadn't ever known before. Worse, he didn't even really know why. Or maybe he didn't want to admit why. Something had been nagging him about the block of flats though; something was happening there that he hadn't sussed, hadn't put together yet.

The phone rang.

Frank picked it up.

"Hello?"

"Sir, Hopkins." Hopkins was one of the specialist search team that was checking out the flats. Diligent officer, really good guy. "I'm going to need you to come down and have a look at something,"

"What is it?"

"A vat, it looks like it had some sort of corrosive substance in it. We found it in the roof space above one of the flats."

"Like an acid?" Frank asked.

"Yeah, but that's not all, there's a little bit of material in there. We weren't able to salvage much, but it looks to me like some sort of wood. The acid or whatever it was, wasn't the strongest I've ever seen, and it's taken its time on it. I think this might be a handle from a machete. If there was metal, it's been completely corroded."

Frank's heart sank. Had he let the cat out of the bag too soon?

"Sir?" Hopkins was still there, he remembered.

"Could it be the murder weapon?"

"It's going to be pretty impossible to tell. It's been messed up pretty bad, and we won't get anything concrete out of it. It could be, probably is given the circumstances, but no lawyer in the land will have an issue dismissing that."

Frank nodded, relieved, then realising Hopkins couldn't see him, carried on.

"Is there anything in there we can use?"

"We'll check the place completely, but so far nothing. If this is linked, I'd suggest it means we know our guy got out a long time ago."

"Yeah, I feared you'd say that." Frank frowned. "Thanks, Hopkins, keep me in the loop."

The world went quiet when Frank hung up. He had been played, he had been beaten, and now he was an accessory to the murder of a UK politician, and it was all so obvious to him now. He hadn't cared, he hadn't done anything. It was an indictment on what he had become. So soft, so spineless. That was why they had picked him, Frank was forced to admit, because they thought he was the one who was most likely to go along with them. The most to lose, so close to the end of the game. Thea had been right all along.

He thought of Thea.

He stood up, grabbed his coat, and left the office.

21

Thea's phone rang. She looked down and saw Frank's name. She slipped her phone onto silent and ignored it. She wanted to keep her focus on what was happening now. The call from Jack Quinn had been unexpected, and she half-suspected that it was a trap. The problem was, she half-believed him, so she had to go with that. All the same, hope for the best, prepare for the worse. In her car, she always carried a Taser, something she'd had with her on a couple of early jobs. She placed it down the interior pocket of the driver's side door. Just in case.

She saw Jack arrive in a grey Audi saloon. He circled the carpark, past some boy racers, reconnoitring them all. Clearly convinced they were nothing more than bored youths, he parked his car next to hers, pointing the opposite way, so their driver's side windows were next to one another's. He wound his window down.

"Not got your friend with you?" Thea scanned behind him.

"No, working alone on this one," he said.

"What have you got?" Thea was as blunt as ever.

"There's a man, an assassin, who's come to the UK. To do what, we're not one hundred percent sure. Reuben Arrowsmith has been paid to protect him, we think." He explained what Mo had discovered and that Erik was probably Vic Bartram's killer. Thea listened and found herself, against her better judgement, believing every word, knowing it all to be true.

"Of course, evidentially, you're probably going to be up against it, unless you can find something in those flats."

"I'll check in with my AD; he's leading the operation for us over there." Thea plotted what to do next and then thought about Frank's call to her. Perhaps he had discovered something. She ought to call him straight after.

"Good," Jack carried on. "The problem is, we get the feeling Reuben is just a patsy. Someone who plausible deniability can be attached to if everything goes sour in whatever it is they're planning. That's why you were pulled from the investigation on him."

"Wait, that wasn't you?"

"Wasn't us. We let you do your job, and if you can convict someone, go for it. It's when you can't, we come in. Like I said, if we can find something you can use in a court of law, it's yours."

"So, who was it?"

"Best guess, whoever is working to get this over the line."

"You mean that its someone in our government? Our secret services?"

"Yeah," Jack said grimly.

"I almost believe you."

"That's a start."

"And what do you want me to do?"

"I want you to start looking for this guy." Jack pulled out his phone, quickly found a picture of Erik, and passed it to Thea between the two cars. "This is Erik Andryiv, international assassin, all-round bad egg."

Thea took the phone and studied the picture. "Do you know where he is?"

"He was being holed up in one of the flat's Reuben uses for his girls."

"Marianne's," Thea said, remembering the unanswered door.

"We think so, but we think he's long gone. He should be. Like I said, this guy is a pro. A damn good one, and we need to turn up the heat."

"How hot?"

"Put his face out there. Making him visible to everyone minimises the way he can operate. Right now, he's a ghost, but if you put his face everywhere and let people know he's about to carry out an imminent terror attack, then he's going to get spotted really quickly."

"And half a dozen other people who look a little bit like him," Thea pointed out. "People profile first, pick out the fineries later. That's what we're dealing with."

"That's a price we have to pay on this one."

"It's a shitty price, and it'll cause panic."

"Good, as I said, it'll make it harder for him to do whatever he's planning."

Thea looked at the picture and then at Jack, then back at the picture.

"Fine, I'll push his face out there, but we get him. Not you."

"I don't care who gets him, just as long as we stop him."

Thea believed him. She nodded. The deal was made.

* * *

Reuben was driving, so he put Bowen's call on speaker. He didn't like doing that, but he knew he couldn't afford to be pulled over, not now. It would have been more than a minor inconvenience.

"Hello?" he announced.

"I need a favour." Reuben noted that Bowen didn't ask and that piqued his anger even more.

"Don't do favours, we do jobs." He knew he was being obtuse, but he couldn't help himself.

"I need a job doing then."

"Where?"

"I've sent you the address, can you get there in time?"

"I'm in the middle of something, pal, out of town," Reuben explained, not even caring about Bowen's reaction.

"Can you send a man?"

"What sort of job?"

"Waste removal."

"When?"

"Right now."

"Jesus, Bowen, we're not special ops, we're fucking gangsters. We can go around and mess someone up for you, but if you want my boys to be playing cloak and dagger, bloody cold assassins, and all that shit, you're barking, mate. You want the job done right, get someone who can do it right, someone who knows the game. I ain't bottling nothing, you hear, but I ain't putting my boys in a stitch that I can't be a part of."

"You're refusing?" Bowen now sounded a little angry, and it was the first time Reuben had felt he might have rattled him.

"No, we don't refuse, I'm just giving you a…" Reuben searched for a term he hoped might bring it home to Bowen. "Let's call it an operational assessment. My boys are not hitmen. You want someone whacked in a hurry, they can do it, but it will be messy, and the fallout could hurt all of us. You have other resources, hell, you could even do it yourself. A damn sight better than my boys can on the hop."

"That's not the point."

"You hired us because we're good at what we do. There are some things you are better at, though, and that takes a lot for me to say, trust."

There was silence from Bowen for a moment.

"Maybe you're right," he finally conceded. "I'll be in touch."

The line went dead. Then Reuben made another call.

* * *

Thea had a voicemail when she finished her meeting with Jack. It was from Frank, and she listened into it as he sheepishly mumbled his way through some half-explained apology for not being the cop he should have been and that he had something he needed to talk to her about, but not on the phone.

A quick call back to his mobile rang out, and Thea started her car to drive back home. What Frank wanted, she really didn't know. As far as she was concerned, they had put everything behind them the other day and he'd already apologised for his lack of effort then. Maybe he was drunk? Who knew? He sounded a little off, the call was a little rushed. True, he wasn't slurring, or singing, two of Frank's common tells when he'd had a drink, but there was something about his voice that sounded out of the ordinary.

All the way back, her head was working through what she had agreed to with Jack. She hadn't lied, she had begun to believe him, especially when he had said that they would let her take the collar if they had the proof. There was a definite energy about him that betrayed his enthusiasm for trying to do the right thing, for wanting to bring people to justice. What bothered her was what would happen if they didn't have the proof. Was she setting herself up for abetting these people?

Dismissing the possibility of failure and resolving to double down her efforts, Thea felt better. She would negate the need for this to go down any other way by getting what she needed for a conviction. She could concentrate on doing whatever was needed, to end this vigilante group when all this was over. It had become a quest for her to do that now, something she had destined herself for the moment that Lowri

Graves had come to visit. It had been a challenge that she had decided she was going to take.

The carpark at the apartment building she lived in was underneath the block of flats. Night was falling now, and numerous fluorescent strip lights cast a slight green and yellow hue on everything they illuminated. Thea approached the bay that was attributed to her flat. She saw Frank's car parked up in her visitors slot. Clearly, whatever it was that he had to tell her couldn't wait.

She pulled her car in next to his, got out, and began to walk towards the entry door which led to the foyer, that then gave access on into the individual apartments. She glanced briefly back at Frank's car, just as she got to the door. It wasn't a planned glance, just an unconscious one, but she spotted something, something that didn't make sense. She stepped back towards the car, her mind beginning to race.

The engine from her car creaked and ticked as the heat seeped out into the air of the garage, but other than that, everything was quiet. There was no one else in the garage, only her, alone. She crept closer to the car. Now she heard her heart beginning to pulse stronger as she got nearer to the car and the visual clues she had seen began to make sense.

There was some sort of mark on the driver's window and a glittering inside the car. The glittering was from glass, broken glass, that had fallen into the car when the driver's side window had been broken. The mark was a dirty, deep red, almost brown, that splattered across, from left to right as Thea looked at it, spreading outwards, wider and wider, in the same direction the glass had fallen.

A bullet had shattered the glass. The reddish-brown stain was blood, and slumped across the driver's seat and passenger seat was Frank, dead, a hole in his head where someone had shot him at point-blank range.

22

"You're convinced there's more people like Glover out there?" David and Mo were talking at Mo's desk. David had come over and sat next to him when he saw the analyst had returned to work unexpectedly, eager to make sure that everything was okay with him. Mo had been through a lot, the first time he'd been under fire and as far as David could ascertain, the first time he had seen someone killed. He'd been impressed by Mo's resolve, but also concerned that it was him throwing himself into his work in an effort to hide from the reality of all the things that he was facing. David knew that, after all this, it was imperative to get Mo the right help. There were demons in his head, but for now, he was functioning, he was focused, and he had a goal.

During their conversation, Mo had said that he felt a degree of guilt for not being able to save Kristian and that he wanted to save some of the others who had no doubt been behind the cyber-attack. There was a chance that the people who killed Kristian had underestimated the way that hackers worked. They hadn't reckoned on him leaving a tag in place. They probably still didn't know that existed. Mo could exploit that to find others and warn them before they, too, became the victims of a clean-up crew.

"I know there are more out there. Come on, it's a cultural thing, disaffection and all that. They'd have been lining up to do this sort of work if they felt it would screw up the system in some way. They just wouldn't have stopped to think about the fallout."

"Keyboard warriors," David sighed.

"Yeah, if you want to label them, they are, but they're just kids usually. Kids with an issue they want or need to confront and they're smart."

"How come they never came to you?"

"Maybe I didn't fit the bill. I'm not as outspoken as some of the other people out there. I'd rather observe and work out what's going on."

"So, how are you going to bring them out into the open?"

Mo pulled a face. "I'm going to need to go through Kristian's system and see if he has any contacts."

"Will it work? Will they talk?"

Mo looked at David earnestly. "I don't know, but if we can get to the people they hired, we might save their lives, and we might stop this."

"Isn't there a chance they might shut up shop on you if you tell them what you do?"

"They might, I might get nowhere, but it will at least put them on guard."

"Okay, do what you've got to do. I trust you."

"Thanks, boss," Mo said, turning to the computer and getting back to work. It felt good to help. To do something, but still ,there was a fear that he wouldn't be able to help these other kids, the same way he couldn't help Kristian.

* * *

"Fucking hell, Yannick." Reuben looked down at the dead Frenchman.

There had been no other choice. Eventually, the other four had figured out what Reuben and Fisher already knew, and despite early protests, Yannick had eventually admitted, that yes, he had spoken to someone. He tried to pass it off as

230

warning them off, by pointing out to them the security arrangements that Reuben had in place. It had all been in vain, and now he was dead.

Reuben had pulled the trigger. He had taken him, tied up in the boot of a car, to a quiet part of the Thames Estuary, a track just north of Cliffe Pools. It wasn't overlooked, wasn't lit by anything, just a dark, dirt track to the water's edge.

The 4x4 he had taken from the pool of cars they kept had bounced its way to near the river's edge, and then he had got out, walking around to the back and opening the boot to reveal Yannick, nicely and securely trussed and under a thick blanket.

With the boot open, Reuben had ordered him out, and they had picked their way to the side of the river. Yannick, to his credit, had accepted his fate. There was no attempt to run, no pleading now, just a grim knowledge that this was how it ended. He had kissed his cross, knelt by the river, and then the shot had been fired from the silenced pistol that had finished the job.

Reuben had wrapped him back in the blanket, weighted a few rocks in it, just enough to take him down slowly, and then pushed him out into the water. The tide would play its part here, taking him away from the land and out towards the North Sea, part of the design behind Reuben picking the time, knowing it would coincide with the changing of the tide.

The drive back had been uncomplicated, and Reuben had done his best not to think about what had happened. There was no point beating yourself up about these things when you were alone. He knew when he wanted to talk about it, and he knew who with.

By the time he arrived home, it was almost one in the morning, but Nisha was still up. She knew that something was happening, she had seen the signs countless times before and she let Reuben dictate the pace. If he needed her, she was there; if he needed to be left alone, that was fine too.

He slumped on the sofa in their living room, face drawn, and sighed. Then he looked at Nisha, genuine sorrow in his eyes.

"Why the fuck did he have to do that?"

Reuben sobbed.

His head slumped forward, and he clasped it, shuddering in his hands, unleashing the emotion of what he had just done.

Nisha moved tenderly over to him and put her arm around him. He bowed his head in his hands, wiped the tears away, and then looked up, talking to an invisible audience in front of him as Nisha cuddled in and listened.

"Stupid, French fuck. They offered to pay his debts and get him a job in France. That's it. That's all they offered. Jesus. I could have given him that, if I'd have known, if he'd have told me he wanted out."

"It's alright, baby."

"Yannick, man, I didn't want to kill Yannick. Miserable bastard, yeah, but I still loved him. He was still one of mine."

"You couldn't do anything else."

"I know, I know…"

"He left you no choice."

Reuben pushed her arm away and stood up, looking at her, still sniffing away the tears.

"Nah, they left me no choice. They backed him into a corner and forced him to panic. He was scared. You should have seen him when he told me; it was like it took a weight off him. They scared him, they fucking killed him. They made me kill him. I ain't having that. I ain't letting them make me do that no more. I'm finding these sons of bitches, both sides of this shit, and I'm ending them all, then we're out. We're done, baby. I ain't risking you no more."

* * *

The noise jolted him from his sleep, and immediately, Bowen was on edge. The sound of his phone vibrating on the bedside table of the hotel room where he stayed was soft, but to him, it might as well have been the chimes of Big Ben. He was on an operation, he was hyper-sensitised now, and nothing slipped past him.

He glanced at the time as he grabbed his phone. A couple of minutes past two in the morning. The call was through the scrambled app, and the code on the display showed it was coming from his superior. Very unexpected.

"Sir?"

"The police have got hold of Andryiv's face. They plan to release it to the media."

"Do we need to move to a new operative, sir?"

"No, we can proceed, for now. We are concerned about the reaction from Mitchell, however. How much does he know about him?"

"Not a lot, if he does some reading, he might be a little disappointed."

"Then we may have to accelerate our timetable."

"That's not a problem, sir."

The call clicked dead, and Bowen was left in the dark.

23

Thea had worked with an almost clinical process once she found the body. She had called it in and waited for the rest of the team to arrive on scene. She had taken great care to preserve everything, telling the receptionist at the apartment block to close the garage. She didn't even think of the disturbance that might cause her neighbours; it was just time to get on with the job.

The garage soon became awash with the various teams that the NCA brought with them in such incidences, and a forensic tent was erected around Frank's car.

Thea watched impassively as the forensic photographer snapped shots of Frank's body, still lying in place in the car. It would be a while before they moved it, she knew. It had never really crossed her mind before, that period between death and rest, where the body lay in limbo, locked in the excruciating last pose it had found. Now it was someone she knew, it was impossible to get it out of her mind. Was she distracting herself from the emotion, she wondered. Probably.

"Hey."

Thea turned to look at where the voice had come from. A shorter woman, with light shoulder-length, strawberry-blonde hair and green eyes, late thirties, stood next to her, dressed in a smart dark coat and white blouse. She knew her instantly. Grace Adams, part of the NCA's internal affairs unit.

"Hey."

"I'm sorry about Frank." Thea knew Grace meant that. She would be hurting as well. Grace went against the grain of the stereotypical internal affairs agent. Making relationships had been her goal since she had been appointed and she enjoyed a great rapport with most of the team, Frank included. She was an honest and genuine person, people trusted her. It made her job easier.

"You doing the interview?"

"Yeah. Is there somewhere we can go?"

Thea led Grace to the flat and offered her a drink. Grace had a black coffee. Thea considered something stronger, but then decided to follow suit. She knew her night was going to go on for a while now.

Grace had asked the usual questions. What had they both been working on? Who would be upset about it? Why was Frank coming to see her at this time?

Thea answered everything earnestly and in detail. All except the last question. That, she couldn't say.

"You say he called you beforehand?" Grace asked. "But you don't know why?"

"No, I never had the chance to."

"Why not?"

"I was at a fast food restaurant, ordering my food. By the time I'd done, he'd hung up. He left a voicemail, you're welcome to listen. Said it was something he wanted to talk to me about in person."

"And you don't know what that was?"

"We'd rowed earlier in the week," Thea repeated herself for the umpteenth time. She knew it flustered some people to go over old ground, but she knew why Grace was doing it. Cover the story over and over, look for inconsistencies. "I called him spineless for not sticking up for me when I had an investigation pulled."

"Could that investigation have been why he was killed?"

"It could have been. I don't know."

"The investigation was into Reuben Arrowsmith. Has he form for going after cops?"

"No, we'd have nailed him for that. He's capable, but I don't think he would take the risk." Thea may have said it, but she wasn't sure.

"Who pulled the investigation?"

"Frank wouldn't say. He gave me the impression it was Five or someone, though. Just things he said. 'No one in this office.'"

"Were you fucking him?"

Grace looked at Thea.

"No."

Grace smiled. "Had to ask."

"He was a lot of things, but Joyce was his world." Thea suddenly thought of Joyce. "Has anyone told her yet?"

"I guess so."

"I need to see her, when we're done, of course."

"Of course. Let's just go through your day one more time, just to make sure we've got everything."

Thea recounted every detail to Grace, one last time, just as she had every time before. She left out meeting with Jack.

* * *

Valentin Mamedov was delighted. A right-wing thug had just attacked and killed one of the most prominent members of the UK's alt-right, in broad daylight no less, and now, his readers were lapping up the idea that the far-right were turning on each other. There had been a morbid joy from some that this had happened. Valentin knew that sold papers, so he had been more than happy to fan the flames of that sentiment, discreetly, obviously.

He was in his office, allowing himself a celebratory gin and tonic, a drink he'd acquired a taste for since moving to the UK. He'd really tried to make himself as British as a Russian could. There were some things he'd never truly get, some things he would always truly miss, but gin and tonic was an excellent British invention, and he savoured each sip.

He'd had a number of calls throughout the day from people from different strands of the political game, all of them, without exception, expressing their dismay at the murder of Vic

240

Bartram. All of them, without exception, had detested in his life. It was Lord Mitchell, however, who had called him offering to do an interview on the subject. This was the perfect time to bring all the parties together, according to Mitchell. As a senior member of the House of Lords, he wanted to take that job on personally and wanted to do the interview directly with Mamedov himself. A chance to really drive home the idea of the left opening its arms to the right and trying to build bridges, Mitchell had proclaimed.

The end of divisive politics. Mamedov snorted at the idea, but he would give Mitchell his five minutes.

* * *

School was always a drag for Kat Quinn, but today it had been even worse. All anyone had wanted to talk to her about was Calum and what had happened to him.

At first, the very thought of talking about Calum, no matter what had happened to him, had made Kat angry. Why would she want to talk about him? But as the questions had carried on, she had begun to realise something. She actually cared about him. She was actually bothered about what had happened.

241

The clock seemed to tick even slower as the day wore on, and Kat was longing more than ever to get out of there. She hadn't seen Isaac all day. They didn't share classes, and he'd managed to get himself detentions through his breaks for swearing at a teacher. He was, she had to admit, a bit of an idiot.

The way he had been shown up by her dad hadn't helped his cause either. He'd embarrassed himself. That wasn't what Kat was looking for in a man. Her dad was already a macho idiot, and seeing Isaac trying to do the same had been a massive turn off. She would probably have to end it. Just not today, not after the day she had been through. Tomorrow, probably.

With the final bell, Kat had made her way to the back doors near the gym where she and Isaac always met. It wasn't just them; all of Isaac's friends, and sometimes Sasha's, would meet there, so as she approached, Kat wasn't surprised to hear voices.

As she reached the corner to the gym, she heard the boys yelping and shouting. Something had got them excited. Great. Just what she needed.

"He went down like a proper soft cunt, mate. No fucking fight, bruv," Kat heard Isaac boasting loudly, to the hoarse laughter of his friends.

Kat stopped and listened.

"Did he cry?"

"Yeah, like a right fucking bitch. He won't be slagging me off to his old boy again, you know."

Kat did know. She walked around the corner.

"Hey, babe." She smiled, wrapping an arm around Isaac and squeezing him tight.

"Alright, girl, you good?"

Kat noticed that the others looked a little flustered, almost like she had walked in on something. She looked up at Isaac. Credit to him, he was playing it cool. "I'm fine. You?"

"All good, babes, let's get out of here, yeah?"

"Yeah," Kat said. She reached out to his hand, intertwining her fingers in his, and playfully rocking both of their hands over and back. To anyone watching, it might look cute. It showed what she expected, Isaac's knuckles were bloody. "What you done to your hand?"

"Fucked a wall up init," Isaac shrugged. "Teacher was stressing me, so I had to go the bogs and let rip."

"Looks painful." She winced.

"Should've seen the other guy." This brought a stifled laugh from his friends.

Kat just smiled. "Nah, you're just a big softie. You wouldn't hurt anyone."

"You know it, babes." Isaac grinned. They all started the slow and meandering walk home.

All the while, Kat was planning.

24

Seeing Joyce had been something Thea thought would help both of them. They had both shared a relationship with Frank, albeit very different ones, and in her head, that bond with him would be something they could relate to.

It hadn't worked out like that, and as soon as Joyce began to break down, Thea realised the horrible mistake she had made. Thea might have been Frank's colleague at work, but it was clearly work that had killed Frank.

"They said he was in your carpark?" Joyce finally asked.

Thea felt a relief. It had been the elephant in the room, or at least, so she thought.

"He wanted to tell me something. I don't know what it was. He wouldn't say. I have the voicemail if you want to listen to it."

"No." Joyce shook her head. Then she changed her mind. "Actually?"

Thea passed her the phone silently and watched as Joyce listened to Frank's last known words.

"What was it?" Joyce handed the phone back

"What was what?"

"What he wanted to speak to you about." There was an urgency in Joyce's voice as if she was hurrying Thea to the answer.

"I don't know."

"How can you not know? It involved you."

"I'd had a case pulled, and we fell out over it. I don't know what he wanted to say about it. If that was it."

"Would someone kill him over it?"

"I don't know. I don't know who pulled the case, or why, or what he knew," Thea said truthfully.

"What case was it?"

"You know I can't say."

"Please. If Frank died for it?" Joyce looked desperate. It was a look Thea had seen too many times before, in the victims of people she had hunted. They all wanted the same thing. Answers. Not revenge, not justice. Those thoughts were the furthest thing from their minds. They just wanted to know why. All the other stuff came after.

"It was a gang thing in London. Frank wouldn't have known enough about that for them to target him. It was something else. I don't know what, but I promise you, Joyce. I will find out, and I will put them away."

Joyce sat backwards in her seat.

"He's really gone, isn't he?" she croaked.

"I'm sorry." Thea sniffed.

On the drive back, Thea focused her mind on the question that she knew would break this. What was it that Frank had wanted to tell her? Why wouldn't he tell her on the phone? Why had it got him killed?

* * *

The revelation of Erik's photo had certainly impacted his mission. He had planned to do a number of reconnaissance missions, but early that morning he had received an encrypted text. He had been compromised. There had been talk of pulling him from the mission completely, but Erik had managed to make them think again. He was used to dealing with hostile environments, and this one would be no different.

The main adjustment that he had requested to the plan was to send someone else in to do his reconnaissance. It was a shame not to be able to go out there and take in the location himself, to really get a feel for it, but using a live link to a mobile phone, he would be able to get a view of everything he would need to achieve a successful outcome. It wasn't optimal, but it was far from disastrous.

The operation itself would again call for a covert approach, making the use of his photo in an attempt to stall him, nothing more than a token gesture. It showed their desperation to find him.

Not that it wasn't worrying, he had to admit as he watched the feed of the location coming back to him on his tablet. There was no doubt that the very fact that they knew who he was meant that, even after the missions here were over, he was going to have to spend a lot of time looking over his shoulder. Even more so than he did now. The heat would pass eventually, but it would never go away, and one day, someone, somewhere, would catch up to him and end it all. That was always the way it was going to be. This just added another name to the list of people itching to pull that trigger.

"Move left, I need to see the atrium area," he calmly spoke into the microphone attached to his tablet, and the person at the other end did as instructed.

Erik saw the atrium. It was large and flanked by a stack of six mezzanines that overlooked the lobby. It was a perfect spot for the attack, less so for a getaway. He looked down at the paper blueprints his employers had provided for him.

"I need you to go upstairs, fourth-floor mezzanine, show me what you can see up there," he relayed more orders and sat back watching as the footage bounced through the lobby to the elevators, then up and out onto the mezzanine.

Here he could look down on the area where the target would arrive. It wouldn't be immediately apparent where the attack had come from; there would be more than a few moments of chaos and confusion, which would aid his escape. The hit itself wasn't the most taxing; it was the escape that he had been brought in for.

The desire to make each hit look amateurish, in order to maintain the premise that this was a fringe group, gave rise to the bombastic approach he was taking. This wasn't subtle. Lethal, but not subtle.

He looked down at the blueprints, before speaking to his accomplice.

"I need you to walk to the fourth door down and go through it."

Erik pressed a button on his watch and the camera once more bobbled on its way through the building, through the door. Erik liked what he saw. A long corridor, with offices all of which had windows pointing outwards, not inwards to where he would be. He directed the camera operator further into the warren of the building, through more doors, down more non-descript corridors, down a fire escape and then eventually out, into a loading area.

Erik looked at his watch. Walking, it had taken the man a little over sixty seconds. He would need to act much faster. No matter how chaotic the scene below would be, he knew that there would be a quick response by the police to put a cordon up. His escape hung solely on being able to navigate out of that cordon before it was in place. Otherwise, he knew he would be captured or killed.

* * *

Calum ached. His face felt like it had been stuffed with cement. It was heavy and hard in places. He could feel it pushing out of where it should normally be, creeping into the edges of his vision, pushing back against his bones, against his teeth, constantly there, a reminder of what had happened.

He hadn't left his room since he got back from the hospital, save for the occasional trip out to the bathroom. There were too many questions outside of the sanctuary of these four walls, too many people prying, not willing to let him curl up, hide and let it all blow over. He didn't want more conflict, he didn't need police, or his dad, or anyone, sorting this out.

He hadn't really been lying when he said he didn't really see who attacked him. There had been flashes of a person in his eyesight, but the whole thing had happened so quickly. So much had been blotted out of his memory, hidden in some dark recess of his mind, thank God, that if you asked him to describe his attacker, he wouldn't be lying when he told you that he couldn't.

His bedroom offered him near enough all he needed. A TV, a laptop, his Xbox, his books. Not that he could use any of those for too long. His head still throbbed if he concentrated on one thing for any real period of time. He devoured the paracetamol his mother brought up to him, alongside the drinks and food that he showed less interest in.

The whole thing had left him exhausted, and were he bothered to consider his situation, he would have been surprised at how much he slept. Calum wasn't one for naps. Indeed, he was very much the sort of kid who liked to stay up late, but now he spent the afternoon sleeping for at least an hour, and he found that not long after nine, his eyes were fighting to stay awake. With very little fight left in him, he had given in.

Kat had been conspicuously absent at first, he thought, and when she did come in, she had been quiet and uncomfortable. More so than normal. Calum quickly decided she knew something. She was in on it. Somehow. That meant that this was probably something to do with her new boyfriend. Isaac. He was angry at her, still, when he heard her knock on his door.

"Hey," she said apologetically as her head poked around the door.

Calum said nothing in return, which was as good as an invitation in. Kat heeded it and pushed the door to behind her.

"How you doing?" she asked awkwardly.

Calum looked at her.

"I know," she said. "Had to ask."

She sat on the end of the bed.

"What you doing?"

"Dying."

Kat laughed.

"It's not funny," Calum went on.

"Sorry. I just…you're funnier than you think," Kat soothed.

"I wasn't trying to be. It really feels like my head has been crushed."

"Looks a bit that way as well," Kat teased him lightly.

Even Calum could spot the softness in her voice. "Thanks," he said, almost cracking a smile. Then he added, "It was Isaac, wasn't it?" It might have sounded like a question, but it was more a statement of fact.

"What are you going to do about it?" Kat shifted her weight and folded her arms.

"I don't know." Calum looked down. Was she threatening him?

"I get it. Police are just a waste of time, and Dad getting involved, well, I know how embarrassing that is."

Calum looked at Kat, spotting the barb, but decided not to say anything about it. "Exactly, not a lot I can do."

"I know, but I can. If you want. I can fuck his life up."

"How?"

"I have ways."

Calum shrugged indifferently. "Do it."

***

Mo had gone to work on Kristian's computer. He knew everything was on there somewhere, it was just really, really well covered. Kristian had been using Tor to get online, which wasn't like your normal run-of-the-mill browser. It didn't leave a list of sites that Kristian had visited. It wasn't as easy as simply looking at his history, but there were different programmes that had been developed over the years that could cut through even the tightest of defence mechanisms. It was just a case of waiting for something he could use.

A breezy "ping" from his computer alerted him to one of his programmes yielding a result. Mo snapped out of his trance-like state and moved quickly through the windows on his display, to find what it was he was looking for.

What he saw was a list of numbers, the sites that the programme had determined that Kristian had visited. It had then cross-referenced the traffic on these sites with the details of people known to The Regulators. It had pulled one site in particular, where Kristian had signed in a couple of times, leaving cryptic messages. The contents of those messages didn't reveal much, but what Mo needed to know was who the other people were.

His plan was simple but risky. Contact each one directly with a short, succinct message that hopefully had enough impact to draw these people out.

There were four more people who had logged into the same system. One, no doubt, would be the people behind the attack. Chances were that it was the person who logged in the most, Mo reasoned. After all, they would be maintaining contact with four other people, whereas the others were simply reporting to one.

It was clear that there was a predominant user on the site, and so Mo discounted them quickly and instead sent his message to the other three.

The message read;

"Ownarchist dead. Bad guys will kill you too. I can help. Contact me."

Attached at the bottom was a picture of Kristian's body, lifted from the police investigation.

Now, all Mo could do was wait.

25

"I'm sorry about your partner," Jack said. "This is a dangerous game we play, sometimes the wrong people get hurt."

It was a token gesture of an apology, he knew that. Frank probably wasn't the wrong person. He was exactly the right person for whoever had pulled the trigger. Jack was certain Frank had known something and he was on his way to tell Thea. Jack was sure of it, it was in his gut. It was the only thing that made sense.

Thea looked nervous. Jack hadn't seen her so quiet before. Something was bothering her. *Does she think I did this?* he wondered.

"I think Frank was bent," she said finally.

It wasn't exactly what Jack was expecting, but it certainly gave everything a lot more context.

"What makes you say that?" He kept his poker face in place.

"His phone was gone, lifted from the car." Thea handed him a small tablet computer that he started skimming through. It detailed the preliminary notes from the investigation. "We checked what it had been used for. The calls were all standard, but his data allowance didn't make sense."

"Encrypted calls?" Jack finished off the revelation.

"That's what we think. It was all going through an app that we can't identify. Is it something you use?"

"Us and most other secret service agencies the world over. Some top-end terror cells, criminal gangs. A whole host of people. A lot of whom would kill a cop."

"Could you ID it?"

"Our techs can try. Did he ever say anything about someone he might have been talking to?"

Thea raised an eyebrow.

"Of course not," Jack acknowledged.

"Like I said to you, he said that whoever had pulled the plug was way up the food chain and was someone I'd never get to."

"Which lends a bit of credence to our fear that it could be someone within the UK government, or at the very least, one of the corridors of power."

"A scabby, shitty little corridor with no windows on what's actually going on in the world," Thea lamented. "I mean, seriously, where do they get off on the idea that killing people is in some way for the best for the country?"

"Bigger pictures," Jack said, knowing full well it was a decision he'd had to make and live with, many a time in the past. "Sometimes you are faced with terrible choices, and you make the lesser of the two."

"Seriously?" Thea didn't hold her disappointment.

"I'm not saying that's what they did here, just, in other cases."

"You tell yourself that."

"I have to."

Thea looked at him for a moment, and Jack saw her resolve soften. For a moment, he was certain she would ask him about where he had been, what he had been through, and he regretted showing that small sliver of vulnerability.

"I'm not going to ask," she said finally.

"I'm not going to tell." He shook his head solemnly. "Seriously, our world, it sucks, and I'm sorry you've been dragged in."

"Well, I ain't going anywhere yet, not till we've got someone. You got any theories yet?"

"The videos make us think it's someone looking to destabilise the extremes of right-wing politics, so probably someone on the left, who wants to capitalise."

"I thought the left was all about tolerance and acceptance?"

"It's a message that's losing. Like I said, sometimes people will compromise themselves for a greater good, or at least what they perceive to be."

"I can't buy that. I can't buy that someone, who thinks they're on the right side of the line, decided to start a terrorist group. Vic Bartram, sooner or later, would have fell on his own sword. They all mess up, so what was the rush? No, there's more."

* * *

The death of Yannick still weighed hard on Reuben, and he had been working hard to try and uncover who had got to his man. Door knocking at Yannick's block of flats had produced a rough description of a man, tall and well built, maybe brown hair. It was a start.

He had hoped that Yannick's phone would provide the biggest clue. He had used it to contact whoever it was he had betrayed him too. The number was scrambled. Reuben had passed it on to one of Bowen's people, who had worked on it, but ultimately found the encryption impossible to crack. At least, so far.

Bowen had asked to arrange a meeting with Reuben. Reuben had agreed, knowing the possibility that he was being summoned into a trap, but also that he couldn't say no, not now he was this far in. Certainly not given how he had turned down Bowen the last time out.

Now he was here, inside the back of a van with no windows, being driven around London for nearly an hour, in a range of directions to ensure there was no one tailing them. It also meant he wouldn't be able to work out where he was.

Finally, the van stopped and backed up, the rear doors opening into a loading bay of what looked like an old factory. Standing on a concrete platform was Bowen, who smiled when he saw Reuben.

"Apologies for the drive, I can't imagine it was the most pleasant experience?"

"I've been on the tube, pal, I know luxury and I know cattle."

Bowen laughed. Reuben wasn't sure if he meant it or not.

"Come on, we need to talk, make sure we're all on the same page."

"Sounds like a plan," Reuben agreed, and he followed Bowen into the building.

Bowen settled on a dusty looking office that wouldn't have been out of place in an episode of *Minder* or something. Ramshackle shelves and crooked filing cabinets lined the room, while a tatty desk lay in between the two of them as they seated on cheap plastic office chairs.

"It's been a busy couple of hours, as I'm sure you know, and I think I need to apologise for trying to put that job on you. I appreciate now what you were dealing with and why you wanted to make sure we used the right people," Bowen explained, a smile on his face like he was appraising a business partnership.

"It's all good, we all do what we have to." Reuben waved his hand casually. "I just hope you got the result you needed."

"I think we did. And your issue, your employees. Can we guarantee their loyalty from now on?"

"As much as any man's loyalty can be guaranteed. They all know the price. It's on them to decide if they want to pay it, isn't it?"

Bowen nodded. "No, I can imagine they do, and I assume you're not in the habit of suffering fools."

"No, nor are you in the habit of inviting me round for a chat and a cup of shitty tea, so let's get to the real reason I'm here."

Bowen smiled slyly.

"The people who turned your man, we think they're part of an international vigilante organisation that we're trying to crack. We have a few links as to people who might be involved, but this lovely lady here is the most likely candidate." Bowen pulled his phone out and showed Reuben a photo of Lowri Graves. "She works for the Home Office, officially, but off the books, she seems to like interfering in things that go beyond what would normally be considered her reach."

"You mean, she's another one, just like you, who wants to take matters into her own hands," Reuben countered, looking at the photo.

"I suppose you could put it that way, but you're on our side, and she's decidedly not, so the time for the ethics debate on this is short."

"What do you want me to do with her?"

"We want you to take her, break her, and find out what she knows. Then kill her."

"Sounds fair. I suppose you have intel on when best to do it?"

"We do, and we'd like to suggest a time when we believe that enough eyes will be elsewhere so that you have less trouble."

"Works for me. Get your people to give the details to Fish, he can sort the op. Me and her will have a little chat about poor old Yannick."

"Wonderful, thank you. Mr Arrowsmith, you continue to be a most useful asset."

"I figure it helps my cause."

Bowen forced a smile this time, a quick snap of one. Reuben spotted it, knowing instantly that the poker face had slipped and that Bowen had a plan for all the loose ends. It was just a shame for Bowen that Reuben had a better one.

26

Annie was scared. She had seen the message online. She hadn't wanted to believe it, but if what this person was saying was true, then she was at risk too, so she did the only thing she knew how to. She dug for the facts.

It hadn't been easy, because she didn't know who Ownarchist was. They had spoken, using both IRC and VOIP services, but they had never seen each other's faces. She knew he was a he, but she didn't know his name. He just liked to be called Ownarchist. She liked to be called Carmage. She had never seen him, but in a way, she sort of loved him, or maybe she loved the idea of him. It was hard to say. Online relationships were often all-consuming and emotionally draining, such was their intensity.

It was one of the reasons why she searched so hard to find the truth. That and self-preservation, which was an even bigger part of it, but when she had found the proof, her love for him had been the real reason she had wept. For that moment, she had forgotten her own safety, her own fears, and she had cried for the loss of Ownarchist, or Kristian, to give him his real name.

She had cried longer than perhaps she should have and she silently berated herself when, finally, she began to start rationalising all that had happened. If Kristian was dead, anyone else who had shared in this project was next in line. The person who had warned her, whoever it was, clearly didn't know who else was involved, but she did. Annie had spoken with Kristian, she had spoken with Raven, and she had spoken with EeQual. Now none of them were responding, they had all gone quiet.

Was she the only one left? It seemed scary, but it seemed true. She knew she had only one option. Run.

Packing a bag with just the bare essentials and taking with her a thick money belt she kept under her bed for just such an eventuality, she was soon out on the street. Cap on, hood up, head down, doing her best to remain hidden. She would walk out of the city, avoiding areas where she knew there was a high number of cameras. Her first stop would be a small guesthouse in Esher, South London. She had marked it out years ago as a place to hide for a night. She had never researched it, never looked at it online, she just knew it was there, because she passed it every couple of months or so on her way to see her aunt who lived on the coast in Havant. Statistically speaking, it was unlikely that anyone would deduce that as a place for her to hide out, so she was happy that one night there, at most, would be secure.

What she did need to do, however, was get in touch with the user who had alerted her to Kristian's death. The problem was that she had no idea who the user was. She'd seen them a few times in some of the chat groups that she used, talking about a couple of hacks they'd been in on. She knew from what she had seen that they knew what they were doing, but they had always stayed on the outside, almost like they had been waiting. Not really partaking. Like so much right now, that scared her. Perhaps that was the trap that they had lain well in advance. Perhaps she had secreted herself so successfully that the only way to flush her out was to use this potential escape as bait. But she knew she had no choice.

She needed to find a way to confirm that the user was one of the good guys and could keep her safe. So, she had straight up asked for proof.

"Need to know who u are?" she had written.

Now as she walked through the streets on a twisty, indiscriminate course that took her in a meandering path towards her destination, she called into where she hoped she would get the answers.

Kingston University was busy, and she would no doubt be seen by countless people. There was also a myriad of CCTV cameras looking across a range of facilities on the campus, but Annie had a plan.

Using a route she had carefully crafted over the years, she approached the university dodging the cameras, finally making her way into the main building. She took off her cap and dropped her hood. No one would know to look for her here, and she would soon take care of the cameras.

She approached the library of the university and was faced with an electronic barrier that opened when a student passed their university ID over the scanner. She took a small white card from her pocket, which had her face on, but not her name. The name was fake, the address was fake, it was a dead end that would lead nowhere.

She made her way to a spare computer and logged in using a fake user ID and then took a small SSD from her bag and plugged it into the machine. A few seconds later, a window appeared on the desktop, and she selected the programme she needed and waited.

The hack was a pretty routine one, designed to open up any number of flaws on a network system as large as that at a modern university. Within seconds the programme had negotiated with and accessed the security system for the whole university. Annie worked quickly, setting up a programme that would ultimately blanket all the university systems with a ransomware package. No one would be able to view the security footage for days at least. Plenty of time to make good her escape. Simple, but effective.

Her tracks covered, she began to work on finding out if she could trust the hacker who called themselves Crassus.

This was a much harder task. Crassus was an expert, he had used the same protocols she had used when he joined the IRC, which meant she knew he was as good as invisible. But he was reaching out to her, he had broken his cover, and she knew that he would have left a trail.

She settled down and began to search. She figured she could give herself an hour at most. Then she needed to be out.

* * *

Erik entered the foyer of the building he had seen on the video. It was as he recalled. He strode in calmly his face exposed a little, poking out from underneath a motorcycle helmet, but not enough so that any of the security cameras he had marked out would be able to get a glimpse of him and run him through any facial recognition software.

Beneath the helmet, he had dyed his hair, trimming it down low, as well as letting his stubble grow further, enough to fool anyone who was only taking a casual glance at him. Law enforcement was one thing; they were taught to look at members of the public and try and recognise a face in a crowd. He knew that the receptionist he was about to talk to would not be so well trained and wouldn't even really be looking at him. She would just see a face she thought she recognised, mull it over maybe briefly, before moving on, convinced he was just a regular courier who she had seen a handful of times before.

He approached the desk calmly and handed over a parcel, wordlessly, as if it was just another part of his day.

"Thank you," beamed the receptionist, looking at the address label and beginning to get up to take the package to the relevant cubby hole.

"No problem," Erik replied and feigned to walk away and then turned back briskly. "I'm sorry, can I quickly use your loo?"

He used the English term, even though it was a weird word to him. What sort of a country nicknames their toilet?

"Of course." The receptionist smiled at him. "It's just over there on your right, second door along."

"Thanks." Erik smiled apologetically, then made his way to the bathroom. Inside it was empty. A row of six urinals attached to the wall on one side and a row of four cubicles opposite. There was a cleaning rota on one of the walls. He scanned the times and dates, happily noting that the last slot was already checked. There wasn't another inspection due for a good half an hour, which would probably translate into much longer if the cleaners here were like the cleaners at any other large facility. Check sheets could be forged and written up easily, and no one was likely to be going around on the hour checking them. They were just there to keep the more hygienically minded customers happy.

He opened the plastic frame of the check sheet and pulled out the piece of paper. On the back, there was a printed sign that read "Toilets closed. Cleaning in progress." He took it, opened the door to the corridor, and seeing no one was around, he placed the sign on the door, before closing it once more.

He didn't need to think about which cubicle to use, he already knew from the blueprints. The second one in from the door would best suit his needs. He entered and locked the door behind him, removing his helmet and attaching it to a sturdy clip on the side of his bike leathers.

With a surprisingly agile leap, he climbed up onto the seat of the toilet and took a small electric screwdriver to the metallic panel of the air conditioning unit above him. One by one, he took the screws out, always listening to hear if anyone would ignore the sign and come in anyway. They didn't.

With the final screw out, the panel dropped, and he caught it with his empty hand, then slid it into the ventilation shaft. The space above was small but large enough for him to get in and navigate to where he needed to be. He placed both hands up and into the vent, finding the lip and working his fingers across as far as they would go, gripping as best he could. Then he began to pull himself up, slowly, surely, until he was completely in the vent. He pulled the cover back across, slipped the screws backwards, knowing it was highly unlikely anyone would ever think to look at them. Then he was gone, into the maze of vents, making his way slowly, stealthily, towards the fourth-floor mezzanine where he needed to be for his next job.

* * *

Mo was monitoring the IRC channel, looking for a sign that one of the other hackers hired for the job had found his message and managed to get themselves safe. So far, it wasn't

273

looking good. Three of the people who frequented it hadn't logged in for a while, and so right now, his job was to try and trace them, to see if they were okay. Of the three people who had been missing from the channel, he'd found two. Both were dead.

That left one person, but that one person was giving Mo hope. Carmage. The chats that they had shared, albeit brief, had revealed someone who didn't really trust the outside world. That might have been working in Carmage's favour.

He had left a trail as best he could. Tags and fragments of code embedded in places that he hoped would allow them to piece together who he was. Carmage was a hacker, someone who saw patterns, spotted flaws, and knew how to exploit them. He was banking on that happening here.

His IRC pinged.

"51363-0364"

Mo looked at it. He didn't know the user, but he was pretty sure they looked like coordinates. He quickly opened a map up and typed them in, adding in the decimals where he thought it made sense. It gave him the corner of two roads in Esher, a small town in Surrey, south of London, at a point overlooking a golf course.

A meeting point.

"When?" he typed back.

"Two hours," came the reply.

Mo quickly fired back a brief, "okay," and then was out of his chair looking for David. He quickly found him and brought him up to speed.

"Ok, I'll send a pick-up team." David nodded.

"No, they won't go for that, they'll see it coming. Let me do this," Mo pleaded.

"What's to say they'll come to you?"

"I've left them so many clues to work out who I am, if they're really good enough. They should know my face, even if I don't know theirs."

David frowned. Mo knew his better judgement was telling him not to send Mo, especially after what he had been through, but Mo had made it impossible to leave him out of this.

"Fine," David said.

"Thanks, boss." Mo beamed, shaking David by the hand, which surprised them both.

27

Adam watched from the doorway as Laura painted in the nursery. He had been against the idea of a green bedroom at first. He was having a little girl, he wanted there to be pink somewhere, but Laura had put her foot down and insisted that just because their child was going to be a girl, didn't mean that they had any right to assume that she was going to like pink. A nice bright green would add vibrancy to the room and to the new life growing up in it, she'd argued successfully.

Laura hadn't heard him come in and he was happy with that. It was a moment of calm, in what had otherwise been a chaotic couple of days. Laura knew nothing about his life. He wanted to keep it that way, forever. She knew he did a dangerous job, thinking he worked in a form of close personal protection. She probably had her suspicions that it wasn't exactly what he said it was. The money was too good, the answers to elusive, and she wasn't dumb.

Finally, she turned around to see him, arms folded, smiling inanely at her.

"How long have you been there?"

"Long enough," he smirked, stepping into the room towards her. "Been busy?"

"Someone's got to get us ready for when she comes." Laura's hand reached for Adam's, placing it on her stomach.

"Not a lot going on there at the moment," he commented.

"Only at night, when I'm trying to sleep. Kid's got it in for me."

"Sorry."

"Not yet you're not. Not nearly enough," Laura laughed.

* * *

Jack had slipped home as well, hoping to get his head down for a couple of hours. It had been non-stop, and with the added stress of Calum's incident, he knew he needed to bed down and get some sort of rest. Clearing his head enough so he could do so was going to be a challenge, but he knew he needed to.

He opened the door and walked into his house, heading for the kitchen to get himself a quick drink, spotting Kat sat at his table, idly watching a video or some other distraction on her phone.

"Oh, hey." Jack didn't break stride, although he was a little surprised to see Kat here. "What you doing?"

Kat put down her phone and looked at him. "I'm here to help you."

Jack raised an eyebrow and walked over to the table sitting opposite her.

"Okay."

"I mean it."

"I can tell."

"I know who hurt Calum."

"Then tell me, that would help."

Kat rolled her eyes. "Would it, Dad? Really? You beating up a kid, that's helping?"

Jack sighed, knowing she was right, but feeling at pains to admit to it. "Okay, so how are you going to help?"

"Well, you can't hurt this kid, but I can."

Jack looked at his daughter. Her eyes were firmly set on his, no blinking, no wavering, just intensely focused, forcing her message into him. He knew the look, it was his.

"Is he a big guy?"

"Dad, not all fights are with fists. Haven't you learned that by now?"

Jack couldn't tell if she was being sarcastic, or she truly was incredulous. He decided not to press and find out.

"No, they're not."

"Exactly. So, I need you to help me get some things, and then I'll do the rest."

"How much trouble could this get you in?"

"Me? None. Him, with his record, a lot."

Jack nodded slowly.

"Okay," he said, knowing he might sleep a little easier now with one less thing to worry about.

* * *

The gates outside one of Reuben's warehouses rolled open, and a van swung out and onto the road. Reuben and Fisher sat up front in the van. Fisher was driving, Reuben was the eyes. He had been given a location and a time to be there. The plan was simple. There would be a small window between Lowri leaving her flat and reaching her car, in which they had to grab her. She would be in a hurry, so she wouldn't be as careful as she was going to need to be. It was an easy snatch. Then the fun would begin.

* * *

Erik was in place. He checked the time. Less than five minutes until the target arrived. He took the backpack from his bag and opened it, checking the contents. Three M67 fragmentation grenades. More than enough to cause the necessary devastation. It was a sloppy style for a hit, not what he'd go for normally. The grenades had a casualty radius of fifteen metres and a kill radius of five. He hoped the first two would either finish off the target or render him incapacitated enough to be finished off by the third. Some might call it overkill. It was meant to be.

Three minutes till the target arrived. He viewed the scene below. It was quiet. The offices that adorned the premises had been shut down, and most of the workers had gone home, which was something that he took a little light relief from. He might be a hired killer, but he wasn't a monster he told himself, although if someone innocent did get hurt, he had been told it would play into the narrative he was meant to be creating.

The key thing behind creating a terror threat was to make it terrifying to the general public. The killing of a politician that most didn't care for, albeit done as a prologue, was not enough to cause the sort of mass panic that was needed for the whole thing to be a success. Erik thought of the smiling receptionist and felt a twang of guilt. He looked over and was happy to see she had been replaced by a burly security guard. Security people accepted a certain degree of risk he decided. Maybe not hand grenade attack risk, but all the same.

Less than two minutes.

28

Lord Leighton Mitchell stepped out of the car, grumbling as he arrived outside the front of the Moorcutt House. It was a tall building that stood on the north bank of the Thames, just east of the Millennium Bridge. It was a multi-function building, made of glass and concrete pillars that rose from the ground upwards, enclosing the structure and holding it upright. Its main use was as office space, but it also had several meeting rooms that some of the more private and elite groups in the capital liked to use for their encounters. Privacy was assured, and it was the sort of place where people like Lord Mitchell might be expected to be seen, without drawing question.

"I don't know why he wanted to schedule a meeting so bloody soon," Mitchell grumbled. "We can talk tomorrow, rather than cram it all in now. Honestly, bloody hacks these days, they're all about the here and now. World's still going to be here tomorrow."

Bowen was walking alongside him as they headed towards the entrance. "I know, sir, but he was insistent, and we want to make the most of the opportunity. We have an agenda, don't forget."

"Yes, well quite. Still, not bloody cricket, not that they have it in Russia. And it shows."

They both walked in through the double doors that led to the glass foyer, and Bowen looked around at the scene. He saw Mamedov and an assistant sat on some chairs in the waiting area, just away from the reception desk. A couple of security guards stood near the barriers that lead to the inner portion of the building, and they prepared subconsciously to greet their guests and usher them through. He looked up to the mezzanine, seeing what he expected to, and then he tapped Mitchell on the shoulder.

"I just have to take a call, sir," he whispered, turning before Mitchell could even register a protest and heading back out of the building.

Mitchell went to say something, but didn't, turning again to Mamedov, who was now up and walking towards them.

"Bloody hell, Valentin, you couldn't wait, could you?" he ranted as he stormed towards the Russian tycoon, who's face went from warm grin to confused look, quickly.

"What do you mean?" he asked, opening his arms out in a show of ignorance. "You called me here."

The two of them continued to approach, both for a moment considering the other's insistence on not being responsible for the meeting. Had they not been so preoccupied, they might have taken more than a quick glance at the sound of something metallic bouncing on the floor just behind Mitchell and then another, similar noise behind Mamedov. Mitchell was half-looking at the first, twisting slightly, albeit more through uninterested annoyance, when the second noise made him instinctively look in front. Caught between the two, he never really noticed what the shapes were, merely shaking his head and carrying on.

There was a flash. That was the last thing that Lord Leighton Mitchell or Valentin Mamedov ever saw.

The noise of the twin explosions greeted Bowen as he stood talking on his phone, his body pressed up against a concrete pillar. Glass flew from the front of the building, scattering out onto the tarmac in front of the building, setting off car alarms. Then came the dust cloud, a small one, that blew out from the foyer. There was no third explosion. Two had done their job.

Bowen stared out at the street as pedestrians cowered, blood pouring from some of them where the glass and debris had found a victim. "It's done," he said to the caller. "Release the second video."

* * *

Lowri got the call just a few minutes later. A senior member of the House of Lords assassinated and a right-wing group immediately claiming responsibility. This was Erik Andryiv. Chances were, he was still in the area. Moorcutt house was just fifteen minutes' drive from where she lived. She was already on the phone to David.

"I'm going to get there now, try and coordinate with the police," she said, pulling on a coat quickly and then opening her door.

"Okay, I'm sending Adam and Jack to meet you there. I've got Raf positioning drones already. Hopefully, we'll catch a lead."

"I'll call you when I'm on site." Hanging up, she came out of the door, closing it behind her, and half walked, half ran to her car.

She placed her hand on the car door, just as she saw the two men one on either side. She knew instantly she was in a bad position. Her only chance was to strike first. She came back on her foot, reversing the direction she had been travelling in, throwing her left arm out, catching the first guy in the neck with her forearm. He gasped, dropping to his knee, but not down completely. The moment he stumbled but didn't fall, Lowri knew the game was up. The blow had been good, but it had lacked the accuracy it needed to put him out of the attack completely. She ploughed on regardless, hoping for a break to come her way. People made mistakes, and these weren't trained attackers, they were simply heavies. Arrowsmith's crew. Their faces flagged in many files she'd already read.

The second guy was closing now, and he brought a clubbing blow, mostly with his forearm and fist, down across the back of her head and neck, rocking her brain down with the weight of it, making her see stars and buckling her knees. It hurt. It hurt a lot, but Lowri knew she had to keep going.

She staggered a step, bouncing into her car, which helped keep her upright, but also pinned her in behind her attackers. She rolled on the door, knees bending to dodge the second man's follow-up punch, which skimmed off her head and over the roof of the car. It left him exposed, a big target in his abdomen, and Lowri had the time to pick her spot and deliver a sharp strike into his kidney that this time put the intended victim down.

Time was against her. The first attacker had regained his composure and saw his chance. The car was a weapon, he knew that, and he slammed himself into Lowri, his heavier body crushing into hers, forcing the air from her lungs as she hit the car, sandwiched between attacker and her vehicle, the metal behind her denting. She heard the window crack and shatter and then she was down on the ground, face first into the grass verge that ran roadside on the street. She tried to push up, but she felt a heavy hand on her head, then she was forced down, into the ground, into the dirt, into darkness, out of consciousness.

29

Mo was driving to Esher, completely unaware of all that was happening. His mind fixed on one thing now, getting to Carmage before anyone else did and trying to find that lead which would bring the whole thing together. He had already started to convince himself that Carmage was going to do that. After all, they'd managed to survive where the others hadn't and keep completely invisible in a way that no one else had. They were definitely a cut above.

He found himself in the quiet town with a little over half an hour to spare. He knew he had a team shadowing him, but he'd not seen them, which impressed and reassured him in equal measure. If Carmage was as good as he thought, there was every chance a backup team would cause them to spook and disappear.

Esher was a real slice of a different side of south Greater London. The home of Sandown racecourse, green and pleasant, based around the crossing of two minor "A" roads that both ultimately fed the A3, spreading out like spokes from a central point. The golf course where he was to meet Carmage was on one such spoke that headed near enough due south from the centre. He drove his car along it, finding a place to park up, before getting out.

Mo wanted to be bold. He wanted Carmage to see him; it was the only way to gain enough trust for them to step out, but he also knew it was a risk. He couldn't rule out that whoever had got to Kristian, and all the other people in the IRC channel as well, could be waiting to take them both out and close that chapter completely. He thought back to Kristian's house, and for a brief moment, he wanted nothing more than to step back into the car, drive away, and disappear, but he composed himself, closed his eyes, then walked over to the front of the golf course. He stood by one of the tall stone pillars that marked the entrance and waited.

* * *

The scene at Moorcutt House was chaotic. Emergency service vehicles were scattered around the building, fanning out from around the wrecked entrance like the debris field that had spewed forth from the mouth of the explosion, littering the street around it with glass, masonry, and body matter.

Bowen had been led away and into a car and whisked back to a safe location to be debriefed by the security services. He would stick to his story that he had simply been lucky, that he had taken a routine call from a subordinate and stayed outside. That much was true, technically. A subordinate had called him, but that was all part of the plan. The story would be checked, and it would match.

CTU was in charge of the scene, and a secure cordon had been placed around the area. A thorough search for the suspect was underway, although, with every second, the likelihood of apprehending him nearby slipped further away.

Jack and Adam parked at the edge of the cordon, their grey Audi slotting in next to a host of marked and unmarked cars, whose occupants were beginning the painstaking process of piecing together what had happened. The media was on site too, and Jack and Adam were careful to keep their faces away from the cameras as they approached an officer at the cordon.

"IDs?" his question was abrupt but perfectly weighted given the situation.

Jack and Adam flashed up their civilian IDs. It wasn't something they used a lot, but through their links within the government, The Regulators had secured a number of "contractor roles" that allowed for their agents to gain access to crime scenes where there were concerns that something was happening outside of the law. It was always a risky tactic because it meant exposing themselves to people and organisations who would either have to act should a vigilante organisation be found on site, or were openly hostile to their being there.

"Who are you reporting to?" the officer asked. Standard procedure was that a contact be needed on site, to maintain and preserve the integrity of the scene.

"Lowri Graves. Home Office," Adam stated, and the officer nodded before bending his neck to his radio and muttering something that was lost in the din of the scene. He waited a few seconds before a garbled response came through. The officer frowned.

"Sorry, she's not on site."

"Are you sure?" Adam asked.

"Everyone's tagged in and out. She's gonna know the drill as well as anyone. She's not on site."

Jack placed his hand on Adam's shoulder, and the two of them turned and took a couple of steps away. "She should be here, she had a head start on us. Something's up."

"I don't like this at all. We're not just one step behind now, we're losing this." Adam grimaced.

Jack already had his phone out and the number dialled. David picked up.

"Go ahead," David answered.

"Graves is missing."

There was a pause as David processed the information.

"Stay on site. I'm going to see what we have. I'll get back to you." David hung up.

* * *

Raf had been working through the masses of CCTV footage from around the outside and inside of Moorcutt. He'd already tagged the assassin. A man who rode in on a motorcycle and then disappeared into the inner workings of the building and never returned. His face was never on camera, but analysis of his build and height had suggested he was a potential match for Andryiv. Not that it mattered, he'd yet to find him leaving the building. There were a number of blind spots, and no doubt one had been exploited, so he was widening the search as quickly as he could.

David marched briskly to his side. "I need your help. Lowri is missing."

"Missing?"

"She never made it to Moorcutt. Have we got a drone in the air anywhere on her route?"

"I can get one over her house in three minutes," Raf was already sliding his chair across to an adjoining terminal and began to bring up the interface to operate one of the fleet of drones.

"Do it," David said, "and bring all our teams in, including the ones we sent with Mo."

Raf nodded, opening a side panel that sent electronic orders to all field units, giving them an urgent recall, then he returned to the drones. Selecting the one he wanted, he inputted the coordinates of Lowri's house, which was a pre-set in the system, as were all their addresses, then turned to David.

"What do you think happened?"

"I don't know yet."

"You okay?" Raf asked genuinely.

"I'll be fine." David's eyes were affixed on the course of the drone as it darted across the London skyline, it's onboard radar ensuring to keep it away from any air traffic above the capitol.

They stood in total silence as the city quickly coursed beneath the drone and then the camera began to tilt, angling down towards the ground, birds-eyeing over the house, circling slowly.

David's face twitched, a quick, almost imperceptible show of emotion. "Her car is still there."

He stepped away from the desk, heading towards his office, then he turned to Raf.

"Trace every vehicle in and out of there. All of them…"

"What about Andryiv?" Raf asked.

"The whole of the British counter-terrorism force is on him. You're on finding who took Lowri."

* * *

Lowri shook herself awake. She was attached at the wrist and elbow to the frame of a metal chair, forcing her forward, hair draping down over her head, her legs also bound to the legs of the chair. Thick layers of duct tape held her tight. She flexed her fingers but couldn't find a rough edge to try and work from.

She looked around the room. It was a small, disinteresting place, with metal shelves that held a couple of bland-looking boxes. Probably some sort of storeroom, often used for interrogations. A hosepipe, connected to a tap over a dirty sink was in one corner, but there were no rubber sheets, no tarp or anything below her. Whatever was going to happen here might be messy, but it wouldn't be an endgame, she assured herself.

Forcing herself through the pounding in her head and the haze of her memory, she tried to make sense of what had happened. She remembered nothing of the first few moments after being attacked. She had briefly woken in a van. She had felt the cold metal on her face as she lay in it and felt the motion of the vehicle swaying her as it went around a corner. It had turned her stomach, a wave of nausea, from the concussion she knew she must have, causing her eyes to roll back, and she had blacked out once more.

Vaguely, she recalled being hoisted up, rag-dolled from the van and to this room. She couldn't count on being certain how far she had been taken, it was all a blur. While she had tried to regain her faculties, they hadn't come in time. She had drifted as they secured her, but now she was coming around, she felt the pain in her head that reassured her she was alive, that she was going to live. Now she could begin to analyse and plan her next move, one she hoped would bring her closer to freedom.

Aside from her, there was no one else in the room, but she could hear the muffled sound of hushed conversation from just outside. Quiet, relaxed, probably not even about her. Just men chewing the cud, spitballing about life. Everyday chit-chat, for an everyday job. Not their first job.

As she sat, the chatter outside died, a resigned "let's get down to business" tone took over and the door opened. Two men walked in. She recognised them instantly from the reconnaissance files on Arrowsmith's crews. Terry Carter and Umar Hassan. Carter was the biggest of the two, a white man, into his fifties now, bald head, thick arms that bulged under a tight black tee. The epitome of English muscle. Hassan was a slightly smaller man, but on any other given day would be classed as big. Egyptian in dissent, thick dark hair and stubble, with broad shoulders and a sneer on his face.

Carter stepped forward.

"You're gonna love us by the end of the day," he grinned, slapping her very lightly across the face as if playfully patting a partner. Then with a sudden rip downwards with his hand, he pulled her blouse from her, jolting her forward, the chair pulled and scraped along the floor with her.

Carter winked, and Hassan sneered some more. "Not bad for an older bird, like," he cooed from where he stood.

"She won't look this way soon enough," Carter goaded.

Lowri said nothing. She did nothing. She looked impassively as if nothing had happened. Don't let them see your anger. Don't let them see your fear. Maintain control.

Before anyone could say or do anything, the door opened. Reuben walked in. He stopped, looking at the scene in front of him, a scowl spreading quickly.

"The fuck is happening here?" his voice grew as he spoke, the final word punctuating the sentence thunderously.

"Just…you know?" Carter stuttered.

"Yeah, I fucking know, I fucking know alright," Reuben paced slowly towards Carter as he spoke, "and haven't I fucking told you all, a million fucking times, that we are all

297

sorts of cunts, bad bastards, evil mother fuckers, you name it, but we are not, I repeat, we are fucking not rapists and perverts. That is a line I will not, and you will not, cross. Now, the two of you, get the fuck out of here, before we get irreconcilable."

Carter flicked a quick glance at Hassan, and the two of them scurried out, heads bowed. Reuben followed them out with his eyes, disgust on his face, his head shaking as the door shut. Was it just a show Lowri wondered? Was he about to play good cop with her? Stranger things had happened.

Reuben looked at her.

"For that, yeah, I'm sorry." Reuben nodded, stooping to pick up the ripped blouse and draping it carefully over Lowri, trying to give her some dignity back and being careful not to look anywhere other than her eyes. A deliberate ploy, Lowri noted.

She said nothing.

"Let's be straight, though. You're here because I was told to bring you here, to ask questions and, more importantly, to ensure I get answers," he sighed, walking back to the other side of the room, then leaning against the wall, one leg crossed over the other, arms folded. "The problem you're going to face is that I've been forced to do something that I can't forgive myself for, and I've got a feeling that as the day wears on, I'm going to find out that you were a part of the reason for it. See, I had a friend, bloke who worked for me, who turned on me. I had to do what I had to do, to protect myself, to protect my family. I killed him."

Reuben's voice raised as he said, "I killed him," driving home with an excitable energy that unsettled Lowri, his eyes widening just a little more than would be normal. He carried on.

"I think I'm going to learn that you, or your people, were the ones he turned to, and if I do, I don't know what's going to happen. I can only make one promise, and that is, that I will have my revenge."

Lowri looked up at him, her eyes fixed on his.

"We turned him. It was us. It was me," she said.

30

Annie had seen the car pull up. She had seen the man who called himself Crassus, but whose real name was Mo Younis. He lived in a two-bedroom flat in Dalston, supposedly paid for by his job working as a freelance IT engineer. She had watched him walk from the car and take up a position leaning disinterestedly against the nearest of the two pillars that lined the driveway that led down to the golf course.

There she had let him wait. He was early, and whilst that might have held a tactical advantage, in that anyone else who might have wanted to intercept the meeting might have missed an early appointment, she also wanted to make the most of that time to look out for any patterns in the traffic, in the pedestrians, in the faces that passed, to see if anyone anywhere was watching and waiting. She wasn't a spy, she wasn't a field agent, but she was very paranoid and very, very analytical.

There had been nothing. No one who had tripped her radar. Mo was alone, it seemed, and she felt more reassured that she could trust him. The tree she was hiding in wasn't comfortable, and she had to work hard to remain hidden. Now was the time to come out.

She pushed her way through the foliage, the sound of the rustling leaves at first not causing Mo to notice, but as it persisted, she saw him look, then spot her, as she dropped to ground level, disappearing behind a wall.

She placed both hands on the wall and pulled herself up, scrambling over, unsure of what to expect when she crested the top. What greeted her was Mo's smiling face, warm, genuine, if not a little perplexed.

"Hello," he beamed.

"Hi," she puffed, the effort of clambering down the tree and then over the wall a little more than she had anticipated. She dropped down to the floor, then dusted herself down. "Let's move."

Her head dropped, and her hood and cap were back on as they marched purposefully into the golf club grounds, sticking close to the edges near the wall and in the tree line.

"I've got to say, I'm real impressed," Mo huffed as he struggled to keep up with Annie's wiry frame.

"Why?" she asked.

"I couldn't find you, I mean, you were a ghost and finding people is what I do."

"I didn't want to be found."

"Neither did the others."

"Of course they did. The tags, the bragging, they wanted people to know."

"You know they're dead, right?" Mo looked at her.

"Yeah."

"You know I didn't kill them?"

"Yeah. I mean, not directly." She never looked up, her head was down, she knew where they were going, and she needed Mo just to follow it seemed.

"What?"

"You didn't kill them, your side didn't, but if your side didn't exist, there would be no need to kill them," Annie explained it like it was the most obvious thing in the world.

"Wow, I mean, thanks." Mo's tone was a mixture of disbelief and offence, and she felt a little guilty. For the next minute, they strode on in silence until he finally asked, "Where are we going?"

"I need to make sure we're not followed."

"Okay."

"I have a place to hole up for a little while; I need to show you something. You'll want to see it."

"What is it?"

"It's their plan. I know what they're doing next. I want to stop it. A lot of people are going to die if I don't."

* * *

Calum wanted to be anywhere but here. The school was full of people, all of them had eyes on him, he could feel it. Word of his beating had got around. It was a school, it always did. Even if it hadn't, even if by some unbelievable quirk of fate, the word hadn't got out, his face displayed a vibrant testament, even now, with the swelling greatly reduced, the cuts beginning to heal, and his eyes fully opened. He still looked like a victim, and with every new stare, snigger, and question laced with what he knew was false sympathy, he felt the wounds more and more, till they were almost an unbearable weight on him, crushing his confidence further and further.

It was not unusual for him to talk to no one in the course of a school day, and it was not usually a hard task. He enjoyed being invisible, but now that had been taken from him, and he found that people wanted to know what had happened. Some of them looked concerned, but deep down he knew that there was no concern there, only, at most, a scornful pity reserved for people like him who were below the societal norms.

There was one person he longed to see. Kat. These last few days she had been a genuine friend to him, and he'd found a love and affection there that he didn't realise they had shared till this point. Like all siblings, he knew that they loved each other, in the sense that they were near enough duty-bound to do so, but the last couple of days had brought them closer together in a way he had never believed possible. They had actually liked each other. He had actually loved her, and he felt a safety with her, in the way she had repelled Isaac.

A promise had been made as well, by Kat, that Isaac would get what was coming to him, that she would end Calum's fear. And he was full of fear. It had only been her words that had managed to get him over the threshold and into school because he knew, sooner or later, his path would cross with Isaac once more, and he had no idea what he was going to do about it.

Now, though, with Kat, his formidable sister on his side, he knew he would be okay. He knew that Isaac would get his.

It was for that reason that Calum was breaking with a tradition of his, one of his golden rules, and heading into the canteen at the school. Like most school canteens, it was the hub of teenage activity throughout lunchtime and the only place Kat would be seen if she was to stay in school over lunch. He was hoping that she had, he was hoping that she would be there and that he could find a security with her. He knew she wouldn't let him down.

It was an incredibly brave act for Calum to open the doors to the canteen and step in. Here was everything that made him nervous, that put him on edge. Teenagers, all of them loud and excited, converging in a cacophony of chatter that collided into him and made his head pound and rattle. It was dizzying and petrifying and exhilarated him all at once, but he knew he needed to find his sister. He needed to find that sanctuary that she offered.

He looked all around the room. There were hundreds of faces, hundreds of kids, all in the same uniform, or at least their personal variation on that theme, but only one who could help him. Finally, he saw her, tall and blonde, standing out in the crowd as she always did.

She wasn't alone, not that she was likely to have been, but still, Calum's blood ran cold. She was with her friend, Sasha, but there was a group of boys around them, and Kat was laughing happily with them. With one in particular. That one, whose chest she lay her hand on as she laughed, was Isaac.

Calum felt the betrayal, felt his world collapsing, and left the canteen.

* * *

Thea had seen the shout go up for the Moorcutt job, but it hadn't interested her. She wanted to be somewhere else. She wanted to see Frank, and so she had headed out to the morgue, waiting patiently to be admitted, and now, waiting patiently again as Frank's remains were located and space set aside.

Finally, a polite young doctor, more than likely a student on placement, came and escorted her into a room with a row of freezers on one wall. Frank had already been removed, his face poking out from under a white sheet, eyes closed peacefully, the bullet wound cleaned up, the damage made to look as minimal as it could.

"Jesus," Thea sighed.

"Ms Watts." Thea looked over towards the voice to see the main doctor, who she had worked with in the past, Carl Palmer, making his way carefully towards her. "I'm sorry about Frank," he added as he offered her a hand to shake.

"Yeah, he was." Thea took a split second. "He would have wanted this job done, of all the jobs."

"Of course, we've done all we can with the medical side. It's what it looks like really, point-blank range shot to the head from a nine-millimetre. Professional job. Do you have anyone in mind?"

"We're following a thread linking this to an organised crime gang we've been monitoring for a long time," Thea explained honestly. It was the only way to convincingly justify her being there, and although she knew it was a risk exposing the story just a little bit, it was one she had to take. "I can't go into much more at this point."

Palmer nodded. "Listen, I'm telling you this because I know Frank wasn't just your partner, he was your friend too."

"What?" Thea asked.

"I had a call, from the MoD. I'm to report anyone who visits asking about Frank. Anyone."

"Who would ask about Frank?" Thea found herself answering her own question silently in her head.

"That's what I didn't get, but they wouldn't tell me. I got an official letter, names redacted, re-stating the order. Even you, I have to tell them you've been in."

"Has that ever happened before?"

"Yeah, strangely enough. I had a body in here, six months back, a real strange case, just the torso. Same order, same letter near enough."

"Who was the body?"

"A soldier, I can dig out his details if you want?"

Thea nodded, working through the possibilities. "Could you do that, and could you also keep that off the record. I don't mind you saying I was here, but for both of our asses..."

Palmer nodded. "I think that's probably for the best. Give me five minutes."

Thea waited. Five minutes later, Palmer was back, and Thea had a dead soldiers name. Joseph Thomas.

* * *

"I got the van," Raf said excitedly from his station.

David was next to him in seconds. "Where?"

"Going in and going out of the area around Lowri's house. I ran the licence, it's definitely one of Arrowsmith's. Time matches up and everything. This is it." Raf spooled through the footage so David could see the van going down a road that led towards Lowri's then reappearing less than ten minutes later.

"Can you trace it?"

"I'm working on it now," Raf's fingers were a blur on the keyboard as he tried to narrow down the location of the van, "give me a couple of seconds."

London was adorned with a myriad of traffic cameras, most of which had ANPR on, but many more that didn't, and it was those that didn't that he was now working on, feeding their footage through a subroutine that did the work of the ANPR on the raw footage at this end.

The system was quick at pinpointing all known movements of the van in the last two hours, and within moments, a route appeared on the screen.

"Okay, I've got where we know they were, there's a few blind spots where we haven't got them, but I should be able to cross-reference everything with known locations used by Arrowsmith, to give us the most probable destination." Raf panted as he worked, the map zeroing in, working through the data being fed into the system, before finally settling on one spot. "There!"

"Where is it?"

"It's a small yard in Battersea. I'm sending the address to all teams."

David picked up the phone and pressed a button, the speed dial putting him through to Jack and Adam.

"We've got a location, you should be getting it now," he said, before adding, "Get there in time."

31

He needed a smoke, after all that had happened. It wasn't a lie, the day had been nerve-racking and then exhilarating for Bowen, the culmination of expert planning and timing that had led to the next step in the plan being followed through.

It had been a shame to kill Lord Mitchell. He had been a useful asset, but his weakness had been his belief that there was a greater moral purpose for all of this and the endgame, when it came, would have shocked him. They had discussed it, even agonised over it, but in the end, it was decided that Mitchell had to go. He could be worked into the narrative as well. Two birds with one stone.

Now though, the pressure would be greater. The leaking of Andryiv's face had complicated matters further, and Bowen was keen to ensure that no lucky citizen should get the chance to bump into their man before completing the job. Afterwards didn't matter, he didn't know enough to implicate anyone, and what he did know would lead to a dead end. If he could make good his escape, all the better; if he couldn't – well, that was an occupational hazard he always had to contend with. Out of professional courtesy, Bowen and his associates had decided that Andryiv wasn't a threat moving forward and would be allowed to walk.

Cigarette lit, he took out his phone and, after a furtive glance to ensure no one was eavesdropping, made a call.

"Yes?" came the voice at the other end.

"It's me. Is our man good?"

"In situ, waiting for delivery."

The line went dead.

* * *

Annie took Mo to the bed and breakfast. It was a thirty-minute walk on the meandering route she plotted. Mo had suggested going back for the car, but she had resisted the idea firmly. She wanted to keep away from any roads for as long as possible.

The room she had rented was plain but cosy. An old-fashioned double bed, with a dark wood bedside table and matching cupboard, as well as a small table that a TV on it, that looked barely capable of receiving the newer digital signal, let alone giving the sort of picture that many were used to.

Annie had said nothing. She had simply taken off her cap and hoody and pulled a laptop from under the bed, placed it briskly onto the bed, and turned it on. She turned to Mo.

"What I'm going to show you is what they had me working on. I don't know where this was for, or when it was for, but I know it will kill a lot of people."

"I have to ask, if you knew it was going to kill a lot of people, why did you do it?"

Annie sighed. "I didn't know what it was at first, before I did it. I looked afterwards."

"So, what is it?"

"It's what I did." Annie looked at him and stopped.

"What?" he asked, trying to mask his nerves and sound as reassuring as possible.

"I turned off the radiation detectors at Dover."

Mo wanted so hard to hide his fear, to hide his anger, but he knew he couldn't, he knew his face would be a visual canvas of all those things and more, and he saw Annie recognise it as her head fell to the canvas. All he could say was, "Holy shit."

"I know, I'm sorry, I... I..."

"What did you think you were doing?" he exclaimed, regretting it before it had even finished forming in his mouth and adding. "You have to help me stop this."

"I'm sorry, I..."

He saw the tears form in Annie's eyes. He knew he should have hugged her, but what she had done, it was all too much for him.

Mo rubbed his hands across his face and sighed. "We'll fix it," he said. "It's what we do."

"I've felt so bad since it happened, I've done all I can to stop them," Annie sobbed. "I've been following their movements online, tracing everything they've been doing."

Mo pulled his hands down and looked at her, suddenly back in awe of her again.

"You've traced them? How?"

Annie sniffed, forcing back the tears. "It was easy, I mean for me, I mean they're using a TOR based VPN, but it's based on old miltech, so the number of computers using that across the globe are limited and the likely places where it would come from. I mean, you got GCHQ, Chicksands, the usual London haunts, so it was just a case of getting a subroutine in there to compare the data."

"That worked?"

"Not at first," she sniffed. "I was looking in the wrong place. I found it though, it's in the house."

"The house?"

"Of Commons, or Parliament, I don't know what it's called, but it's there. Whoever is doing this is in the freaking government, so you gotta promise me, as soon as you can, you get me out of this country."

* * *

It took Jack and Adam less than ten minutes to make it to the yard.

Traffic was light and very much on their side, but still, a degree of caution had to be utilised as they raced towards the scene. Their car wasn't equipped with the sirens and lights of normal law enforcement vehicles, so they couldn't alert any pedestrians or other road users to their progress, and so both were focusing on the road ahead and the environment around the car, to maximise safety, whilst still driving as quickly as possible.

Another unit was also on the way, a van of four men, all heavily armed. They were to rendezvous just outside the location and then go in. A drone was already in place over the building and had confirmed the van was still on site from its circular orbit, 25,000 feet above the city, it's electronic eye locked onto the yard below, well out of view.

Jack pulled up a street away from the yard, and the two of them sat in contemplative silence for a moment.

"Front or back?" Jack asked.

"Heads I get front, tails you do." Adam pulled a coin from his pocket.

"Hands of the gods?"

"Only way. I don't want it to be my fault if you take one going in," Adam shrugged, flipping the coin. "Heads it is."

"Okay, and just so you know," Jack looked at his partner, "I could totally live with making the call if you got shot."

"Heartless man, damn heartless." Adam shook his head as the van containing their four colleagues arrived.

Jack and Adam got out of the car to meet them. They both had 9mm SIG Sauer P320s Tacops, with extended magazines carrying twenty-one rounds, instead of the normal seventeen, which they had drawn, but held close to their sides. It was the model of gun that the US Army had ordered in early 2017, an effective handgun that was reliable and accurate, as well as relatively easy to conceal. The perfect choice for The Regulators. The four men from the van were all dressed in casual-looking clothing. Sturdy boots, nothing loose fitting, dark neutral colours to blend better with the environment.

"Two to the front with me, two with him," Adam said.

"If we can take any of them alive, we do so," Jack added. "We need their intel. We're still playing catch up."

"What about Ms Graves?" one of the men asked.

"She would value intel over her life. If you want to save her, you best make sure that we have someone we can talk to as well, because she will be pissed off otherwise," Adam warned.

The two teams split and headed for their respective ingress points. Adam's team held back for a moment, minimising the risk of being seen, whilst Jack's team went to work on the gate. It took them less than thirty seconds to cut the hinges out of the gate and move themselves up to the door and place the breaching charge.

"In position," Adam whispered confidently into the comm unit.

"Roger, in position. Raf, keep that eye above us," Jack replied, bringing in Raf who was running the drone still and would be offering tactical support should anyone approach or leave the building.

"All set back here," Raf responded.

"On my mark," Adam began the count. "Three, two, mark."

The doors at both sides of the building were flung open by the breaching charges, flapping loosely on their broken frames as wood and debris splintered around the teams. At each end of the building, the first man was already moving, stepping into the doorway briefly to toss in a stun grenade. They both went off in near perfect synchronicity, showering the inside of the building in bright burning magnesium flakes as the teams swarmed in.

It was Jack who led the way at the back and saw the first hostile, Umar. The force of the flashbang had thrown him to the floor, his gun already out of his hand, and Jack saw the opportunity. Umar was getting up, trying to, his legs wobbling from the blast, no idea what was happening. Jack charged, dropping his shoulder and ploughing Umar into the wall, knocking any stuffing left in him from his body, falling on the man, pinning him, gun wedged under his jaw.

"GO! GO! GO!" he urged the rest of his team forward. "One hostile detained," he reported.

* * *

Adam was leading his team now, at a steady but quick walk through the building, pistol drawn, waiting for movement.

It came as he rounded a tight turn which opened out into a small office area. A figure lurched out from behind a filing cabinet at the end of the room, next to a door to what looked like the central part of the building. Adam instinctively ducked before the figure had taken aim. The shot cracked and whistled above him, past the rest of his team.

"Contact," Adam called, before levelling his pistol where the figure had appeared. He was still a long way from the filing cabinet, and other than a small table and desk, there wasn't much in the way of cover.

"It's over," Adam called out. "There's another team coming around to flank you, step out."

"Fuck off!" came the reply, before another volley of shots came around from a wild hand behind the filing cabinet. They all missed their mark, loose and hopeful at best, scared and desperate more likely.

Adam looked again. No cover. Open ground to the filing cabinet, then the shooter, then the back wall. There were a few bits of office furniture on the wall, another tall filing cabinet, a low set of drawers, and a fire extinguisher.

Stepping back behind the cover of the comer, Adam took a breath, visualised the room once more, all the things he had seen, putting them in their places, going through his motion in a split second, and then he stepped out and fired.

His shot found its target, hitting the fire extinguisher with an unmistakable "ping" that quickly turned into the "crump" of the pressurised gases inside bursting free and engulfing the shooter. There was a scream of panic, or maybe pain, and then he was dancing out in the cloud of gases that were quickly dissipating around him, his gun still waving around, firing off a wild shot back towards Adam.

It didn't, and it left Adam with little choice. He returned fire. The man fell as three bullets ripped into his chest. He didn't move again, and after a quick pause, Adam moved over to him, kicking the gun away. He felt for a pulse. Nothing. He looked down at the man's face and recognised it instantly as the man who had killed Kristian Glover. Justice.

Standing up quickly, he moved to the door, the other two men fanning out behind him, taking cover against the frame, then taking the handle. He nodded to one of the other men, who stepped across the door, against the other side of the frame, then Adam opened it, and his colleague raised his gun, scanning the room.

It was empty.

No one there.

Save for an empty metal chair, with cuttings of duct tape wrapped round the legs and frame.

32

Some people's parents left them packed lunches. Others left them notes telling them how much they loved them or wishing them well for their day.

Not Kat Quinn's. Her dad had left her something else. It was just what she needed.

All day long at school, she had felt nervous. Someone would know what she was up to, someone would look in her bag and see what she had planned, and then she would be the guilty party.

But they didn't, and the bell came, and kids everywhere started to stream from the school.

She wasn't meeting Isaac tonight. Tonight was basketball training, and Isaac didn't miss basketball. It was the only thing at school she had ever seen him get passionate about. All the same, she was still heading to the gym.

Having killed ten minutes idly browsing through the library under the pretence of a quick burst of revision, she finally made her way to the gym building. The last of the stragglers were long gone from the school grounds, and no one saw her as she opened the doors and walked in.

On the right were the girls changing rooms, but she headed left towards the boys. Holding her breath, she opened the door. *Please let no one be in there,* she prayed silently.

The changing room was deserted.

Moving quickly, she searched for Isaac's bag. It wasn't hard. Isaac was far too lazy to pack his belongings away properly in one of the lockers. His clothes were strewn by a peg, only his jacket hung in place. It was the only piece of clothing that wasn't uniform. Underneath it sat his bag.

Quickly she undid it, taking the package her dad had left for her and hiding it deep at the bottom of the bag. Her plan needed it to stay there till the morning. She was certain it would. Isaac wouldn't be looking for his exercise books when he got home, and the package was small and light enough to easily pass unnoticed amongst the debris found in a teenager's bag.

Heart racing, she closed it up, trying to place it exactly as she had found it. Satisfied, she stood and made her way to the door, stepping out and nearly colliding with Mr Evans, the head of PE.

"Miss Quinn? What are you doing?" his eyes widened as he spoke.

"Sir, sorry, these were in my boyfriend's bag." Kat pulled a tampon from her pocket and thrust it towards her teacher. "I really need to go," she urged.

Mr Evans floundered for a moment. "Of course, sorry, go on."

Kat raced past him, into the girl's changing room. She darted into the nearest toilet, slamming the door shut, then leant back against it. Her body was shaking with adrenaline. Thank god her dad had told her to make sure she came up with a reason for being there if she was caught.

She composed herself, waited a while, and then exited. Mr Evans was gone. The foyer to the gym was empty again. Now all she could do was wait.

* * *

Mo looked at the data that Annie had collected. He didn't doubt her for one second, but she had insisted on showing him her working out. Perhaps for validation, perhaps because she was proud of it, but what she had done was indisputable. She had proven that the leak had come from inside the Houses of Parliament, just where inside it was another question. Despite that, he could tell that she didn't trust him. That bothered him.

"Listen," Mo began, "I need to be honest with you about what happened to the other guy."

"Ownarchist?"

"His name was Kristian," Mo corrected, and Annie nodded. "I was there."

Annie stopped for a moment, her body tensing. Mo saw her fear.

"I wasn't involved in killing him or anything, we were there to help him, like I'm here to help you, but we didn't get out of there quick enough. They found him, found us, and we couldn't stop them killing him."

Annie nodded again, slowly this time.

"I don't want that to happen again, to happen to you," Mo went on. "So, you need to come with me."

"Uh-uh, no, I don't want to." Annie shook her head firmly and pushed back on the bed away from him. "Not until I know all the variables. I mean, I just don't know what I'm getting into."

"No, but I can tell you what you're getting into if you don't come with me."

"You can't. You couldn't find me, they won't either."

"I needed to find you quickly, they can take as long as they want now. You're always there, and until you help us, you're in danger. Once you tell us what you know, it doesn't matter to them if you're dead or alive, at least not until after the dust settles. Then, they will come for you, and they'll have a lifetime to find you. Not hours, not days or weeks, but however long it takes to make you pay. The only way you get to have a normal life is if you help me get them."

The way Annie looked at him, Mo knew she was working through what he said, a giant computer in her head, running through the probabilities and outcomes, before finally reporting back that, yes, he was right.

"Fine. We'll do it your way," she agreed reluctantly.

Mo grinned, a warm, genuine grin, hoping to ease some of Annie's reluctance. "Great, I need to call my guys, find out where they're at, and then we'll make our way back."

* * *

They had been driving for an hour. Reuben had said nothing to Lowri from the moment she had told him that she was responsible for the killing. She had hoped to bring out an angry response in him, but one never followed. He had stared at her for a moment, she had seen the hatred in his eyes, and she had waited for the attack to begin. It hadn't. He had simply turned and walked out of the room.

Now she was in a car with him, her hands cuffed down to the side, on the runners of the chair. Her arms were starting to ache now, stuck in that unnatural position, but Lowri was trying to focus on the future and how she might escape. Being in the front of the car meant that every action was watched. Had she been locked in the boot, she may have been able to do something, but here, she sat in silence next to Reuben. It meant that every moment they shared was a moment of menace, and as calm as she was keeping herself, she knew that he was attempting to intimidate her, to scare her, before he killed her. It was making for an uncomfortable journey, but in no way was it intimidating her. Perhaps he was hoping to elicit something from her, some titbit of information that meant he wouldn't be going back empty-handed. She wasn't going to give in to him though, and by now, his need for revenge far outweighed anything else.

Already she felt she had made a smart move. The interrogation had been called off, so whatever plan Reuben was meant to be following, he had gone off-piste. Now they were simply progressing to the endgame, so on a wider spectrum, that worked for the integrity of the mission, not that she intended to talk.

She also wasn't going to get hurt nearly as badly as she would have been during the interrogation. Small mercies, of course, but one to be thankful for nonetheless. Lowri had seen what torture does to people, and she didn't really fancy her last hours to be taken up in a similar way.

She wondered where they were going. There was obviously some reason why Reuben had chosen to take her from the first location. It was clearly an emotional response, but emotional responses had a habit of backfiring. He had lost the security and control of the space he had before, and he was taking her somewhere else. Maybe that end location would be secure, but there were going to be moments on the journey at the very least, where possibilities would be opened up. It was inevitable, and she intended to make the most of them.

* * *

Fisher watched as Umar was escorted into a van by two large men, both of whom he assumed would be armed. He didn't know what had happened, but he knew it didn't look good, so he hunkered down in his seat and waited to see who else they bought out.

It wasn't a long wait. Two more men came, wheeling a tall box, a little over six feet tall, he figured. It reminded him somewhat of a coffin. They placed it into the back of the van. Then came another two men, who stopped briefly to talk to one of the first, who was now sat in the driver's seat of the van. It was a brief chat, simple instructions, nothing they didn't already know, before they headed off, getting into their own car. Finally, both vehicles drove away.

Fisher pulled out his phone and dialled a number, Reuben's number. No one picked up, so he dialled another.

"We might have a problem," he said, before listening to the response and then hanging up his phone.

The road was quiet now. The van and car both out of sight, but Fisher still decided to err on the side of caution. He waited for another minute. Finally, he got out of the car and made his way to the small unit, carefully assessing every step as he approached, wary of any lurking dangers that might lie in wait for him.

Getting nearer, he could see that the front door was ripped off its frame and he guessed the same was true of the back door. This was a rescue mission, trying to get back the woman they'd taken, but where was she? Where was Reuben?

He entered the building. He could still smell the gunpowder and magnesium in the air. He knew what had happened. A full-on assault, to take the woman back and to take prisoners, judging by Umar's survival. He pulled his gun out. He didn't want to be one of their prisoners. He couldn't be one of their prisoners.

Slowly he rounded the corner to the office area outside the room where they would have been holding the prisoner. A fire extinguisher had been shot and exploded. There were blood splatters on the wall and floor nearby, and he figured that someone had been hit. Looking at the amount of blood, mortally so. There was no body. That must have been what the box was for.

In the holding room, the chair was empty. No prisoner. No blood. No Reuben. Fisher thought back. The men coming out of the building didn't look happy. They weren't resigned, but they were definitely facing a problem, which meant the woman hadn't been there. Reuben had taken her. He needed to find out where. He picked up the phone again and dialled Reuben. It rang.

Then there was an answer.

"I'll speak to you when this is done," Reuben snarled. The line went dead.

Fisher sighed. The woman was as good as dead. He just hoped Reuben got her to talk first.

* * *

"Okay, so I've got a car registered to Reuben Arrowsmith being picked up on ANPR not far from your location. Heading east out of the city towards the A2, then again when he's actually on the road." Raf was on speaker phone so that both Adam and Jack could get the intel.

"How far ahead of us is he?" Adam asked.

"Twenty minutes, give or take, but he's travelling at a nice leisurely pace, so I assume he doesn't want to get picked up. Plus, he's got the usual traffic slowing him down."

"Can you plot us a route that will give us a clearer run?" Jack leaned over the steering wheel from where he was driving, angling himself toward the phone.

"Traffic is rough everywhere," sighed Raf. "I'll do my best to ensure that he gets hit with every traffic light I can, but you're still going to have to motor. If you want, I can put a marker on his car, so that he might get pulled by police."

"We don't know what the situation is with Lowri." Adam shook his head, even though Raf couldn't see. "We don't want to put someone else in the firing line as well. We need to handle this ourselves."

"Okay, I'll keep you posted on his whereabouts."

Adam hung up the phone and looked at his partner who had a steely, determined gaze on his face. "You alright?" he asked.

"I hate chasing shadows," Jack snarled.

"It ain't my favourite game either."

"We've been looking at this the wrong way all the time. We've been chasing the tail of the dog; we've never even got close to the head."

"Need to give this dog a bone."

"No shit. So, whatever happens, we take him alive."

"Whatever happens?"

Jack looked at Adam and said nothing. Adam went on. "You know Warner isn't going to like that."

"Is he thinking with his head?"

Adam shook his head. "No, I don't think he is."

"Exactly. Lowri would sacrifice herself for this and Reuben is the closest thing we have to a lead to the top. We should have lifted him ages ago, and now people are dead. Innocent people."

"That Nazi wannabe was hardly someone worth crying tears over," Adam pointed out.

"We ain't here to pick apart people's politics. He played by the book, he deserved to live. And Mitchell, he was a good man, by all accounts. We take Reuben, we take him alive, and then we break him apart."

"

33

The traffic was tricky. If he had been a paranoid man, Reuben might have even felt it was a deliberate ploy to slow him down, but he wasn't. He just took it to be one of those things that was sent to test him in life. Soon enough, he was free of the city, out onto the M2, where once again the speed limit signs conspired to keep his speed limited, despite no obvious need for traffic calming.

The motorway was a short part of the journey, and the woman stayed quiet. He didn't speak to her. Hell, he didn't even know her name. Did he need to? He wasn't sure. Would it make him feel a bit better to know the name of the woman who had caused him to kill one of his own? Probably not. She was nothing to him, just an act of revenge and the order had been clear, find out what she knew, not who she was.

Going back with no information still troubled him. He knew he was playing a dangerous game here. Whilst it was true that he didn't know who was at the top pulling the strings, he knew Bowen was a man not to be trifled with. The fact that he hadn't been able to extract any information weighed on him like a black mark on a school report. He would have failed, even if he simply said that the woman had resisted all methods and then died during torture. That would be an admission of not getting the job done, and Reuben did not like *not* getting the job done.

"You want to tell me anything before the end?" he sneered at her, knowing it was a token gesture and feeling angry at himself that he had let his rage, his quest for revenge, get in the way.

She said nothing. It stung him harder. Had she known that when she told him she had been responsible for Yannick's death? Was it all a ploy, a sacrifice to save a bigger picture?

The fear of being wrong ate at him, but he forced it down, forced it back inside himself, not allowing it to take root. He had plotted a course of action, and whatever the outcome, now he had to see it through. They were almost there now anyway, it was almost over for her, there was no way back.

* * *

David was with Raf, keeping tabs on the chase. Jack and Adam had closed the gap, but the news they were getting from Raf wasn't hopeful. The more Reuben had been slowed by the attempts to slow traffic, the more aggressive his driving style had become, and the gap, whilst it had narrowed, wasn't enough. Now he was off the M2, heading north towards the Thames estuary and it was becoming clear what he was aiming for. A drone was over his car, well out of view, but it could do nothing other than observe. Reuben had to be kept alive.

The route he was taking now had only one way in and out. That was in part good news. They might not make it in time to stop him killing Lowri, but they would make it before he could get away. They would take him in and break him. David was already visualising that.

"You're just five minutes behind him now," Raf reported as they passed through the small suburb of Cliffe Woods.

It wasn't going to be enough.

They were running out of road.

Lowri was running out of time.

* * *

Lowri bounced in her seat as the car bobbed its way along the dirt track that led to the water's edge, her wrists pulling against the metal of the cuffs that held her to the chair, biting into her flesh and leaving them red and raw.

In front of them, as the light began to dim, lay the Thames estuary, a busy channel, that took traffic in and out of London from the North Sea, then on to Europe and the rest of the world. The current was strong, tidal, and would move anything out with it, taking it into the deeper waters of the sea, or washing it up on one of the many mud flats. There it could lie undiscovered until eaten by the wildlife or buried for all time under a thin veil of sediment and silt.

The suspension creaked and moaned a little more as the BMW made clear its mournful protest at the route it was being taken down. This was not what it was made to do, and it was letting them both know.

At the end of the track, lay a gate. Reuben pulled up just short of the gate, and they sat in silence for a moment, looking out at the river in front of them. The moment seemed to span forever, a never-ending reach across time, taking Lowri from the moments of her life to the instant of her death.

"Let's go," Reuben said coldly, getting out of the car.

He came around to the passenger door and uncuffed her, her feet first, then right hand, then left, then he stepped back, drew his gun and motioned for her to get out.

"I don't want to carry you," he said, "but I will if I have to."

Lowri complied, getting out of the car slowly, mechanically, her motions steady and measured. She tried to look calm to Reuben. All the while, he looked anything but to her.

"That way." Reuben stepped backwards, giving her an arc, and motioned with the gun towards the gate.

They walked, in single file, Reuben just behind Lowri, his gun levelled on the centre of her spine, heading slowly towards the water's edge, processional in their movements. No rush to reach to the end of the line. The light was fading faster and faster, and a dull murk was enveloping both of them, making it hard to see the uneven ground in front. Lowri found her feet stumbling as she moved forward.

"Keep going," came the growl from behind.

They reached the gate, which lay just twenty feet from the river bank. Lowri could imagine that she might just tumble into the water if her body fell the right way. Neither of them would really control that, that much was sure. It would simply be gravity taking over, as all of her functions stopped as the bullet cut through her brain, blocking out all the signals forever.

"Open it," ordered Reuben. His voice was still hushed but menacing.

Lowri opened the gate, let it swing in front of her, and then stepped through, Reuben close behind, scanning around him for any possible witnesses.

Then she stumbled forward. Just a little, not enough to make her go down, but enough to cause her to wobble. She stopped and stood straight to compose herself, as Reuben, just a fraction behind her and distracted by his reconnaissance of the area, found himself walking right up to her back, his gun nuzzling into her spine, just left of centre, touching, not much.

But enough.

Lowri span to her right, and suddenly, Reuben wasn't aiming at Lowri anymore, his shot was pointed across the water, deep into Essex and beyond. Completely pointless, completely out of play.

The darkness helped her, she knew his eyes would struggle to pick out a fast-moving shadowy figure. Quickly, she was on his side, then her arm came up, reaching under his gun arm and pulling it up, coiling up and around his throat, forcing his arm straight into the air. He fired the gun, but the shot was out of panic, it was never a threat. Before he could even begin to compute what was happening, Lowri was pulling him down

339

to the ground, her left hand twisting his right arm, forcing him to drop the gun as they struck the ground.

Reuben tried to scramble free, but Lowri was strong, far stronger than he had imagined, and then she rammed the gun, hard, under his jaw.

"Fuck!" Reuben exclaimed in anger, headlights appearing in the distance, wobbling their way quickly up the road towards them. He knew he had been beaten.

"Now I ask the questions," she hissed.

* * *

Nisha waited patiently. Reuben's yard had been unusually quiet today, but she had wanted to find him. His phone had been off, which was unusual, but not completely unheard of. It meant he was in a moment that he didn't want shaken from. Sometimes she wished she could shake him. In fact, she knew she could, so did he. That's why his phone was off.

His stubbornness, she lamented, was what would get him killed. It was a huge part of why they had got here, but he needed to reign it in sometimes, especially now, when they were so close to getting what they needed to get out and begin afresh, as someone else, someplace new, somewhere good.

She sat in his chair, behind his desk. It was all designed to make him look more powerful. A big oak desk that was far too large for anything he would ever need it for, designed to cast an illusion of grandeur, to separate him from those who worked for him. Reuben was always keen to keep that hierarchy intact, and this was just one way of positive reinforcement.

The chair was grand too, the most expensive leather swivel he could find. It reclined, rotated, rocked, gave him the power to change his position when he saw fit, to better cast that image he needed to reflect. Nisha thought it was comfortable, but not worth the price he had paid. Things like that, she might have to have more of a say in when they were out of this game.

She heard a noise downstairs, as the door to the yard opened and someone walked in. Nisha rose up and walked to the window to see Fisher, alone, walking into the building. She was disappointed it wasn't Reuben, but she was sure if anyone knew where Reuben was, it would be Fisher.

She heard him enter the building and begin to do something downstairs. She could hear the drawers in the filing cabinets opening and things being moved, maybe he was looking for something. She waited. She was in no rush. She had all the time in the world till Reuben returned.

Finally, after a couple of minutes, Fisher entered the office. He couldn't hide his surprise to see Nisha.

"Oh, sorry," he said as he spied her sat on the desk.

"It's all right, Fish. How you doing?"

"Good." Fisher nodded. "You?"

"Just waiting on the boy, you know. He tell you where he at?"

Fisher frowned. "I tried calling," he looked thoughtfully at her, "but he never answered."

"He's got a mission on." Nisha nodded as she thought out loud. "He got a job he's trekking to, and he don't want us talking him out of it."

"Did he tell you what he was doing today?" Fisher moved to one of the drawers, he seemed a little more relaxed than he had when he first saw Nisha, and he began to search through the paperwork in the draw.

"Usual, Fish, he just said he had to grab some bitch who had been causing that Bowen trouble."

"He told you about Bowen?" Fisher pulled some papers out, folding them and putting them into his pocket, his hand hovering as he struggled to get them to go in.

"Yeah, he tells me everything, you know that." Nisha shrugged.

"I guess I do."

Fisher pulled a gun from his inside pocket. Nisha saw it and spent what seemed like an eternity trapped in a terrifying moment of realisation, then Fisher fired. Nisha tried to turn to get out of the way, but the bullet struck her in the side of the head, blowing through her skull, into her brain, and spraying Reuben's impressive desk with dark red blood.

34

It had all started fifteen years ago for Fisher and Bowen. Both men had served together in Afghanistan. They had been part of the 2nd Battalion, Paratroopers, and they had seen extensive deployment out there. Fisher and Bowen had both acquitted themselves well and had found a friendship in each other, which had waned slightly after demobbing.

Bowen came from the sort of background where he never had to fear what was coming next. His family were connected, people within prominent positions. Fisher hadn't had such a luxury and had found work hard to come by, working as a bouncer and security across East London, until he made friends with a young upstart in his gym, who had a vision of greatness that really appealed to Fisher.

So, for a while their paths had separated, until Bowen and his partners had hatched their plan. Fisher's name had been raised by Bowen. Or so he had told him. Fisher knew his old platoon mate would know he was down on his luck, but he made such a case that it was because he was capable that Fisher had accepted.

The plan was simple. They had wanted to find a patsy to cover their tracks. Someone who could be used to get their

344

asset in the country and offer protection off the books. Reuben's group were selected as the perfect candidates for the role. They would have a direct link into the group in Fisher, someone embedded, who would give them a loyalty that they needed to be certain of complete control over the operation and someone who, when the time came, could clean-up house for them.

That was what Fisher was doing now. It had never been the intention of anyone involved to take out Nisha, but she had told Fisher what she knew, and that was too much. A simple calculation went through his head in an instant, and he despatched her quickly and efficiently. Reuben might have been a friend to him over all these years, he might have given him an opportunity, but the main thing that Fisher had learned to work for Reuben was that, ultimately, you had to look out for number one, just as Reuben was doing.

Perhaps it might have been different had Reuben not had his heart so set on leaving and getting out of the game, but with that move, he had taken away the security of everyone who worked for him. He might not have seen it, but that admission was the moment that Fisher had decided it was time to find a new opportunity. When his old friend Bowen had got into contact, it was just a simple decision.

Throughout the whole operation, everything that Reuben had said or done, every single conversation, right down to his plans to turn on Bowen before the end, had been fed back by Fisher. It had all made the eventual betrayal seem that much smarter. Reuben was a man of no particular moral code in this matter, so why should Fisher be? He was being asked to betray one side or the other, why not pick the side that would offer him the better long-term prospects.

Now he had the most important part of his job to do. To clear up the rest of the crew before Reuben returned. He tried phoning his boss again, but no reply. He kept his phone out and dialled the first name of the gang in there, Lyndon Waites, and waited for him to answer.

"Lyndon, it's Fish. I need your help at the office, come alone, don't tell anyone. I think we have a problem."

Fisher hung up. Waites would be along shortly. He would kill him the moment he walked into the office, then he would begin to track down the rest of them. Umar was an issue, his being captured didn't help, but he didn't know much, certainly not anything that could compromise him.

* * *

"You need to come listen to this." Polly raced into David's office without knocking, causing him to look up from his desk with surprise. He had retreated there after Jack and Adam had confirmed Lowri's safety and that they were bringing her back. The relief he had felt had surprised him, and he was sure it must have shown to the others, so he wanted to take some time out to recompose himself.

"What is it?"

"I think Kevin Fisher just killed Nisha." Polly's eyes were wide. She had spent hours listening to the conversations in that office, part of the team that had tried to piece together everything they had heard, looking for a link to pull this together.

"Killed her?" David stood up and followed Polly out of the room, back to the small confined space where she had been listening in and making notes.

"He shot her, I know that much, and now he's calling in someone to help him out. Phone log shows it's Lyndon Waites."

"You think they're planning a coup?"

"Could be, or it could be something more, but, Reuben's girlfriend, when he finds out…"

"He's going to be destroyed," David cut her off. "He's on his way here."

"Reuben? We got him?" They had reached the desk, and Polly passed the headphones to David and started to spool the audio back to the right point.

"Yes, but this changes everything. Let me hear."

Polly played the audio, and David was in no doubt. "Good work," he acknowledged. "Let me know when Waites arrives and see what they do. Could be they try and clean this up."

"Okay."

David stepped up and walked back to his office, closing the door and phoning Jack.

"Jack, are we on speaker?"

"No, sir."

"Good, listen, keep this call one-sided. I think Fisher just killed Arrowsmith's girl. Has he had any phone calls?"

"Yeah, that would be the source of them," Jack replied.

"I thought so. Don't take any of them. I want to break that to Reuben in a controlled setting; I want to turn him on them. I don't want him going off half-cocked and trying to pull something so he can get revenge. I want him here and subdued first."

"Understood, we're on our way."

David hung up. If Reuben was betrayed and if Nisha really was dead, then there was a chance here to make a play that could blow the whole case open, but first, they needed to get proof.

35

He hadn't thought it was possible to be even more nervous of crowds than he was before, but the sight of a mass of children at the gate of the school flushed Calum with fear. Something was happening, he could see that from the buzzing swarm of teenagers and hear it from the excited chatter of their voices, but he had no idea what, and he was certain he didn't want to know either.

As he got closer, he felt his fear abate as he saw two police cars in the school carpark. Something might well have been happening, but at least it was being carried out by the right people, and the fact that the police were there meant that nothing was likely to happen to him.

He saw the police officers eventually, their bright yellow high-vis jackets marking them out through the crowds. Whatever had happened must have happened quickly and must have been dramatic. The lights on the cars were still flashing, and he could see they had someone with them, someone struggling hard as he was part frog-marched, part dragged to the police car.

"I ain't done nothing, you fucking pig, ain't done nothing!" the voice screamed in a mix of anger and fear. Calum knew the voice instantly, and he knew who they had before he could see the face of the wildly thrashing body ahead. It was Isaac.

He slowed his pace, worried again, not because he had done something, but because of an intense dread that his being there would mark him as the reason for the arrest. He didn't want Isaac to feel he had a score to settle, so he held back, pressing himself up against the metal bars of the school fence, and waited, watching through the gaps, feeling the cold metal as he lay his cheeks against the bars, watching them drag Isaac into the car. The crowd began to circle, and the police made the smart decision to move him away quickly, aiding the teachers and other school staff in their quest to regain control of a now extremely over-excited mass of teenagers. Calum began to feel something wash over him. He was almost elated, and the aches and pains that had cursed him since the assault seemed to seep out of him and into the cold bars his face rested on.

Once the car had gone, he made his way into the school grounds, head down, and into the playground. Summoning up all the courage he could, he looked for someone he half-knew, a face from his form, and found a girl called Rachel. Feeling the spit in his mouth disappear, he hoarsely asked her, "What happened?"

"Oh my God!" she excitedly exclaimed. "They nicked Isaac from year eleven. I mean, like, he had a knife and a load of drugs they said. It was mental, they just came in and took him down!" She was beside herself with excitement, but Calum just nodded back, dumbstruck, and then without another word, walked off. Rachel never noticed, she was back to her friends.

Calum walked to class. He was smiling.

* * *

When she had spied the rundown building that Mo wanted her to go into, Annie had felt her doubts come back. There was no way this was the base of an underground resistance. It was tatty, bland, everything it shouldn't be, but then she realised the logic in that disguise, and she had followed him carefully in.

Inside she had been relieved and then amazed. It was true, everything he said. This was a proper organisation, with real resources. She had looked out over the floor of the field office, at the people working at their stations or huddled around each other chatting through whatever strand of the operation they were on, and she saw and knew that this was something she had never dreamed of.

All her ideas of insurrection, or fighting corruption, had been of back-alley movements, or lone wolf hackers, like herself, forming virtual collectives to target companies they felt were operating above the law, to try and hinder and impede them as best they could. That all seemed like silly fantasy, like tickling the belly of the beasts, compared to this.

"Holy shit," she breathed.

"Good, isn't it?" Mo said.

"It's insane."

"Whole world is insane, you know that."

David had been alerted to them returning, and he walked over and offered a hand to Annie, who tentatively took it, holding on meekly as he did the shaking for them both.

"Welcome to our London office," he said firmly. "Sorry, I need to cut to the chase. We need everything you have, all your work, and we need it now. If you're right about what they've brought into the country, we might be fighting for our lives."

Annie shot a worried glance at Mo. "You think they could do it here?"

"It could be anywhere, depends what they have."

"I never…" Her voice trailed off. Mo knew she hadn't thought of the risk to herself and was now longing to be heading back out of the city.

"It might not be in London. Wherever you were heading, you could have been walking right into it. You'd never know," he soothed.

"Mo will get you set up, the two of you will find them," Warner added.

Annie just nodded.

* * *

The car containing Jack, Adam, Lowri, and Reuben pulled up in the parking lot under the building, and the four of them made their way into the very centre of the structure where eight holding cells had been built, as far from any potential way out as possible.

Reuben still had his swagger. His pride had taken a dent, he didn't expect to be bested by anyone at gunpoint, but he had been, and right now, he had felt like a rank amateur. But it wasn't something he would dwell on, at least not negatively. He would learn from it, and he would move on. He wasn't dead, they wanted him alive, and he would make a deal to keep it that way. No problem.

Lowri left them and made her way back to the office floor. Jack and Adam flanked Reuben as they made their way to the cells. None of them spoke. There was nothing to say at this point. Just trying to make him sweat it out, Reuben thought, unaware of the drastic change in his situation that was about to be revealed to him.

The holding cells were set in solid concrete, three-foot-thick inner walls on each cell, no windows, simple strip lighting embedded in the join between wall and ceiling, a small flat-bed made up of a mattress on a concrete protrusion, and a toilet in the corner. They weren't designed for long-term habitation; they were designed to be places of reflection, places where people began to contemplate their predicament.

The door to the cell consisted of two sliding barred gates, each one retreating into a recess within the concrete wall, one from the right, one from the left, and locking in place. They operated by a switch in a hidden control room that overlooked the cells from an adjoining room. Jack looked up at a camera on the ceiling, nodded, and the doors opened with the metallic thumping and grinding of the machinery needed to propel the doors backward and forward.

A slight nudge from Adam made Reuben walk forward, and then the doors closed behind him as he looked at the dull grey interior of the cell. It really was a depressing place, he thought, but he was prepared to use the time to hone his side of the negotiation. They would be back, he knew, as he heard the door to the holding cell area open and close, and when they did, they would find he was not just some dumb two-bit gangster but a man of cunning. A survivor.

* * *

Fisher had despatched Waites easily. The big guy had walked into the office, blundered in almost, completely unaware of anything going on. Fisher had been able to put two bullets into his back and another into the back of his head when he had fallen. That left him with two more to take out before Reuben. Both were at their homes; Fisher had already sent a text to them and told them to stay put. He would visit them both once he had finished at the yard. True, Reuben had numerous other associates, people who worked under him, who Fisher had come into contact with, but he knew he didn't have time to take care of them all. These were the crucial ones.

He walked upstairs to the office again. Nisha still lay next to the desk where she had fallen, her body bouncing off the body of the desk, tumbling down on top of itself. He silently cursed Reuben again for involving her. It wasn't what he had wanted to do, but what choice did he have? She knew, and she needed to be removed. Anyone who could link him to Bowen, or even back to Andryiv, had to go.

He stopped.

The girl whose flat Andryiv had stayed in. She would also need to be removed, as would the girl opposite. More on his list. This was going to be a busy day. He walked over to the filing cabinet, pulling open the bottom drawer, taking out a cigarette lighter before removing some papers, lighting them, and placing them back in.

He did this to all the cabinets in the office. There were five, and by the time he finished, smoke was beginning to fill the room. He headed downstairs and took a can of petrol he had already placed by the door to the main room of the ground floor and began to splash it strategically over the building. Enough to get things started, to make the fire ferocious enough to burn all he needed to. There wasn't a lot that needed to be covered here, but it was always better to be safe than sorry, and besides, it was a statement to Reuben. The bridges were being burned along with the building.

Walking back to the door to the outside, he traced a trail of petrol behind him, stepping outside, still pouring. He threw the can back in, then taking out his lighter once more, pulled some papers from his pocket. He lit them and dropped them onto the petrol trail, which ignited instantly, racing eagerly back into the building and lapping over everything it touched. Fisher watched for a couple of seconds, then turned and left the yard forever.

36

Thea sped through the London streets, the blue lights on her car lighting up the road with their opalescence bouncing off every surface they touched. Something was happening with Reuben's empire, and she was desperate to know what. A colleague had tipped her off that one of his properties was on fire. Everything they knew he owned was on a watch list. Anything that happened there was flagged and processed appropriately. Thea had to get there quickly to find out what was happening.

It was always in Thea's mind that this was somehow connected to Jack and Adam. She wondered if this was their work, that perhaps Jack had gone back on his word to turn Reuben over to her and that they had waded in and done something drastic. As much as she hated Reuben, despised his very existence, she didn't want to see him dealt with this way, not while there was still a chance to put him behind bars.

Four fire engines were already on site and battling the blaze when she arrived. The flames had been doused, but still, the building smoked and smouldered and an acrid smell hung in the air, mixed in with the sound of the pumps on the fire tenders, which were still blasting jets of water into the shell of the building. Downstairs was gutted, that was clear. Blackened scorches reached out from every charred door and shattered window, but upstairs, whilst smoke still cascaded out of the windows, didn't seem to have suffered the same searing heat damage as below. She knew from the intelligence that they had gathered, that upstairs was where Reuben did his work. She hoped something had made it through the fire that could be used against him.

Getting out of her car, she walked quickly up to the white-helmeted watch manager who stood deep in conversation with one of his colleagues next to one of the tenders. He saw her coming and turned to greet her as she flashed her badge at him.

"Thea Watts, NCA," she said.

"Aldous Green," he replied. "You guys got here quick."

"We've got the building on a watch list," Thea explained. "Have you found anything of note?"

"I should say so. Come on." Green ushered her quickly towards the other side of the fire tender, which had been obscured from her view as she arrived. As they got around the corner, Thea saw two black tarpaulin sheets lying across what were clearly bodies, on the street, just outside the fence.

"They were inside?" she asked, although she knew the answer.

"Yeah, but I don't think they were killed by the fire. I mean, I'm no pathologist, and the big one is so burned up you can't see, but this one." He bent down to the smaller bag and pulled it back. "That to me looks like she's been shot."

"She?" the word jabbed at Thea, and she almost choked as she said it. There were numerous women it could have been, but all the same, Thea knew, even before Aldous had pulled back the sheet.

"Nisha." Thea couldn't contain her shock, and she knelt to look at Nisha. Nisha's body had been tarred with the soot and ash, but she hadn't been decimated by the fire. The wounds on each side of her head were still clearly visible.

It was the last thing she had been expecting to see. She thought she might see some of Reuben's men. Maybe even Fisher and, at an outside chance, Reuben himself, but not Nisha.

"You know her?" Green asked.

"Yeah. She was involved in this, all this. Sorry, but that's all I can say. Can I see the other one?" Thea stood.

"For all the good it will do you," shrugged the Watch Manager.

The second body was bigger, almost definitely a male, but Thea couldn't work out who, other than it definitely wasn't Reuben and probably wasn't Fisher. Maybe someone like Waites or the charmless lump, Terry Carter.

"We got the ambo coming to pick them up," Green offered.

"Do you think you'll find anymore?"

"Hard to say, I wouldn't rule it out, but we've had a pretty thorough look around. We got a call of people being trapped, so we went in and did our best due diligence, you know."

"Yeah, of course."

Thea stood up and walked away from the bodies, her eyes on the burning fire. She couldn't get that question out of her head, she had to know for certain. She took out her phone and dialled Jack.

Two rings and he answered.

"Did you start the fire?"

"Wasn't us. It was Fisher."

"Fisher?"

"Yeah."

"You know Nisha's dead? Shot in the head it looks like."

"We thought as much. We've had his place tapped; we heard the shot. We're the ones that called in the fire, Thea. I told you, we have rules."

"Shit, Jack, what the hell happened?"

"I don't know, working theory, Fisher was paid to turn on Reuben."

"Fisher's stupidly loyal, I mean like rabid," Thea protested. "He wouldn't turn for money, not on Reuben."

"Then it's something else, but he pulled the trigger."

"Jesus." Thea sounded exasperated. "When Reuben finds out, this is going to kick this off to another level."

"That's what we're banking on. We're going to tell him shortly," Jack said calmly.

"Tell him?"

"Yeah. We've got him locked up in our facility downstairs. We're just putting together our plan, then we're going to tell him what happened."

"Jack, I need to be there. Whatever he says after that, I need to hear it," Thea pleaded.

"You can't, we're falsely imprisoning him, technically. You come here, your case is over."

"Then let him go, let me have him. Let me tell him. You promised me."

"I know I did and I will give him to you."

"Now, Jack. I need him now. I need to be the one to tell him," she urged.

"Okay, I'll see what I can do. Stay reachable," Jack said, then he was gone.

* * *

"I don't like this." Lowri shook her head. "This Watts is unstable. She's a firebrand, she doesn't follow protocol."

"Neither do we," Jack snorted, not hiding his annoyance. He had expected David to offer the strongest opposition to his plan and for Lowri to be onside from the off, but she had dug her heels in.

"We do, but we follow our own," Lowri snapped. "She is only in it to get Reuben, you can't lose sight of that. The intel we've just received is that there's a nuke out here. It could even be here in London."

There was a moment's pause as Jack and Adam let that sink in. Neither showed any emotion, but Jack felt the shock tingle through him as he thought of his family. He knew Adam would be feeling the same. His mind kept working forwards, however.

"The only way we get to do that is turn Reuben loose on the streets anyway. She's got nothing to hold him on, no charges, not yet," he insisted.

"I'm not convinced either," David weighed in, as Jack knew he might. "There's a real chance we lose him in the wind."

"Then send him with a chaperone," Adam offered.

"A chaperone?" Lowri echoed.

"Sure. That Watts trusts you," Adam nodded at Jack, "and she'll trust you even more if you deliver Reuben, but do it on the proviso you're his shadow while we find Fisher. After that, they can do what they want with each other, but this way, we get our input, and the cop gets to feel his collar a little."

365

There was a moment of quiet. Jack looked at Lowri and David and saw they were thinking about it. Giving Reuben up was a risk, and perhaps he did trust in Thea a little more than the others would like. Adam had come good on this one.

"Fine by me," Lowri consented.

"Then we do it." David still sounded hesitant, but he would always have to follow Lowri's lead.

"One proviso." Lowri raised her finger. "You need to ensure that we don't lose the bigger picture here. If she gets in the way of us finding who's behind this, you remove her."

"I'll set it all up," Jack said. "I won't let this go south, I promise."

37

The cell doors had trundled open. Reuben hadn't moved. The two men who had marched him in there returned and stood at the doorway as if inviting him out. He looked at them once, disinterested, and then away again. In they came, calmly, but still in control. They lifted him from where he sat on the bed and walked him out. Whilst he didn't resist, he didn't help them either.

He had expected to be taken somewhere and interrogated, but as the walk went on, they found themselves at a security checkpoint, where one of the men, the shorter one stopped. The taller one entered some data into a small tablet on the desk, watched by a guard, then continued on with him.

They approached a thick double steel door, which opened automatically. They walked down and into a small carport where a grey saloon car, a Vauxhall, waited. The driver's door opened, and Thea Watts stepped out, Reuben laughed and shook his head.

"Oh, my days, girl, you must be desperate. Linking up with these? You are finished when my lawyer gets done with you," he laughed.

Thea opened the rear passenger door. "Just get in the car, please." There was something in her voice that made Reuben look at her oddly. It was almost pity, almost like an apology.

"Yeah, what's your game here? What's happening, Watts?" he asked, now just a little thrown by her tone.

"In," Jack ordered abruptly, and Reuben slid in the back.

"Thank you," Thea said to Jack as he started to make his way around to the other rear passenger door, before putting her hand on his shoulder, stopping him. "I need you guys to check a name for me. I don't think it's safe for me to run it through our computers," she confessed.

"What's the name?"

"Joseph Thomas," she said.

"I'll get our people to look at it," Jack agreed.

They both got in, and Thea turned to look at Reuben. There was a pause.

"What's going on? Fuck's happening here?" he angrily asked.

"I'm so sorry, Reuben. Nisha is dead," Thea said, just as she had said to countless other people who had lost partners, parents, children in tragic circumstances.

Reuben froze, then sank back in his chair. There was no fight, which Jack had been preparing for, there was no anger.

"We think it was Fisher."

"Nah, nah." Reuben shook his head. "You're trying to twist me here, trying to fuck me over."

"I'm not."

Reuben looked at Jack. "The fuck have you done?"

He tried to lunge at him, but Jack pushed him back into his chair easily with one hand.

"We did nothing more than you on this. I'm as responsible as you are. We all share in this."

"What the hell you on about?"

"Fisher was covering his tracks. He betrayed you."

"Nah, man, I ain't buying that."

Jack pulled his phone from his pocket. "You want to listen to this?"

"What is it?" Reuben snarled.

"It's the recording of what happened. We've been tapping your office."

"How the fuck did you do that?"

"Do you want to listen or not?"

"Nah, nah, you're messing with me, it ain't happened, she ain't dead." Reuben held firm in his belief.

"I'm afraid I'm going to need you to identify the body." Thea was still sounding soothing and sympathetic. It shocked her to find she meant it as well.

"Identify the body, get to fuck, will you. Yeah, let's go, man, let's go there now, call your fucking bluff, show me the body, cuz you ain't got no body, ain't been no killing. My girl is fine."

"Call her," Jack proposed.

"Gimme that phone." Reuben snatched at Jack's phone, pulling it away. As he did, Jack pressed play, so that Reuben held the phone in his hand as the recording played. It burst out of the phone and stopped him in his tracks as he heard first Nisha and then Fisher, speaking in his office. As he listened, the realisation began to set in. He could hear the escalation in

Fisher's voice that Nisha had missed, the curiosity in his questions that led him to his one option. Reuben knew it, recognised in an instant what was coming and shouted out, "No!" but it was futile. The shot rang out, and there was the sound of something scraping on the desk, then silence.

Reuben sat ashen-faced in the back of the car looking at the phone.

No one spoke.

Reuben looked up to Thea, doing all he could to hold back the tears, not wanting to show this weakness to his enemy, but knowing that very same weakness had been exploited already by someone who he thought was a friend.

"I need to see her," he croaked.

Thea nodded, starting the car.

* * *

Kat walked into her brother's room. He was lying on his bed, watching TV. He was smiling, which she was glad about.

"You look happy," she remarked.

"What do you want?" he asked, smirk evaporating.

"Just came to see how you were." Kat wandered slowly into his room. "Some day at school, wasn't it?"

"I bet you're gutted." Calum sat up on his arms. "I know you were back with him."

"You saw us?"

"Yeah, in the canteen."

"You never go in the canteen," Kat said with surprise.

"Well, I saw you both."

"Not everything you see is the truth, you know, Calum. Just ask yourself this; how unlucky would that idiot have to be to come into school with a load of class A and a knife, then get caught randomly?"

Calum pulled a face. "I don't get it?"

"You will," Kat said. She smiled and left the room.

* * *

Mo and Annie were given the name, Joseph Thomas. It took them just seconds to get a hit.

"Jesus, that bloody Lord who was killed today, his assistant, bloke called Joseph Thomas," Mo said excitedly.

Annie looked at the screen, a picture of Lord Mitchell's aide appeared on the screen. His name, indeed, was Joseph Thomas. "Is it the same one?" she asked. "I mean, it's not a ridiculous sounding name, I bet there are a few Joseph Thomas out there."

"I don't like coincidences Annie," Mo typed quickly, "but, you're right, we should check."

He opened the file of the dead soldier. A picture came up. It wasn't the same guy.

"Ah, shit," Mo grimaced. "I thought we had him."

"Let me check something." Annie slid in next to him, making him move his chair across so she could get at the keyboard. Her fingers were quicker than his as she inputted some commands into the computer. "You don't believe in coincidences, I don't believe in face value."

She leant back, and the computer screen flashed up a link.

"See?" she said.

"Whoa." Mo read the information. "Joseph Thomas served in the same unit as Kevin Fisher."

"Another coincidence?"

"Told you, I don't like them." Mo shook his head in disbelief.

* * *

Erik saw the van pull up outside the warehouse where he had been holed up since the assassination of Lord Mitchell. Moving locations had been a drag, but stay too long in one place, and the law of averages says that you're going to be spotted, which he couldn't afford. He prepared this location prior to the attack, setting up a small provision store in the roof space of an old disused hosiery factory. It had been due for demolition but, due to an ongoing legal challenge about the historical significance of the building, was now left to rot, it's only significance being that it was becoming a blot on the local landscape.

He had squirrelled himself away in one of the old storerooms, barricading the doors to ward off any potential bum or squatter who might have similar ideas, but he had been assured that security on the site would mean that no one would get close enough. That security had been bought by his employers and ordered to patrol everywhere, except the area around the storeroom. Whilst they didn't know it, they were operating as his own personal bodyguards. True, they wouldn't be willing to put their lives on the line, certainly not for little more than minimum wage, but they offered security against unwanted intruders and a delaying tactic against anyone a little more official.

He had arrived by way of a delivery truck. No one had seen him arrive, and now, no one would see him leave. All the security firm would know they were doing was their job in the first place, just a little more vigorously for a few pounds more.

The van would take him and the bomb to a staging area, near to where the final attack needed to take place. Now they were inside twenty-four hours of the operation, and it was the right time to move up. Placing the device was going to be problematic, and with timings absolutely essential, Erik knew that there was little scope to get this wrong. Set up too early and the whole thing could be discovered before it was time, set up too late and Erik ran the risk of making himself a statistic, a number on the body count.

He watched the van reverse up to what once served as a loading bay and went back to the storeroom, retrieved his bag, and cleared away any sign that he might have been there. Satisfied, he made his way downstairs, into the loading bay and into the rear of the van. The driver would never see his face, nor he the driver's. A very acceptable arrangement.

In the back of the van was a briefcase. It was small, silver, smart looking. He picked it up, feeling the weight. The Soviet Union and the US had manufactured a number of these during the Cold War but destroyed their stocks. Israel had staunchly denied ever creating any. It had been theorised by many that this was a lie. Few knew the truth. Erik. He was holding one right now. Based on the American design for the MK54 SADM, or Special Atomic Demolition Munition, it was a fully functioning, devastatingly powerful, easily portable, nuclear bomb.

38

It was a different morgue to where Franks was being kept. This one was situated at a hospital a little way outside of the city, nearby the NCA offices. Most of the crimes that ended up on their slate would have specialist pathologists working on them, and there was a need to keep things all close to hand. It was smaller than most of London's more prominent hospitals, a private place, where people paid to be away from the hustle and bustle and usual trappings of an NHS hospital. It was a far more peaceful and serene setting than Nisha had been treated to in the moment of her death.

The three of them walked through the hospital in silence, passing only the odd porter or nurse on their rounds, before reaching the morgue. A receptionist greeted them and signed all three of them in efficiently. They were shown through a door into a waiting room, where they were told they would be collected when they were ready for identification to begin.

They waited. For all three, it seemed uncomfortably long, each for their own personal reasons. Finally, a white-gowned assistant arrived and calmly stated, "We're ready."

There was a moment of pause. No one seemed eager to get up.

"We don't need to go with you," Thea said, and Reuben nodded, then stood and followed the assistant.

Thea and Jack sat in awkward silence waiting.

"Are you going to give me him?" Thea finally broke the silence.

"He's here isn't he?"

"You're not going to screw me?"

"No," Jack replied. "But you've still got nothing on him."

"He'll talk now."

"He will because he wants to get Fisher. As long as that carrot is there, he'll talk. It's still not going to help you, because his word alone isn't a case."

"I can put him away."

"Or you could let him ride it out and solve the bigger case."

"I've told you all along, I want Arrowsmith."

"That's fine." Jack pushed himself back in his chair casually. "Thing is, the people who he's after, they turned off the radiation detectors at Dover docks a couple of days back. You might get Arrowsmith, but there might not be a court in London left to try him in."

"A nuke?"

"We don't know."

"Shit, you can't handle this on your own, this needs everyone."

"Reuben's orders, ultimately, have been coming from someone inside the government. We traced it back to the Houses of Parliament. Don't get me wrong, we've already put the right people on alert, the words out, but no one is being told. Ask yourself why?"

"Panic."

"Exactly. What government is going to tell ten million people there's a nuke out there. Shit, might not even be here in London. It could be anywhere. That's near enough seventy million people suddenly in a blind panic. You want to go further? It might have been on its way out of here. Someone might be using this to smuggle nukes out of the country, although, it doesn't really fit with what's happened so far.

Whatever it is though, Thea, the top people know and they don't want anyone else too. I'm just telling you so that you make an informed decision. I won't stop you doing whatever you want to do, not my place, but just think about it."

"People need to know," she insisted.

"And that could force their hand, make them take action sooner."

"Or it might make it strategically impossible for them to reach their target," Thea countered. She could barely believe that there was even a thought of keeping this under wraps. "Things like this can't be covered up."

"How many times have you heard about something like this before?" Jack asked.

"Never."

"Yeah, never. You think someone has never tried this? You think we haven't been this close before?"

Thea looked at his face. It was resolute, grim, as he revealed this secret from the darker world in which he lived. She suddenly realised she knew nothing about him, nothing about his life so far, and that scared her.

"My God," she whispered.

"It will be found, and you can help us. Let Reuben loose, let him find Fisher. Then when it's done, do with him as you please."

"In this state, he could do anything, and then I'd be complicit."

"I know, I'm asking you to risk a lot, but if we don't do this, we might lose even more. Anyway, what would you even hold him on? He's a suspect in what?"

Thea leaned back in her chair looking at the ceiling, her head resting on the wall behind her, hands drooped between her legs. She looked beaten.

"Fine," despondently she agreed. "We do this your way. If we must. But if it goes south, you better find a way to get me off the hook."

"I won't let this come back to you, I promise."

Thea closed her eyes. She knew he wouldn't, she was just worried how he would stop it.

* * *

Reuben's world was over. He had known they weren't lying. True, there had been hope, but that hope had been extinguished with the first lift of the sheet that covered Nisha's body and the sight of her hair. She was unmistakable to him, her everything burned into his memory forever. Now, that was all she would be. A memory. His reason for living was gone, and he wasn't so vain, so foolish, to not realise that this was his fault.

He had told her too much; the recording proved that. Fisher had been left with no choice but to kill her. It was the same sort of attitude that Reuben had used throughout his career, something he had fostered in the man who he had trusted with his life until less than an hour ago. Reuben had created this situation, this inevitability, and he would live with that forever. It would kill him eventually, he knew that, but for now, he would suffer.

Another person who would suffer was Fisher. The traitorous son-of-a-bitch would be dead within the day if Reuben chose to make it that quick. No one was going to stop him. Not Watts, not the big lump with her. He promised that to himself as he walked back to the waiting room where they both still sat. He stood and looked at them both as he walked back in.

"I have to kill that cunt," he said matter-of-factly.

"Fine," Jack shrugged. "He deserves it. One proviso though. I get to ask him some questions first. Nothing more, nothing less."

"Deal," Reuben replied, before looking at Thea. "You down with that?"

Thea said nothing. She stood and looked at them both. "Let's go find him."

* * *

Fisher had to admit this was the part he felt least comfortable with. Marianne and Ursula were both good girls, but there was a chance that both of them could pass on something regarding Andryiv. He couldn't let that be the case. They were loyal to Reuben, not him, and he was well across that line now. He would have to be quick, and he would have to be effective.

He went to Marianne's door first. She wasn't as gobby as Ursula, he would feel worse about killing her. She would probably cower and beg, whereas Ursula would fight back, and if she put up a fight, he'd leave with less remorse. Any potential commotion with Ursula would result in Marianne being warned. Simple common sense.

He knocked on the door and waited. Behind him, he was sure that he would now be watched. The two girls looked out for each other, so he turned and looked across the way to Ursula's door. She would see him and relax. He tried to look as casual as possible, not easy, for someone who wasn't used to being casual.

Marianne opened the door, a little surprised to see him. "Hello?" she asked innocently.

"Marianne, Reuben asked me to come in and check a few things. He was worried that the flat might have been bugged," he lied.

"You mean when that man came?" Marianne was already opening the door anyway. Why wouldn't she?

Fisher stepped in, looking around as part of his act. "Maybe. Care if I take a look around?"

"Yes, please do." Marianne stepped aside and then fell in behind Fisher as he strode into the living room.

"Did he go into the bedroom?" Fisher asked.

"I guess he went everywhere."

"Can you show me?"

"I didn't see where, but, okay, I show you around." Marianne had always been compliant, always done as she had been told, Fisher thought. It had been drilled into her, her whole life. A man speaks, you listen. From the beginning of her life to the end. How helpful, he mused.

She opened the door to the bedroom and went to walk in, but she didn't make it. Fisher brought the butt of his gun crashing down on her head and she crumpled instantly, a muffled gurgle from her mouth as she slipped out of consciousness.

Fisher stepped over her and lifted her up onto her bed. The covers were pink and satin. Very garish he thought. Hardly a spot for a corpse, but still. He lay her face up on the bed, blood already beginning to seep from the wound, then he took a pink pillow and placed it over her head. There was no fightback, the blow to the head put pay to that. She just simply slipped from unconscious to oblivion. From living to dead. From being a problem to a problem solved.

Fisher waited long enough for it to be done, then he waited some more, holding the pillow firmly in place with his gloved hand. He lifted it and bent forward to hear for any gasp of breath. Nothing. She was gone.

He stood up and took a quick look around. Satisfied, he made his way out of the flat, shutting the door behind him, ready to pay a visit to Ursula. Had he stayed a few seconds longer, he might have heard the buzz of Marianne's phone.

39

"I am coming! I am coming! Give me a fucking minute!" Ursula screamed from inside the house as Fisher knocked for the third time. She knew he would know she was there, but she desperately wanted to stall him as long as possible. Before he had called Marianne, Reuben had called her and warned her that Fisher was coming to kill them all. She had wanted to run, but as she reached the door and peered through her eyehole, she had seen him exiting Marianne's flat, and her heart had sunk. She knew her friend was dead and she also knew she wouldn't be able to escape undetected.

Running back into the flat, she had considered her options. She thought about climbing out onto the small balcony and trying to dangle herself down to the next floor, or even climb up to the one above, but she didn't trust herself to make the gap when she looked at it. The best thing to do, she had decided, was to delay Fisher's entry and then put up the biggest fight she could.

"Ursula, it's urgent," Fisher had shouted back through the door.

Of course it's fucking urgent, she thought to herself. *You want to fucking kill me quickly so you can get away before Reuben rips your head off, you bastard.*

"I'm just getting out of the bath, damnit. I'll be two minutes," she hollered angrily. She didn't know if he would believe her or not, she just hoped he would for at least a minute or two. Eventually, though, he would come through that door.

* * *

Thea, Jack, and Reuben were on their way, but they wouldn't get there quickly enough, so Jack had called in Adam. He was now just minutes from the flats, alone, but armed and prepared. He knew that Fisher was going to be in or around Ursula's flat. Ursula had told Reuben that she had seen Fisher going into Marianne's flat and Marianne hadn't answered her phone, so it seemed, sadly, that they were going to be too late to save her. Ursula's safety was a secondary concern as well. It was merely a case of getting to Fisher and apprehending him.

He was three minutes away according to the Sat Nav. He wondered if Ursula could keep Fisher at bay long enough?

***

"Ursula!" Fisher banged on the door and shouted. He was drawing attention to himself, he knew that, but he was angry, and he was worried. She must know something. Maybe Reuben was back and had tipped them all off. He needed to get this done and get it done quickly. Marianne hadn't been warned, so Reuben was probably still a long way from here. He just needed to tie up this loose end, then he could think about his old boss.

There was no reply now from inside the flat. It had gone quiet. Ursula had run out of things to shout and was probably getting herself ready to fight back. A further complication. He stepped back, then lunged forward, lifting his right foot and, using the momentum of his whole body, brought it smashing through the door.

There was no noise inside. No light. The blinds had been drawn to try and help her hide. Smart move, Fisher thought.

He stepped into the corridor and padded forward, taking his phone out and using its torch. He scanned left as he approached the door to the bathroom. He opened it, shining the light into the small room, flashing it from side to side to make sure no one was hiding in it. Nothing.

He moved forward. On his right, the wall gave way to counter space, as the kitchen of the flat began the impressive studio living area. The work surfaces were clean and smooth, nothing on them. He peered across, looking down to the floor as best he could, looking to see if someone lurked there, waiting to take advantage of the dark. Again, no one. He edged further forward through the shadows, semi-illuminated by the light seeping subtly through the blinds. She was in here, that was clear, but where? Time was running out; he had to find her.

He stepped past the sofa and into the centre of the living room, then decided to check the bedroom. She would be in there, the furthest point away from the entrance, so in her mind probably the safest part. Not the truth, as it was the furthest from the exit, which she would need to get too.

He didn't see the small table that sat next to a chair. It was too dark, and the table was too low. He caught it with his right knee.

He stumbled, not sure what it was. His first thought was that it was Ursula, and his hands grabbed for it. Feeling the hardness of the table, he realised his mistake.

Then he saw a shape bolting away from him. He knew it was her. He lunged forward, diving to grab her, tumbling forward, over the same table and into the dark.

He saw the flash of Ursula's legs in the murky light, and he reached out a strong arm, not quite grabbing round a leg but doing enough to trip the escaping woman. She tumbled to the floor, kicking out in desperation, trying to scramble away.

Fisher jumped onto her back. She squirmed beneath him, trying to twist and turn out from under him. He knew he didn't quite have the grip he wanted, and in the dark, it was hard to see where she was, but he managed to feel his way, bringing his knee up and driving it down into the bottom of her spine, trying to pin her in place. She kicked and bucked some more, trying to throw him off, trying to break free, but his weight was too much. Now he was on top, he could exert all his power over her.

He thought about reaching for the gun and shooting her, but the noise would have alerted someone, he was sure. He simply reached forward and placed both hands around her throat from behind. It wasn't hard, his hands were big and thick, and her neck was slender. Although she struggled, it wasn't hard for him to get his hands in position, and he squeezed hard, hearing her rasp.

She was struggling frantically now, and he felt her right arm slap against his side uselessly. He squeezed harder. Then, something else hit him, something that felt different, something that felt wrong.

It never dawned on him she might have been holding a weapon. It was arrogance, in the end, that killed him. He looked down to see the flash of a knife coming out of his side and then quickly being forced back in, with a wet slap and squelch, as it cut into his kidney deep inside him. He loosened his grip involuntarily and fell backwards as the strength suddenly sapped from him. The knife went in and out, in and out, in and out, three more times, quickly, each one with more venom than the last, as his strength sapped and hers swelled. He fell back and looked at the ceiling, confused and beaten.

Then something else happened, someone burst into the room holding a gun. Already Fisher was losing consciousness, he could hear the man screaming at Ursula to stop, but the words didn't make sense. He watched through a glaze as the man pulled Ursula away and then leaned over him, pressing his hands on his wound, trying to stop the flow of blood. It was no good, Fisher knew he was done. He could feel life ebbing away quickly.

40

"He's dead," Jack spat.

"What do you mean dead?" Reuben's voice was already straining.

"He went for your girl, and she defended herself."

"No, no, I want that bastard, I want him," Reuben snarled.

"We all did," Jack lamented.

"Fuck!" Reuben roared, kicking out at the seat in front of him in rage, jerking Jack who sat in front and turned to face him.

"Hey! Listen, get a grip will you! Get a goddamn grip. You want the people responsible for this?"

"Fisher was responsible for this and me. No one else," Reuben seethed.

"What about the people above him? The people who he betrayed you for?"

"What are you doing, Jack?" Thea interjected.

"We've got no link to the guy called Bowen now, other than you." Jack was pitching to Reuben now. "He probably wants you dead, needs you dead, like he needed Nisha dead."

"You want me to bait him?"

"The guy probably has a nuke. Yeah, I want you to bait him," Jack explained.

"A nuke?" Reuben's eyes widened noticeably, and Jack confirmed what he already suspected, that Reuben was a pawn.

"Yeah, Reuben, a nuke. You were used to get someone into this country and to protect them, while they set up to kill more people than have ever been killed before in one go. What did it cost them?"

Reuben shook his head and looked away.

"I know what it cost you," Jack went on.

"Five fucking mil," Reuben muttered.

"You must have known they were serious?" Jack pointed out.

"Nuke serious? Nah, not a chance, bruv. Not a fucking chance."

"No, I believe you, and I'm gonna make a bet on two things. One, you don't want that nuke going off, because you're a businessman, not a psychopath, and two, you want these people because you can't have Fisher."

Reuben stared coldly back at Jack "Yeah, that would be a good bet to make."

"Then help me out here. Get me to these guys."

Reuben looked at the two of them, and Jack could see a process going on in Reuben's head. He felt hope. Reuben knew something, and he was on the precipice of delivering.

"Cut me a deal," Reuben shrugged.

"No deal," Thea cut in.

"I wasn't talking to you, love. You ain't got nothing on me, not a damn thing more than you had a month ago, which was the sum of shit. No, you, big man, you cut me a deal."

"What sort of a deal?"

"I seen your place, I figure you want to keep me in a cell like that for the rest of my days. I don't want that."

"No one would," Jack agreed.

"So, one, you make sure you cut me loose."

"That could work." It wasn't unusual for The Regulators to deal in such ways. Bad people did bad things, and justice didn't always prevail, but there was always a scale where offences could be weighted and deals could be struck. The weight of Reuben's crimes to the threat of a nuclear device being detonated wasn't even comparable. "What's two?"

Reuben looked at Jack with a stony gaze that almost, but not completely, hid the evil intentions that lurked somewhere within his plan. "When we find Bowen, and we will find him, the three of us go get him."

Jack shook his head. It wasn't the request he'd expected. A part of him had figured Reuben would want to be the trigger man, and if it were possible, Jack would have seen no issue with that, but taking Thea as well? Where did she play into that? It could still be that Reuben wanted to pull the trigger, but with Thea there. She would finally have something on him. He looked at Thea and could see that she too was finding the logic hard to fathom.

"Fine," she said, perhaps coming to the same conclusion Jack had, that here was a chance for Reuben to finally incriminate himself.

"You don't need to be there." Jack knew how this was likely to end, and aside from the personal risk, it put Thea in an unenviable professional position. "This could go a lot of different ways."

"He says he knows how to find them. I want that. More than anything else. Fuck the danger, fuck my career if I have to, fuck whatever comes. We stop this bomb."

Jack had to agree. There was no other play. "Fine."

"I'll give you Andryiv now, but we need to start moving out of the city. I don't want to take any chances, and I know where that cat's been. I want out of here if he's got what you say he's got."

"How are you going to give him to us?"

"You need to ping a mobile. A Nokia 515 to be precise. Got 33 days of standby life that sturdy little number. Marianne, God bless her soul, she did me a solid while our visitor was here. See, I ain't never been anyone's mug, and I knew from very early on that I was being set up to be one. Our young Mr Andryiv had a thing for girls from back home, you know, back in the USSR and all that, and Marianne seemed to fit the bill. He spent a fair bit of time with her, enough time for her to secrete a Nokia 515 in his bag. Snipped a hole in it, stitched it up, turned off the vibrate and the ringtone. There you go, ladies and gents, a lovely little tracking device. You ping that phone, and you'll find out where he is, or at least where his bag is.

Given that Marianne reported that it seemed to have most of the tools of his trade in it, I figure it's with him near enough twenty-four-seven."

* * *

Reuben passed the number on to Jack, who passed the number on to Mo, who pinged the phone. Within seconds he had a real-time location on the phone, and constant pinging meant that they saw that it was on the move in central London. A drone was despatched immediately, carrying radiation detection equipment that would be used to verify if the weapon was with him.

"I've sent a chopper to Adam. He's heading to the coordinates, but I think we should push this up the chain of command." David watched the screen intently as the drone homed in on small lorry that was currently meandering through central London traffic.

"No, the reaction will be too slow, especially if the call gets into the wrong hands. It only takes one person to stall this, and the bomb goes off. It might expose them to us, but at what cost? Thousands of dead? No, we can't risk it."

"What if we can't get there on time? They could be on their way now?" David urged. "Our people are still fifteen minutes from intercept."

Lowri turned to Raf. "What are our probable targets?"

"It's central London." Raf spread his hands to emphasise the broad web they were casting. "They could be going for anything. I mean, they've gone for politicians, so best bet is the Houses, I guess."

"No, rule that out, they've surgically picked their political targets. And don't forget this came from inside the Houses, the whole thing leads back there." Lowri stood over Raf looking at the screen and the list of potential targets their algorithms had predicted.

"They might be trying to cover their tracks, burn it all down," Raf went on.

"They didn't expect anyone to know that's where they were. They covered their tracks. No, it's not there. We need to work out what they're doing and why. What has been the message with these damned videos?"

"They've been inflammatory," David answered. "And they've co-opted others, others who don't necessarily want to be involved. Naming names."

"It's a smear job," Lowri announced. "They want to kill the alt-right."

"You think?" David saw the resolution in Lowri's eyes and knew she didn't just think, she damn well understood.

"Of course. That's why this is happening, that's why people at the top are involved. It's a bloody stitch up on the far-right groups of this country. They'll find links between them all and bang them up for life, not to mention the fact that the public outcry will bury them. It's a goddamn false flag."

"What's the target?"

"Killing politicians wasn't enough, that was probably a warmup, one from each side. Bartram was a populist right-winger, Mitchell an old school leftie, Mamedov a new school one. You end up with both sides of the political spectrum hating you. Now you just need to give the people who don't give a shit about politics a reason to hate you. You hit something not political, but personal."

"Oh shit!" Raf exclaimed. "There's a goddamn vigil at Speakers Corner for the politicians. A bloody cross-party thing. Thousands of people are going."

"That's the target," Lowri snapped. "Can we intercept?"

"Traffic's a nightmare all over; the place is snarled up because of this damn protest. Cars are going to struggle to close in on them before they get there." The icons on Raf's screen told the story, there was no way they could hope to get close.

"Adam's our only chance now." David looked at the data in front of him. It was far too close for comfort.

***

The chopper pitched down, circling over Hyde Park. The whole area was teeming with people, most heading towards the vigil. A needle in a haystack, Adam thought as he surveyed the scene.

"You got to get me down there," he called out to the pilot over the din of the engines.

The pilot shot an annoyed glance back. "Are you kidding?"

"Just get me low enough to jump then."

The pilot shook his head but did as he was told. Adam saw people looking up as the helicopter got nearer to them. Slowly they began to step back as it came lower and lower.

Adam undid his seatbelt and slid open the door. People were pointing up at him, shocked. He sighed. This was going to smart.

He jumped.

There was still about twenty feet to go when he did so. He rolled as he landed, doing his best to minimise the blow, but it still hurt.

He didn't have time for that though. He was up and running in seconds. He had always been a good runner, someone who could hold a good pace for a long time, and now, with the stakes as high as they were, he was dodging through the people, heading east along the top edge of Hyde Park, hoping to get there in time. He knew that there were now two drones ahead, one to capture the radiation count from the bomb, the other to send real-time pictures back to the field office, to allow them to coordinate the operation. He hoped that it would give them enough of an edge to stop the attack. If not, he was dead, he knew that much, and so were many thousands of others.

The area around the park was full of protestors, most of them standing around, holding placards, talking eagerly with each other, at this point, still waiting for the keynote speakers to begin and the rally to reach its fever pitch. It made movement a little easier than fighting the tide, but still, there were numerous people standing in places they shouldn't be, or idly crossing the street in front of him, determined, it seemed, to hinder his process in saving their lives.

He darted between them, hoping he still had time. The type of bomb meant it had to be planted manually. It had a fifteen-minute timer, as standard, but that didn't rule out the possibility it might have been tampered with to shorten the fuse, or maybe even able to be detonated by hand, which was unlikely, given the lack of political motivation for Andryiv. There was also the risk it could be triggered remotely, which was deemed far more possible as a fail-safe, should Andryiv suddenly develop a hitherto unseen conscience.

Every available precaution was being taken to limit that possibility. The drones were jamming mobile and radio signals in the area, which was causing a little discomfort among the police ranks that Adam could see as he raced towards the scene, but hadn't yet registered in any resonant way with the protestors. Hopefully, it could be lifted soon enough before knowledge of it spread and risked becoming something else.

He could see the corner now, and he scanned for Andryiv across the mass of heads, placards, and vehicles.

"Where is he, Raf?" he barked breathlessly into his com as he neared the location.

"The phone is just two hundred metres the other side. It's stuck in traffic. Hold on…" Adam heard Raf respond.

"Drone has a spike." Raf could see the readouts from the first drone, and they were telling him without doubt that radioactive material was now out in the open. "Just going to get the other drone in place for a visual."

Adam was off and running. "Is it Andryiv?"

"Yeah, I got him." The excitement in Raf's voice was clear. "He's carrying a silver briefcase. That's got to be it. That's good, there's only one type of bomb it can be. We can disarm it, but we need to get it."

The crowd was thicker now, and Adam had to really work hard to get through them, sending several protestors sprawling as he tried to draw the straightest line towards Andryiv.

It felt like a lifetime before he heard from Raf again, which he had to assume meant he was moving in the right direction, but with every shuffle through a crowd, he knew he was getting closer and closer to missing his chance, to the bomb going off. Andryiv could have already started the timer. They couldn't lose him. If they did…

"He's coming straight at you, past the fountain." The birds-eye camera was still feeding Raf real-time pictures.

Adam saw the fountain. He still couldn't pick out Andryiv, but he forced himself ahead. "Don't let me go past him," he ordered.

"I won't." Raf could see the two of them closing towards each other now. "He's the other side of the path to you now, dead ahead, fifty feet, coming straight at you."

"I need to get behind him, tell me when we pass." Adam stayed on his side, eyes dead ahead, acting as nonchalantly as possible. He didn't want to spook Andryiv. If he tried to take off running, the sheer weight of numbers between them would make a foot chase a hard task.

"Okay, hold on, he's coming up in three, two, one, now!" Raf counted Adam in, and as soon as the word "now" came through, Adam spun and moved in the other direction, working across the path.

Ahead, Andryiv's head was clearly visible, Adam could see him. The plan was simple: step in behind, identify the case, check for any wires that might serve as a dead man's switch, then two shots to his back, and break with the crowd, bomb in hand and hope for the best.

He was now three people behind, then two, then one, then he could touch Andryiv if he wanted. He could reach out and grab him around the throat, fire the shots, and be done. But he didn't. He looked at Andryiv's hands. Then he looked again.

"He's not got it," he hissed and turned back on himself, head down, hoping that Andryiv hadn't turned. "Where the fuck is it?"

"Shit, he had it, he definitely had it," Raf panicked.

"Can you see it on the radiation detector?"

"No, the system isn't that precise, I know it's there though, it's definitely there."

"He dropped it; walk me through his route. It has to be here."

Adam walked quickly, scanning every bush, every stretch of floor.

"He walked pretty close to the fountain, it could be in there?" Raf offered.

Adam said nothing. He sped up and saw the fountain. "Shit."

In front of the fountain was a mountain of discarded bags, coats, unused placards, all dropped by the protestors who no longer wanted to carry them.

"It's like a fucking jumble sale. You need to get everyone here now. Let him go if you have to."

"He can't have hidden it, he never stopped moving, he must have just dropped it."

"Which means the timer was running before he got out of the van." Adam realised that their time was getting shorter and shorter. "Where is he now?"

"He's doubling back along Bayswater towards Marble Arch station."

"The Underground, perfect bomb shelter. We've got minutes at best."

Adam looked at the mountain of bags. Raf was right; if Andryiv hadn't stopped, then the bomb hadn't been concealed. There was no time, no need.

He walked along them, as slowly and meticulously as he dared, looking for a hint of something that didn't look like a scruffy duffle or a "No More Hate" placard. Nothing. He reached the end of the row, nothing.

"It's not here. We're running out of time." He could feel his heart racing, he almost felt hopeless.

Raf was going back through the footage. "He definitely had it before the fountain, hold on…" He span the footage forward a couple of seconds. "Ripples! In the water, it's in the fountain."

Adam jumped over the bags and into the water. "Where about?" he shouted as he thrashed through the cold, bubbling water.

"Right in the middle. You're right on top of it."

Adam looked down. There it was, a silver briefcase. He pulled it out, forcing his way back through the water as more and more puzzled onlookers watched this bizarre scene playing out in front of them, blissfully unaware of the danger they were in.

"I got it!" Adam said, placing it down on the edge of the fountain. He tried the clips, locked. Quickly he pulled a lock knife from his inside jacket pocket and jammed it in hard, forcing the mechanism with a strength born of fear and panic, popping it open with a sharp crack and displaying its contents. "Have you got any idea what to do?"

Inside was a long metal rod that pointed down towards a metallic box that Adam knew would contain the nuclear material.

"I got the schematics in front of me," Raf said, his voice effortlessly calm and professional. "There should be an electronic board in the top right corner as you look at it?"

"Got it," Adam said scanning the components. "It's got four wires coming out. You want me to cut them?"

"Just rip that son of a bitch out. That's the brain. That goes, the bomb stops."

Adam didn't ask twice, he just did what he was told. There was no other choice. He reached in quickly, felt his fingers biting into the mixture of plastic and soldered metal, and ripped. It cracked and came out.

Adam looked at the bomb. "Now what?"

"That's it. Should be."

"How do we know?"

"If you're dead in the next ten minutes, I guess I'm sorry."

Adam laughed. "You tosser." He slumped backwards, still in the water. Then he laughed again, looking up at the people who stood watching him, amused by their perplexed looks. He laughed again, relieved, then he stood up, closed the briefcase and made his way through the crowd.

"I need a beer," he muttered to himself.

* * *

Andryiv sat down on the carriage of the Underground train, a small miracle in itself, he thought. He had let his beard grow and wore a hat and sunglasses, which he assumed would be more than enough to stop anyone from casually glancing at him and recognising him from his photographs. Plus, this was London, no one ever acknowledged anyone on the Underground. It was the safest place to be.

He checked his watch. He had six minutes to spare as the train began to move off and into the safety of the vast network of tunnels that ran under London. In two minutes, he would be at Bond Street, then two minutes after, Oxford Circus, and a couple more to Tottenham Court Road. The bomb would be going off at some point around then, which would have him clear of the initial blast and, if he hustled quickly enough south, well out of the way of the fallout. It had been close, but they had pulled it off. He sat back, and for the first time in what felt like a lifetime, he tried to relax.

He didn't notice the two men who got onto the carriage just before the doors of the train closed. He had for the first time in his professional life, switched off. He did notice when they stood in front of him and looked down on him. He fixed them both in the eyes, one at a time and saw them both slightly lift their jackets to reveal their weapons, ever so slightly and only to him.

Erik Andryiv sighed and closed his eyes. He placed his hands on his legs so they could see them and accepted his fate. There would be no blast as they arrived at Tottenham Court Road and there would be no hustle south and for the Channel. Instead, Andryiv would ride the Underground to the end of the line in Epping, where he and his two new companions would stay on the train till everyone else had left. Then they would walk slowly to a convoy of three 4x4s that waited there to ferry him off and out of existence, as far as anyone else would ever be concerned.

41

"They got it." Jack felt the tension evaporate from his body as he relayed the message back to Thea and Reuben.

"Told you," Reuben said, no hint of emotion in his voice. "Now, let's go get our man."

"You haven't told us how we find him yet," Thea pointed out.

"And I can't believe that I'm sat in this car with two people, one a cop in one of the most prestigious, most highly thought of organisations in the UK. The other, I don't know what he is, but I've seen how he works and where he works, and I can only begin to guess at the money you lot are pumping into it, and I'm the only one who cracked who he was." Reuben was almost angry in his delivery; he didn't seem to be taking any joy from this. If anything, he was disappointed with them.

"You're smarter than us, we get it," Jack shrugged, not rising to the bait.

"I'm not smart. I'm cautious. Fisher did the vetting on him, so maybe in that respect, I'm even considered stupid, but he said he knew the guy. Someone from his army days," Reuben explained.

"Maybe he wasn't lying?" Thea looked to Jack.

"It was all a dead end, there was no one called Bowen in his army days. He might well have been there, but he clearly had a different name," Jack pointed out.

Reuben laughed. "Course he had a different name, he ain't no rank amateur. You lot must be though; didn't you work him out?"

"No, enlighten me."

"What, you never watched *Bullseye*?"

Bullseye was a TV programme that aired on Sunday nights in the UK. It was part quiz show, part dart challenge. Teams of two, one selected for their dart prowess, the other for their general knowledge skills, battled across both disciplines to win prizes, most of which were second-rate, apart from the prizes that were revealed when a team failed to take it home. It coined the catchphrase, "Let's have a look at what you could have won." The host of the show was Jim Bowen.

It took less than two minutes to pull the information together. Lieutenant Joseph Thomas and Lieutenant Kevin Fisher served with another man, Lieutenant Paul Rushe, who was indeed nicknamed Bullseye, on account of his expertise on

413

the rifle range. His photo was pulled up, at which point there was little chance to deny that Paul Rushe was now Joseph Thomas, aide to the late Lord Leighton Mitchell.

"I don't get it?" Jack was confused still. "Why Bowen?"

"Code names," Thea answered for Reuben. "He thinks he's a smart arse, so he went for something cheeky but obvious."

"You got me down to a tee, girl," Reuben nodded. "Ain't no way I'm discussing someone like him, when God knows who is listening. One slip word or something and we could all be in it. So, we used a codename. I mean, come on, obvious init when you think about it?"

"Startlingly so." Jack glowered at Reuben, knowing that he'd bested them on that. They'd underestimated him. It was probably one of the reasons he'd been chosen, an unpredictable element that kept them on their toes.

"Why did they kill the other soldier?" Thea was still piecing it all together.

"These people needed a clean skin to get past the security clearances needed to become Mitchell's aide. Thomas was probably nothing more than the wrong man at the wrong time," Jack offered.

"It seems excessive."

"These people live by excess, I'm afraid. Whatever they wanted to do came at a cost. That cost is mounting up by the second."

* * *

Jack had relayed the information back to the office and details were being dug up constantly. Rushe seemed to have disappeared after leaving the army. He had an address, he had a national insurance number, he had a bank account where money sometimes was moved in and out, but nothing out of the ordinary. Other than that, he didn't exist. A couple of utilities in his name, but that was all. He never bought food, never bought clothes, never bought appliances. He was a ghost. All apart from one thing. Paul Rushe owned a car.

The address was a modest house in Ipswich, not far from Colchester, where the battalion was based. A team was despatched immediately to investigate, but the theory was that it would be a shell, nothing more. The car wouldn't be there though. Its plates had already been run through ANPR, and a number of hits had come back, all placing it in and around central London. Mo had left Annie to try and build up a route to see if he could piece together where the car had been.

"This guy's cocky," Lowri mused as she looked at the data Mo had dug up so far. "He thinks he can get away with it, whilst still goading us."

"That'll be his biggest mistake." David was with her scanning through the same data on a separate pad and pacing around the office. "Arrogant people slip up. We've been treating him like someone who wouldn't, but now we know he has. We need to investigate all the links here. Get his whole squad in. If he reached out to Fisher, there is a chance there are other people in his unit who he reached out to."

"The car is still our best bet. There might be places it travels to regularly. If we can locate one, we can get there. Otherwise, we're making a slow play, and we have to work on the basis that he's looking to disappear."

"Fine, send the details to Jack, check out the house, we might catch a break."

* * *

The bomb hadn't gone off. Which meant Andryiv had failed. Fisher was no longer answering his phone as well. It was, as they would have said back in the day, completely fubar.

"What do you need me to do?" Bowen asked his handler.

"Stay calm, we will extract you. Make sure there's nothing left that can tie anyone and then head to the exfil."

"Do you think I've been compromised?" The pain of failure had hit him harder than he might have expected, had he ever contemplated failure. Now it had happened, he had realised he should have done because there were certain tracks he was having to quickly cover and it was compromising his escape.

"Take no chances." The line went dead.

He knew he should have prepared for this. It was his fault that he had left certain things in place, but which to tackle first? The house, or the car.

42

Annie almost crept up to Mo, she was so nervous. When he had asked her to work on the car alone, she felt like a giant spotlight had been shone on her and that everyone was watching. It scared her to be so exposed to people she didn't even know existed and could therefore not trust, but she had got her head down, hoping that this one last job would be the one that brought her safety and freedom.

"I found the car," her voice croaked timidly.

"Great work!" Mo beamed, pleased that she had taken on the task and completed it.

"It's in a carpark, least, as far as I could tell. Your system pinged up something about a cross-reference?" Annie was referring to a little pop-up message that had appeared when she accessed the location. She didn't know it, but the system was designed to automatically pull together vital pieces of information and was always looking for a link between things. Sadly, no one had programmed it with data on 1980s game shows, although that would surely change.

"It did." Mo quickly tapped a few buttons and brought up the feed from Annie's screen. "Oh shit," he said. "I need to call Jack."

* * *

Jack took the call. Mo warned him from the off he needed to keep it one-sided. He told him what he knew, and Jack uttered monosyllabic responses. Mo promised to let him know if the car started moving. Jack said he was certain it would.

* * *

The car had to go first. He'd left it in too obvious a place. If anyone ever found out what that cop knew, it would be a disaster for all of them, not just him. He'd probably end up paying with his life. Failure on the mission, he would probably get away with, if it resulted in a failure, that was. The seeds had been sewn and just because this set piece hadn't been executed, didn't mean that there weren't many more opportunities to stick the sword into the alt-right. They were a threat to global security that needed to be eradicated. Populist politicians needed to be exposed for what they were so that the established systems could be preserved. Those who had enjoyed power previously could keep on doing so for years to come. That was his task here. Stop people defecting to the far-right and keep their votes going to the places they were needed. No, he hadn't messed this up enough to be worried about his own safety. He would be fine.

The parking garage was much as he remembered. No cameras, no one around. He made it to the car, got in, turned the key, and drove out, heading for home.

***

Annie and Mo both watched as the car pinged up on ANPR after ANPR, threading its way North, just as they had expected. They let Jack know, and he began to plot an intercept. This was the endgame.

"You know, you don't have to stay, I mean, here on the floor. I guess they'll want to debrief you, but this bit, well, I don't know how it's going to go," Mo said.

"This is the guy who tried to kill me, right?" Annie looked at a still image of the car from one of the ANPR cameras, Bowen's face obscured behind a sun visor so that only his chin and mouth crept into view.

"Best guess, or at least the one calling some of the shots."

"I'd like to know what happens to him. I'd like to be able to sleep tonight."

Mo thought back to what had happened to Kristian. "Yeah. Me too." He nodded before adding quickly, "You know, you done really well here, given what's happened. You ever want to get involved in the fight, this might be your way to help win it."

Annie turned away and looked across the room. "No," she sighed, her voice somewhat distant, before turning and looking at Mo sadly. "All of this, it came from people who have it all already. They want to preserve the world as it is, and the world as it is still sucks. You guys are the enemy. You're not the good guys. You break the rules and you kid yourself it's for the people."

Mo went to reply, he went to defend himself and his colleagues, then he thought of Kristian.

He said nothing.

* * *

They parked on a street that backed onto Bowen's house and waited. Bowen was being tracked by a drone, so they could stay well-hidden until the moment was right.

"When we go in, I lead, you two wait." Jack was worried about leaving Thea with Reuben, but he knew there was something in this for Reuben. What worried him more was that Reuben wanted to get to Bowen. It seemed to be the only play that made sense; he'd missed out on Fisher and was still out for revenge.

"Fine, but we come in when you secure him," Thea agreed, looking at Reuben who simply said nothing and nodded. "I want him alive, I don't want any of this gung-ho vigilante shit," she went on.

"I'll take him alive, and we can work out the details of where he goes next. If you can put together a case, I promise you, he's yours."

"And if I can't?"

"He comes with me, he can't stay on the streets." Jack knew there was no way Thea could put together a case. He knew that Reuben wouldn't incriminate himself and he knew that, with Andryiv picked up by his team, there was little or no proof of what had happened. The bomb was in their hands as well. It was the safest choice while the extent of Bowen's network was still unknown. He wasn't the top rung of the ladder, and therefore, someone in power was going to come gunning for him the moment he was in the system. He wouldn't make it through the week before some mishap happened in custody. Just another unexplained death. Happened all the time. He wanted to help Thea, he wanted to give her the case, but he couldn't.

43

Bowen pulled onto his street, a quiet little cul-de-sac built in the 1960s. It was the last place anyone would think to look for someone involved in a plot to set off a nuclear device in London, yet here he was, home, for the last time.

He scanned the road ahead and saw nothing untoward. Same cars he always saw, on the same drives that led to the same houses, owned by the same people, most of whom had been here for a lifetime, seeing their kids grow and move on, before retiring for the quiet life in this small part of suburban British bliss.

He parked the car right at the end of the drive. Shortest distance from door to door. He was out of the car and into the house in seconds. He didn't have much to take care of here, just a laptop that needed to come with him, a couple of passports in different names, and the details for a bank account that would keep him secure for however long he had left. Bowen was no idiot, he never expected a long life, but he hoped he'd have a little longer and he certainly wanted to enjoy what he had.

Everything was where he left it, all ready to go on a table in his living room. Straight in and out, he picked up the laptop, which was in a smart black bag, slipped the passports into a side pocket, and then the small slip of paper with the details of the account on.

There was no time for sentimentality, he didn't pause to look around the house. He turned and made his way quickly to the door, opened it, and faced down the barrel of Jack's gun.

"Move and I kill you," Jack growled.

Bowen took a couple of steps back into the house, and Jack followed, gun trained on his captive, never blinking. He took his phone from his pocket. "Call Watts," he ordered and the phone duly obliged. "I got him," he told her.

"Was that the NCA girl?" Bowen looked at him quizzically. "You know they'll never put anything on me."

"I know, but I made a promise to try." Jack motioned with his gun to a simple grey sofa that sat by the wall. "Sit."

Bowen sat down. He smiled. "You know, you might have me, but you can't stop the plan. Ask yourself as well, do you really want to?"

"Quiet," Jack warned.

Thea and Reuben came in within a minute, and Bowen made no attempt to hide his surprise. "Well, this is unexpected."

"Paul Rushe?" Thea asked.

425

"Yeah, among other names."

"You do not have to say anything…" Thea began.

"You don't really want to go down that route with me." Bowen shook his head. "Let's get straight to the point here. What I've done, what I've been part of. It's not a bad thing, really. We're doing the country, the western world, a favour. We're removing the scum, the alt-right, the goddamn Nazis, if we're being honest. We're showing them up for what they really are."

"Is that what Lord Mitchell thought?" Jack queried. He wanted to get as much out of Rushe as he could before it was too late.

"Of course. This was his plan, to a degree. You follow the paper trail, it'll all go back to him."

"By design. Which is why he's dead." Jack understood.

"Of course. He was a patsy. Willing to a point. I don't think he would have really died for his cause, but in truth, someone had to. We're at war, don't ever forget that, with a threat we've not faced in over seventy years. Last time out, millions died, do you really want that again? If you could stop it happening, wouldn't you?"

Thea shook her head. "I had a similar lecture from their boss," she nodded at Jack. "She was preaching to me about the whole need to go outside the lines of the law to make the world a better place. That's what you're saying too, and I'll tell you the goddamn same thing. It's all a load of populist crap. Yours isn't the only ride in town. There are other ways to skin this cat."

"None of which are working," Bowen cut her off.

"And nuking a corner of London wouldn't work either."

Bowen sighed. "So you say, we may never know. However, I think at this point, I'm going to leave."

"Leave?" Jack looked around at the other people in the room with him. "Really?"

"Well, here's the pickle you find yourself in. You aren't going to be able to take me out of here with her here. She's not playing your populist game." Bowen nodded. "And you, my dear, if this guy holding the gun told you that you he was going to give you the evidence to put me away for this, I'm afraid he played you."

"Jack?" Thea looked at him.

Jack couldn't bring himself to look at her. He felt the shame of his broken promise. "They won't give up the evidence. They won't let him go into the system. If they do, he'll be dead within a week, and we'll never be able to get to those above him."

"You son of a bitch," she rasped, and Jack knew she was right. An uneasy standoff began.

"So, if we're down to the last play, you're either going to have to kill the cop, kill the hood, and take me in, or I'm walking out of here." Bowen stood up, dusting down his jacket.

"That ain't completely true, is it?" Reuben said from behind them all.

All three of them looked at him. Satisfied he had their attention, he went on.

"You killed her boss, remember?"

"What?" Thea looked at Reuben, then at Bowen. She didn't see Jack mouth "shit" to himself.

"This boy here, he personally pulled the trigger on your boss, Frank was it? See, he thought that he had no choice. He was told that his hired muscle was all otherwise engaged, and this was something of a time sensitive matter, wasn't it? Something he knew that you didn't want him passing on?"

Reuben smiled at Bowen, who said nothing. "See, that was a lie, people keep on underestimating me. I wanted my leverage, I wanted something I could use to get me out of a rather nasty little pinch I could see coming. So, I sent a boy to put a car in your carpark, Miss Watts. Obviously, I know where you live, took a vested interest in that. I saw your man here arrive, and I saw your man Frank arrive. Not that they saw me, see, I was watching it through my GoPro app, on the little camera I'd got my boy to install on the dashboard. Got some real nice shots on that I can tell you."

Reuben reached into his pocket and pulled out an SD card, handing it to Thea.

"Why?" she asked.

"He saw my face." Bowen shrugged like it was the most innocuous incident in the world. "And he developed a conscience. I think he was going to tell you all about it. You should be thankful I got to him first, or you wouldn't be here now."

Thea went to say something, but then stopped. She shook her head and turned away from Bowen, looking at Reuben.

"Why tell us this? Now? Why wait till we were all here?"

"I got my reasons," Reuben said.

"He wants him dead, Thea, he knows you can't protect him, but he doesn't want me to have him, because like I said, we're all part of the reason Nisha is dead. Which means he won't let me win, and he's certainly not going to pull the trigger himself and end up inside," Jack warned. "If he gets arrested, they'll find a way to get to him, to shut him up. There's too much we need to know."

"I promised Joyce. Frank's wife." Thea could feel the emotion of that moment all over again, the devastation that Joyce as going through. "She has to know justice."

"He will get what he deserves with us, I promise."

Thea shook her head. "Are you going to stop me?" she asked.

Jack looked at her and then at Bowen.

He looked at the gun that was still in his hand, and he knew he had a choice. He knew what he was supposed to do, he knew his orders.

A clean-up team would arrive and take care of the bodies, and the house would be left empty for years to come until everyone ever forgot that a man lived there all on his own. Reuben would be missed by no one. Thea was more problematic, but ultimately, she wouldn't be found and nor would any evidence.

"Your boss, that Lowri woman, she told me that one day I would want to cross the line," Thea went on. "This isn't my moment, I can't do it. Not for this. I can't let him go."

Jack gazed at her, then at Rushe, then at Reuben.

He placed the gun back in his pocket.

"Paul Rushe, I'm arresting you for the murder of Frank Knight," Thea began.

* * *

Jack waited in the house while she cuffed Bowen and made the call for backup. Bowen said nothing throughout, quietly contemplating his fate no doubt, Jack figured.

Reuben had gone to sit down on the kerb outside, his head in his hands. Jack couldn't see for sure, but the way his body was moving seemed to suggest he was crying.

"What are you going to do with him?" he asked Thea.

Thea walked over to the window and looked over at Reuben. He picked himself up, dabbed a forearm to his eyes and started to walk away. "I spent the last eighteen months of my life trying to catch him, trying to break him, put an end to him. I couldn't do it."

"You're going to let him go?"

"I hate him, he's a villain, he's scum, but looking at him, looking at that now, everything I wanted to do him, nothing could punish him like this. And you know I've got nothing on him. Absolutely nothing at all."

Jack allowed himself a little laugh. "I thought you didn't believe you'd cross the line?"

"I didn't pull the trigger, and if I can put him away, for anything, I will."

"But that doesn't mean you don't believe this is some sort of justice."

Thea said nothing.

"What about your investigation?" She finally broke the silence.

"We'll keep digging. This guy is just a rung on the ladder, a really low rung. We've got someone out there who's trying to skew our democracy from the inside out. I'll do anything to protect that. It's what I do."

"Is it really that noble?"

"Noble isn't a word I'd use, but it's necessary. Power corrupts, and people want to cling on. We're nothing to them, don't ever forget it."

A police car entered the cul-de-sac.

"You should leave," Thea said.

Jack placed his hand on her shoulder. "If you ever need us."

"I won't," she said firmly.

Jack nodded and turned away from the window. He headed through the house, out into the back garden, hopped a fence into the neighbours' garden and disappeared.

THE REGULATORS WILL RETURN IN

SHADOW OF MALICE

READ CHAPTER ONE OF THE NEXT BOOK ON
THE FOLLOWING PAGES

VISIT WWW.BENBRUCE.CO.UK TO SIGN UP TO
BE THE FIRST TO HEAR ABOUT THE NEXT THRILLING
ADVENTURE AND IF YOU ENJOYED THE BOOK,
PLEASE DO LEAVE A REVIEW.

THE
REGULATORS

SHADOW OF MALICE

By Ben Bruce

1

It was raining heavily, and he was soaked to the skin. The few clothes, if you could truly call them clothes, offered no resistance to the elements torturous assault on his body.

Not that he noticed.

He didn't feel the rain's icy touch on his skin or the wind slicing through him, cutting into his fragile frame as it sought out the wounds that crisscrossed all over him, making them ache more and more. The heavy rags he wore slapped against the cuts and sores on his body, stinging every time the material found an open wound.

Not that he noticed.

His bare feet scuffed against the wet tarmac, the rough texture of the road had already cut his feet, opening up old wounds, creating new fissures from which blood seeped out, spreading like dark red clouds in puddles and marking his route. He stumbled, knowing that his legs weren't responding how they were supposed to, but not really understanding why. He didn't have time to understand why. He only had one thing in mind.

The streetlights seemed to be looking for him, their pools of light spreading reaching towards him, hoping to snare him, illuminate him, expose him. He knew that he had to stay away from them, but the nearer he got to his destination, the harder it was to stay in the shadows.

Scared beyond comprehension, he continued forward, hoping that he was heading in the right direction. How could he know though? This wasn't a place he knew. It wasn't where he had lived in his whole life. He didn't know where he was; he couldn't even be sure he was still in his own country. Everything seemed strange, everything seemed scary. He just wanted to find his destination. To be safe.

Would he be safe?

He had been told they wouldn't believe him. That they would simply take him and return him back where he came from, but he knew he couldn't believe that anymore. He had believed it for too long. He had to believe something else now.

Maybe it was the first springs of adolescence, or a deeply hidden genetic trait that had come from his forefathers, but he had started to ask questions. Quietly he had tested the limits to see if he could find a chink in their logic. He knew he had let that message keep him captive as much as the chains, locks, ropes, and cells they'd used. Now he was ignoring that message. Something from his life before, something his carer had always told him, had finally won out. "Always trust the police, son," his carer had said. "They're here to help."

He had to believe it was true. If it wasn't, then he would be caught again, and he would be punished. If that happened, he hoped they would kill him. That was better than the life he had lived for the last… how long was it? He didn't know. He didn't even know how old he was anymore. He must have missed so many birthdays. Too many to even count. It felt like a lifetime. It had been a lifetime for him. A lifetime he didn't want to be part of anymore. All he knew was, however old he was, he had lived long enough like that, and if the alternative was death, then that was better than staying there.

Even he knew, despite his young age, that it was a drastic realisation to reach. He had been five - he could count to five when he had gone into the house - and now he knew he was older. Much older. He had been able to tell that by looking at the other children that had arrived after him. They seemed to get smaller and smaller. Maybe they were bringing younger children, that was probably happening as well, but he knew he was becoming one of the older ones and that meant that sooner or later, his time would be up.

He stumbled on, wobbling from side to side, panting as he went, wondering if he would ever find what he was looking for. Perhaps this town didn't have one? That was possible. It didn't look the biggest place in the world. The roads were quiet. All the shops and pubs looked shut. There were no lights on in any of the houses. Perhaps this was just a village. He knew about villages; he had been to some on trips to the petting farm with the foster home before all this happened. Villages had farms, they had post offices, but they didn't always have police stations.

But as he ran on, he became certain this wasn't a village. The buildings seemed to go on and on, and he found himself heading deeper and deeper into the warren of streets. The buildings getting bigger, closer together. This had to be the right place.

Still, the rain poured, the wind howled, his eyes stung. Was it from tears? Was he crying? He didn't know. He hadn't cried for a long time. He had shut that side of himself down a long time ago, allowed it to retreat into himself. A weakness that he never wanted to show anymore. Emotion got you into trouble in the house. It got you hurt, got you killed. He had learned about the hurt and heard about the killed. Some people left and never came back. He had been lucky he hadn't been one. Until now. But this was different.

Finally, he saw what he was looking for. The blue light from the sign glowing, like a beacon of hope, and now he knew he was crying. He gulped as he ran, getting closer and closer, his feet slapping on the wet slabs below, his head bobbling on his weakening body.

When was the last time he ate?

He scrambled up the stairs on his hands and knees and pushed the glass door to the reception room open, spilling inside and falling to the floor.

"Help," he croaked.

The officer behind the desk looked on with shock. "What the hell?" he exclaimed standing up from his desk.

The boy looked up and saw the officer standing there for a moment. It felt like forever, but finally, he moved, opening the door as he scurried towards him, bending down.

"You alright, lad? Can you hear me?" the officer asked, scooping him up in his arms, but there was no response. The boy, exhausted from his efforts, was on the verge of passing out. He felt the relief and the exhaustion hit him in unison as the warmth of the officer's grasp highlighted how cold he had been out there.

"I need some help here," the officer hollered to his colleagues deeper in the station, before grabbing his radio and calling for an ambulance. The child's eye's flickered open, and he looked at the police officer. He closed them again. He was safe, the officer would help him. The police always help people. That's what he had been told.

Trademark Acknowledgement

The author acknowledges the trademark status and trademark owners of the following places and items mentioned in this work of fiction:

Audi Avant
BBC
BMW
Bullseye
Facebook
Ford Focus
Glock
Grey Goose
Guardian
Kevlar
Minder
Sandown Racecourse
SIG Sauer
Taser
Tor Browser
Twitter
UK Border Agency
Vauxhall
Whatsapp
World of Warcraft
XBox

37828547R00261

Printed in Poland
by Amazon Fulfillment
Poland Sp. z o.o., Wrocław